TRUMPET OF THE DEAD

A THRILLER

Kurt B. Dowdle

Black Feather Press
New Lebanon, New York

Kurt B. Dowdle/Black Feather Press
110 Darrow Drive
New Lebanon, New York, 12125

Publisher's Note: This is a work of fiction. Names, characters, places, and incidents are a product of the author's imagination. Locales and public names are sometimes used for atmospheric purposes. Any resemblance to actual people, living or dead, or to businesses, companies, events, institutions, or locales is completely coincidental.

Ordering Information:
Quantity sales. Special discounts are available on quantity purchases by corporations, associations, and others. For details, contact the "Special Sales Department" at the address above.

Trumpet of the Dead/Kurt B. Dowdle. -- 1st ed.
ISBN 978-0692401828

to Ingrid

"I wept and wailed when I saw the unfamiliar place."
—Empedocles

PROLOGUE

The job required a knife. A gunshot, even at night, would've brought them running, churchgoers spilling out doors and leaning out windows. And he knew he wouldn't be able to reload and shoot his way out of the yard, even with the repeater. In his right hand he held the fighting knife, a clip point model he'd stolen from his brother before he'd lit out north. He caught a flash of moonlight off the blade that carried him back to the holler. Night hunting with his brother, the first time.

Music from the church provided the accompaniment to the memory. The sound swelled, pushing upward and out. He saw the cellar door of the church swing open, and the first man emerged, scanning the tree line. Then came the prisoner, shackled hands in front. And behind him another captor. The trio reached the top of the cellar stairs and stepped onto the church lawn. The rescuer crouched lower, preparing for his run. Behind him he heard hoof beats and men shouting to each other. In less than a minute, they'd be in the yard, loading up the prisoner and taking him back.

That left more than enough time for his work. He leapt from darkness, the thundering organ covering the sound of his steps. He drew within ten feet before the first man saw him and raised his pistol. But the first captor was too slow for the blade, which entered just below his sternum. The captor fell and brought the man face to face with the prisoner, who looked at his ally with a flicker of amazement and fear. The man shoved the pistol in the prisoner's hands, and the prisoner wheeled to fire on the remaining captor.

The man said, "Don't shoot 'im," as he fixed his gaze upon the second captor, who knew that judgment day had arrived. The organ reached its crescendo. The man adjusted his grip on the knife and coiled to make the lunge that would fell the final man standing between him and his prisoner's freedom, not to mention his own trip home.

In the instant that he sprang, knife poised to finish the job, the man felt a sharp sting at the back of his neck, saw a blinding flash, heard a mighty blast of trumpets and was himself delivered.

1

"I need your help, son."

Kamp looked up from his work to see a boy, four and a half feet tall, maybe eight or nine years old, staring. Kamp had been focused on sawing planks and hadn't heard the kid approaching on the path from the road to his small farm.

"Say again?"

"I need your help. Son."

Son?

It had been a strange day already, one of those warm days in late October full of half-lit colors at midday, edges rounded with haze. He'd risen early, well before Shaw and his daughter, to sort the lumber in order to build a new slaughterhouse to replace the one that had burned. He had worked carefully for weeks, preparing the ground, ordering some of the materials and making the rest. Kamp had counted all the costs, the tangible ones anyway.

But now that construction was set to begin, he found himself questioning the project and wondering whether he'd ever wanted a slaughterhouse in the first place. As he pondered motives and unexpected turns of events, the boy grew impatient.

"I ain't got all day, son."

Kamp turned his back to the boy and returned to his labors, sawing a plank through and letting it fall.

The kid said, "You know I seen you before."

"I'm working."

The kid walked to Kamp's side. "Let me help you."

Kamp looked at the kid's clothes. He wore a dark green velvet jacket with matching short pants. The jacket had brass buttons, and underneath it, a white shirt with a lace collar.

"You don't look cut out for it."

"Don't let this clown costume fool you."

"How's that?"

"Son, I ain't afraid to sweat."

"Kamp."

"Huh?"

"My name is Kamp."

"Shee-*it*, I know what your name is, and I'll outwork you any day." The kid spat on the ground for emphasis. "Guaranteed."

Kamp studied the boy. The voice and the face didn't match. And the kid's manner didn't fit his age. He didn't appear to be deranged, though.

"How old are you?"

The kid tossed his jacket on the ground and walked to the stack of planks.

"I'll help you out with this, and then maybe you'll listen."

Kamp and the kid sorted the rest of the planks and then sawed them to their proper dimensions. By the time they finished, the kid was covered in dirt and sawdust, his straw-like blonde hair stuck to his forehead with sweat.

Kamp said, "That's all for today."

"Done already?"

Kamp couldn't place the kid's accent. It wasn't Pennsylvania Dutch, and it wasn't British. He tipped his slouch hat back on his forehead, wiped the perspiration from his brow with the back of his hand and sat on the ground.

The kid said, "Son, you got a cigarette?"

Kamp ignored the question and said, "Where are you from?"

"West Virginia."

"What are you doing in Pennsylvania?"

The kid shook his head, disgusted. "Look, you intend to help me or not?"

Kamp took a deep breath and then looked up at the wispy clouds. "What with?"

"You need to tell me first whether you intend to help, then I'll tell you what with."

"That's not the way it works."

The kid balled his fists hard enough to drain the blood from his knuckles as his face went purple. "I come all this way, come to your house, ask you an honest question. I work alongside you, cheek by jowl. And you ain't gonna help, ain't even gonna *listen?*"

Kamp looked over the kid's head, signaling the end of the conversation.

"This is as much about you as it is about me. I know about you."

Kamp raised his eyebrows.

The kid continued, "That's right. Long time ago, years ago I seen you. I seen you plenty. Before."

Kamp rubbed his left temple with his first two fingers. "Really."

"Goddamned right, really. And I seen. I know. I know what's coming back on you."

Kamp said, "I want to help, friend. You're welcome here anytime, especially if there's work to be done. But what you're asking for, I—"

The kid said, "Remember that red felt number you used to wear? Remember that one?"

"No." Kamp stood up stiffly and brushed the dirt from his pants.

"The hat, that red hat you always wore when you an' your brothers was frolickin' up yonder on that mountain?" He motioned to the tree line.

Kamp felt a stab of grief in his throat as he caught a fragment of vivid memory.

"See? You remember. I seen you up there. I was there, too."

They heard the clatter of hooves on the road, and a fine carriage pulled by two horses came into view.

The kid gave a laugh. "You're in for it now. She's a hellcat, this one."

The carriage turned onto the path to Kamp's farm, and the horses pulled up a few yards short of where they stood. The driver, formally attired, climbed down from his perch, but before he could open the carriage door, a woman burst out and marched straight to Kamp.

"What gives you the, the *gall*, sir?"

Kamp removed his hat. "Ma'am, I think you mis—"

She turned on her heel to look at the kid. "He's filthy. And these clothes are *ruined*. Do you see what you've done here, mister?"

"Kamp."

She walked to the kid. "Oh, I know who you are. I've heard stories. And I have a mind to inform the police." She held the kid by his shoulders, inspecting his face, then let out an angry sigh.

Kamp took a deep breath, closed his eyes and exhaled slowly. When he opened his eyes, he focused on the woman. She wore a black, tight-fitting jacket and long black skirt, a riding habit. She was tall and lean, jaw set. Formidable.

The woman stood up and faced Kamp. "Kindly never speak to this boy again, Mr. Kamp. Understand?"

"Ma'am, I don't know him, and—"

"May it remain so."

He rubbed the bridge of his nose with his thumb and forefinger, then looked at the woman's face. She had brown eyes and high cheekbones. But in spite of the intensity of emotion, she had no color in her face. And no blemishes, no scars. Her dark hair was pulled back and hidden beneath a riding hat, adorned with two black feathers.

Kamp put his hat back on and tipped it politely. "Good day, ma'am."

She held his gaze for a moment and then turned her back to him. The driver, who'd stood motionless during the exchange, offered his hand to assist her.

The kid followed behind, and just before he disappeared into the carriage, he turned back to face Kamp, smiled and said, "See you t'morrow, son."

Kamp walked in his back door to the kitchen, fixed himself a cup of coffee, sat down at the table and listened to the silence. Shaw and their daughter had left for a walk in the woods hours ago, and Kamp took the time before they returned to reflect on the day's events.

In the months since he'd completed his year-long stint as Bethlehem's first-ever police detective, visits such as this one had become more common than Kamp would have expected and much more frequent than he wanted. Lost souls and misfits made their way to his doorstep, as if by magnetic force. They'd started coming just days after he'd completed the construction of his new house, arriving one by one and always for the same reason.

They needed at least help, at most salvation, and they'd determined that only he could provide it. These wayward pilgrims perceived that Kamp somehow existed outside the normal functioning of society and because of that, he could be of assistance. What chain of logic brought them to that conclusion, Kamp couldn't fathom, and by the time they got to him, it was usually too late for them to be helped, let alone saved.

In the past year, Kamp had used the money he received from the city, ostensibly for "meritorious service," to build the new house—farther back from the road than the old one—and to pay for the needs of his growing family. Life had proceeded in much the same way it had before he became a detective and embroiled himself in a violent conspiracy that nearly killed them all. But indeed, normalcy had returned, mostly.

Kamp knew he'd never be held in the same regard as before, and truth be told, most people who knew him before already thought him strange. His failed attempt to save an accused murderer from a killing mob marked him as an outcast, and his diligent efforts to expose a number of the city's leading figures as members of a bloodthirsty cabal made him a threat. And it seemed unlikely that Kamp's upstanding and godly neighbors could ever forgive him for fathering a child with a Lenni Lenapé woman to whom he wasn't even married.

And yet, Kamp never considered himself anything like a pariah, as the opinions and prejudices of others touched him little, if at all. When he returned from his service to the city, as was the case when he returned from the war, Kamp made it his ambition to lead a quiet life. As he tipped the mug and drained the last of the coffee, Kamp concluded that the appearance of an odd kid and his domineering mother wasn't entirely outside the realm of the expected and was nothing compared to the wild, jagged scenes that still played out in his mind on a daily basis.

NYX BAUER JOGGED ALONG THE TRAIL on the mountain above Kamp's home, stepping over the patch of dirt where she'd buried her parents' murderer, most of him anyway. She carried the Sharps rifle in one hand and used the other to brush the hair from her forehead.

Nyx passed the shallow grave she'd dug the year before without pausing to reflect, because she was tracking a live animal now and because she knew the man she'd put in that grave wouldn't be coming back. She hustled to the crest of the mountain and stopped. Crouching low, she found another fresh print. She followed it and stepped lightly until her quarry, a black bear, came into view. Nyx felt that heightened sense, the exhilaration she'd never known before she took up a rifle and began asserting her will with it.

The bear didn't notice her, perhaps because the recent chill in the air preoccupied it with the wish for a long, deep slumber and the food it would need to survive. Whatever the case, Nyx moved in silently and more than close enough, then leaned against a maple tree. She raised the Sharps, and waited for the bear to turn broadside and offer her the ideal angle. When it did, Nyx gently squeezed the trigger.

But in the instant between the blast and the moment the bullet did its work, Nyx saw what the bear had been watching. Two cubs came into view as the bullet penetrated and the mother bear collapsed. Nyx stood fixed to the ground, smoke burning her nostrils. The newly orphaned cubs fled for the bushes. She watched the mother bear breathe her last and then Nyx turned on her heel and ran back down the trail.

Kamp heard loud footsteps on the front porch and assumed his family had returned from their ramble. Instead, the person of Nyx Bauer, breathless and in tears, burst through the front door.

She held the Sharps out to Kamp with both hands and said, "Here."

Nyx wasn't one of the people who'd come to Kamp for help during the previous year. In fact, he hadn't seen her at all, in spite of the fact that they'd been bound together for life by sorrow and trial.

Kamp raised his eyebrows. "How you been?"

Nyx dropped her shoulders "I'm upset!"

"I see that."

"Take it. I don't want it anymore!" She shoved the Sharps into Kamp's hand, and he set it down next to the fireplace.

He said, "Well, it's good to see you, anyhow. I was about to fix some supper."

Nyx paused to listen, then looked up the stairs. "Where's everyone else?"

"We're right here." Shaw stood in the doorway with the little girl, Autumn, asleep on her back.

OVER THE MEAL KAMP MADE, Nyx recounted the story of how she'd set out that morning on a hunt and picked up the trail of the bear. She told them about the fateful shot that felled the animal. While she talked, Autumn sat in Nyx's lap, laughing and playing with the silverware.

Nyx finished the story and handed the little girl back to Shaw.

She focused on Kamp. "Did you ever kill something and wish you hadn't?"

Kamp looked over Nyx's shoulder and out the front window of the house. "Of course."

"Did you keep doing it after that?"

"Doing what?"

"Killing."

"I did."

Nyx shifted her gaze to Shaw. "What about you? Did you ever kill anyone by mistake?"

Kamp saw Shaw stiffen, and he felt his stomach go tight. He didn't mind Nyx's direct questions, as he believed he understood the way her thinking worked. He knew that in order to understand a situation for herself, Nyx felt as if she had to inhabit someone else's consciousness. But she didn't know Shaw and either didn't understand the cultural injunction against this kind of direct question or, more likely, didn't care.

Nyx persisted. "Did that ever happen to you? Did it?"

Shaw took a deep breath. "We weren't supposed to kill anything."

"Who's we?"

Kamp changed the subject. "A kid came by today, a boy, maybe eight or ten years old. Blonde hair, like straw. And then his mother came looking for him."

"What did she look like?"

"Tall, dark hair. Angry. Sound familiar?"

"Nope."

The meal finished, Nyx stood up and over the protests of Shaw, cleared the table. They heard her washing dishes in the kitchen sink, then the closing of the back door. Nyx was gone. Kamp looked to the fireplace and saw that the Sharps was gone, too.

Kamp and Shaw listened to the silence, watched the sun disappear behind the mountain and then looked at each other.

He said, "You don't have to say it."

Shaw smiled. "You can't save her, Kamp. You can't."

"I never said I could."

2

Kamp followed the croaking of ravens up the mountain. He could see the trail by the light of the half moon and wouldn't have been able to find the exact spot otherwise. And he was certain Nyx hadn't gone back to field dress the bear. Kamp didn't worry about Nyx, as such. He knew that her life would follow its own trajectory, same as everyone else's, and yet he wished he could prevent suffering, for her and for anyone else unlucky enough to find themselves in her crosshairs.

He pulled cold air into his lungs and felt his legs getting warm. He almost felt healed of the injuries from the previous year, the ones that could heal, at least. The raven calls grew louder, directing him to the exact location where the bear fell. The birds scattered when he approached and promptly perched in nearby branches, squawking their imprecations.

He knelt down and got to work immediately, because the hide and the meat would soon spoil, if they hadn't already. Since the weather had turned cold and dry, he figured he had some time. Kamp pulled the knife from the canvas bag he carried and began skinning the bear's legs as close to the paws as he could get, slicing each wrist joint with a hatchet and then peeling the hide back. Once he'd caped the animal, Kamp began boning out the meat with a butcher knife. He worked as quickly as he could, blade flashing in the silver light.

He also picked up the sound of footsteps approaching from behind, perhaps a wolf or another bear. Kamp crouched low and changed his grip on the knife. He turned and sprang, holding the blade close to the throat of the figure behind him.

The kid stood unflinching with a bemused expression.

He said, "Christ, but you're jumpy."

Kamp lowered the knife. "And you were just about dead."

"Wouldn't be the first time."

Kamp went back to butchering, while the kid looked on.

"I'm startin' t' think you need more help than I do."

"How's that?"

"That meat's fixin' to spoil."

"You know how to field dress a bear?"

The kid snorted, "Course."

Kamp felt a fire starting at the base of his skull, felt the anger rising in his chest.

The kid said, "Gonna hafta work a helluva lot faster n' that. Else yer gonna have maggots."

"Ach, shut *up!*"

"You brought salt and pepper, though, I bet. Let me get going on that hide."

Kamp motioned with his thumb. "In the bag."

The kid fished out the pepper and began working it in. "I suspect yer gonna need my help carrying all of this, too."

"I wasn't planning on taking the hide. You're welcome to it."

"I bring that home, and the old lady'll shit bricks. You seen what she's like." The kid laughed to himself.

"Your mother?"

"Not exactly. She thinks she is."

"Then who is she?"

The kid folded the bear hide carefully and then took a handful of salt from the jar Kamp had brought. He rubbed the salt between his hands to clean them.

"You wouldn't happen to have a smoke, wouldja?"

Kamp ignored the question and wrapped the meat in a muslin hunting bag. With his free hand, he picked up the canvas haversack and headed back onto the trail. The kid scooped up the hide in both arms and followed Kamp.

It was still dark when they reached the house. Kamp opened the bulkhead doors, and they put the meat and the hide in the cellar. Kamp now wished the slaughterhouse was built, in spite of his ambivalence.

The pair emerged from the cellar, and both breathed a sigh into the cold air of the pre-dawn. The kid tipped his hat back on his forehead.

"Now you hafta help me."

"How do you figure?"

"Well, son, Jesus said that iffin' a man com-*peyls* you to walk a mile with him, you oughta go with him twain. I figure I gone at least that far with you already."

"I didn't compel you to do anything."

"You sure about that?"

THE KID LEFT WITHOUT SAYING GOODBYE, and by the time Kamp finished salting the bear meat and storing it in the kitchen, dawn had begun to seep through the windows. He knew he wouldn't sleep and that Shaw and Autumn probably wouldn't be up for hours.

He started a fire, heated a pot of water and washed his face and hands. After he put on a clean shirt, his thin work jacket and his hat, Kamp walked out the front door. He saw a black shape moving back and forth in the front yard, one of the bear's cubs. The cub gave a low, sad cry, calling for its mother, which it must have smelled. Kamp knew that the cub wouldn't leave, and he didn't want

Shaw, or worse, Autumn to discover it in the yard. Neither did he want to kill it.

Kamp went back into the house, poured a bowl of milk and walked slowly toward the cub. He held the bowl out gently and let the cub smell it and then lap it a few times. He pulled the bowl away and backtracked toward the bulkhead doors, descending into the cellar with the bear following. While the cub finished the bowl, Kamp went upstairs, locking the cellar door behind him. He wrote a note—"Back soon. Bear in basement"—and headed for town.

Riding a horse wasn't an option for Kamp, as one of the permanent consequences of having been shot in the head was intense vertigo every time he climbed in a saddle. Driving a wagon produced the same effect, and so he rode the train when he could. But since Kamp had already missed the five-seventeen Black Diamond Unlimited into Bethlehem, he'd have to hoof it.

Kamp never minded marching as long as it wasn't on an empty stomach. And since he'd grabbed a handful of hard biscuits on his way out of the kitchen, he knew he'd be fine. Besides, he needed a long walk to think through the two visits from the kid.

A number of statements the kid had made started a flood of associations in Kamp's mind, memories and feelings that he thought had long since washed away. And even though he'd first met the kid the day before, Kamp was already retracing the causes and contingencies that first brought the kid to his door then returned him again in short order.

Something about the kid reminded Kamp of the local misfit, Daniel Knecht, who'd also happened onto his property, trying to outrun the law. By saving Knecht from a train detective's bullet, Kamp had unwittingly set in motion a chain of events that led directly to the gruesome murders of an upstanding husband and wife, not to mention the execution of the fiend Knecht himself.

True enough, the detective's bullet might have missed Daniel Knecht, and Knecht might have raced to his early grave regardless. And Jonas and Rachel Bauer were almost certainly doomed, even if Knecht hadn't darkened their door. But Kamp couldn't escape the fact of having been a cog in a murderous machine. And before that story ended, Kamp himself had taken lives.

The kid and Knecht looked nothing alike, and neither did the kid seem broken and forlorn, as Knecht had. But still, there was a similar quality, a rootlessness, a sense that both had been cursed to wander. Kamp also reflected on Shaw's point about not being able to save Nyx Bauer, knowing she was right but committing to the girl's salvation all the same.

Kamp knew his thinking would lead to nothing but rumination. Soon, his mood would darken, and not long after that, a full-blown war would erupt in his mind, complete with foul apparitions and endless gore. But Kamp had learned through hundreds of such episodes that physical exertion would keep him in his body and could hold the demons at bay. And by the time he'd walked halfway to Bethlehem, his brain had slowed so that his thoughts kept pace with his steps.

The wind blew away the haze, and Kamp walked the road under a brilliant sky lit with yellow sunshine on a scene of fall colors' full blaze. He breathed the sweet smell of maple leaves and listened to them crunch under his boots. By and by the town came into view, or rather, Kamp saw black smoke billowing from Native Iron and then the stacks themselves and the iron-making plant and finally the buildings, streets, carriages and denizens that constituted Bethlehem proper.

He avoided going to town as much as practical necessity would allow. Kamp assumed that although he was engaged in no quarrels at present, he would forever be regarded as an outsider and a malefactor for what he'd done in the service of the Bethlehem Police Department. And yet, he needed information, and in spite of their shared history, Kamp needed to begin with the decidedly low-brow High Constable, Samuel Druckenmiller.

KAMP REMEMBERED the beat Druckenmiller walked, recalling, too, that the man followed the same path every day at the same time. He assumed the High Constable did this so that every criminal could be certain to avoid getting caught. Kamp also assumed that after the turmoil of the previous year during which Druckenmiller himself was nearly beaten to death, he would return to the same routine he'd followed before the trouble started.

And if that were the case, he'd be making the turn from Main Street onto Market at exactly ten-thirty. Kamp waited on the corner and soon saw the familiar shepherd's crook bobbing up and down in the mass of mid-morning pedestrians. When Druckenmiller saw him, Kamp watched the color drain from his face. The High Constable tugged his hat brim down, trying to look nonchalant and pass by without acknowledging Kamp, who pulled up alongside.

"*Guder mariye*, Sam. *Wie bischt?*"

Druckenmiller grunted, "Morning."

"Need a favor."

The High Constable's eyes darted back and forth. "Christ, Kamp."

"I need you to find some information about a couple of people."

"Ach, I don't work with you no more. And I sure as shit don't work *for* you." Druckenmiller took the silver flask from his vest pocket and took a long pull. He offered the flask to Kamp, who declined.

"I just need a few answers."

Kamp saw color begin to bloom in Druckenmiller's face.

"Yah, a question here, a question there and pretty soon I'm in the hospital again. Or *dead*!"

"A kid came to my house, nine years old or so, rich kid with a big mouth. And his mother. Tall, mean. Kind of a strange—"

"Leave me *alone*," Druckenmiller hissed. He stared at the ground and stopped walking.

"No one's after me anymore, Sam. And no one's keeping an eye on you."

Druckenmiller looked up and faced Kamp. "You don't know that."

"Right now I just need a few answers."

The High Constable sipped the flask again and put it back in his pocket. Kamp saw a familiar twinkle in the man's eye.

Druckenmiller said, "What do I get?"

"I'll leave you alone."

"Yah, what *else* do I get?" He cocked his head to the side.

"Ten pounds of bear meat. Butchered this morning."

Druckenmiller started walking again. "I know the two you're talking about. The kid's name is," Druckenmiller affected a British accent, "*Hins*-dale. *Mas*-tah Becket Hinsdale. And his mother's name is *Mah*-garet."

"Who are they?"

"The wife and son of Raymond Hinsdale, formerly of Massachusetts. They live over by you now, in that stone house with a slate roof, back from the creek."

"I know that one."

"Nice big house. Yah, well, Raymond is now the president of Black Feather Extraction, the outfit that took over after the chief of the last one died."

"Silas Ownby. He was murdered."

"Yah, that poor bastard. Anyhow, this Hinsdale is in charge now."

The police station came into view. They walked up the steps to the door, then paused outside it.

Kamp said, "How do you know this, Sam?"

"You wouldn't believe the horseshit we been through with this one already. You just wouldn't believe it. You think all he's got is a big mouth. You don't know the half of it. Kid's *troovel.*"

"What kind?"

"Breaking into buildings, mostly. And carrying a gun. Course, we can't do much with him on account of he's a *junge* and his father's a big shot. And that mother. Jeezus crackers but she's a piece of work. Don't get mixed up with 'em, not if you can avoid it."

"One more question. What do you know about Nyx Bauer?"

Druckenmiller smiled for the first time as he turned the knob and walked into the police station. "Why, you can ask her yourself. She's right here."

NYX BAUER SAT on the wooden bench in the jail cell, staring up at the small window near the ceiling. She looked much the same as she did when she'd visited Kamp's house the night before. Two scroungy looking men sat on the floor away from her in the far corner of the cell. They kept their distance out of respect or, more likely, she'd intimidated them. Kamp crossed the room.

"Nyx, Nyx."

She snapped from her reverie, reorienting herself to the hard bench, the iron bars and Kamp's voice.

"What are you doing here?" she said, without emotion.

"Business in town. What are *you* doing here?" Kamp knew she wouldn't like the question, and when she didn't answer, he wasn't surprised. "Are you hurt? Is there anything I can do?"

She said, "Go home" and went back to looking up at the window.

By the time Kamp turned around, Druckenmiller had already taken off his boots and propped his feet on his desk. He held up a book to show Kamp the cover.

"Around the Moon. Jules Verne." He pronounced the V as a W.

"What's she doing in there, Sam?"

"Ach, this is a good one. Here, they shoot them all the way into space in a rocket shaped like a bullet with such a, such a *conone*, a Columbiad, ya know, a huge gun and then—"

Kamp raised his voice. "Why is she in the cell?"

Druckenmiller looked up at him with an expression of hurt. "*Ach*, Kamp, why ya always have to be so ugly?" He set the book down and put his feet back on the floor. "She was there when I got in this morning."

"Who was here over night?"

"Who?"

"The cop on duty last night. Who was it?"

Druckenmiller screwed up his face as if he had to work to remember. "Obie."

"The drunk?"

"Ach, we all got our predilections. Obie's just a *hoofty*. But we don't have him do nothing except watch to see none of the jailbirds gets loose till I get in."

"Who arrested her? Who brought her in?"

"New guy."

"Stop dicking around, Sam. What's his name?"

"I got work to do, Kamp."

"Let me read the report. There's a report, right?" Kamp felt the kindling at the base of his skull, and he knew it would only be another minute or so before it erupted.

Druckenmiller sensed it, too. He said, "All I know is it had something to do with the pharmacy. Go ask your friend, Emma."

THE SIGN OVER THE DOOR READ, "Pure Drugs & Chemicals, E. Wyles, Druggist." Kamp removed his hat, went in the front door and saw E. Wyles herself, sleeves rolled up and grinding ingredients with a mortar and pestle hard enough so that her long braid swayed to and fro. She glanced up to see it was Kamp and then went back to work.

She said, "What do *you* need?"

"No good morning?"

He was accustomed to her abrupt manner and her typical mood, and he enjoyed prodding her as much now as he did when they were children.

She looked up and put the knuckles of one hand on her hip. "Good morning, Kamp. What do you need?"

"Heard Nyx Bauer ran afoul of the law last night and that it had something to do with you."

"That's what you heard." As usual, E. Wyles wasn't giving an inch.

"What happened, Emma?"

"I suppose that's her business, not yours. Is there anything else you need? For your little girl? For Shaw?" She finished mixing the compound and carried the mortar and pestle to the back of the pharmacy.

He called after her, "Emma, I didn't think you'd be happy to see me, but I also didn't think—"

"You didn't think. You don't think. Mind your own business. I'm certain that's enough to keep you occupied."

Kamp walked to the back of the store. "I won't drag you into anything. Tell me what happened last night."

Wyles put the mixture she'd prepared into a vial and then put the vial in a paper bag.

She said, "I worked late last night and left around ten o'clock by the back door. When I turned the corner and left the alley, I saw a person, who turned out to be Nyx, smash the window next to the door, unlock it, and let herself in."

Kamp looked at the broken window next to the back door.

She continued, "Not ten seconds later, a police officer ran in the door, baton raised. I rushed back to see what was happening, and by the time I got back inside, the police officer was writhing on the floor."

"What did she say?"

"Nothing. The police officer stood up and put handcuffs on her."

"What did you do?"

"I told him, for god's sake to put them away. He insisted."

"He arrested her."

"He wanted to arrest her for burglary, and I told him that she'd committed no crime."

"And?"

"And another officer appeared, and the two of them took her away. I followed them, naturally, to the police station. I'm going back there now to see that she's released."

"You mean pay her bail?"

"Of course." E. Wyles put on her coat and grabbed her keys.

Kamp said, "One more question." She had a flat expression but raised one eyebrow slightly.

"A Margaret Hinsdale. Or a kid, Becket Hinsdale. Do you know them?"

"Why would I know them?"

"Does she ever come in here? For medicine?"

Wyles shook her head. "Private and confidential, Kamp. For god's sake."

"So that's a no."

"Private and confidential."

3

There wasn't time for Kamp to digest the information he'd learned on his trip to Bethlehem, wasn't time to pick through the particulars of what the High Constable and Emma Wyles had said. Kamp had already been away longer than he wanted to be, and now, as he willed his feet to move faster toward home, he felt for the first time that day the strain of not having slept the night before.

But even though there wasn't time for Kamp to get sidetracked, for him to do anything but make a beeline back to his family, Kamp soon found himself lost in a reverie. It was as if the events of the previous twenty-four hours—the sense perceptions, the work, the people he'd met, all of it—forced Kamp to all sorts of places in his mind. He found it possible to continue to walk toward home, but he could in no way hurry.

Letters began to spin in a cloud before his mind's eye, slowly arranging themselves into words and eventually questions that formed a discrete three-dimensional structure, a locomotive. The questions appeared one by one in something like reverse chronological order. Why had Nyx Bauer gone from dinner at his house to E. Wyles' shop, and why, if Wyles had told the police that no crime had been committed, did they take her back to the police station? How could a police officer have seen Nyx breaking in before Wyles herself saw it happen?

Kamp also wondered about his conversation with Druckenmiller. How much more did the High Constable know about the kid Becket Hinsdale and his mother Margaret? And, naturally, Kamp couldn't resist wondering about the kid's father, Raymond Hinsdale, successor to Silas Ownby, the man Kamp tried to save, only to see him cut in half by shrapnel from an explosion. And as soon as the name Black Feather appeared, Kamp wondered to what extent Fraternal Order of the Raven was orchestrating the show.

He turned off the main thoroughfare and onto the path toward his house. He'd walked this route thousands of times, and his body could guide his steps without Kamp having to think at all. But when the mountain came into view, Kamp returned to his senses, and when he did, he found himself struck with a thunderbolt of grief so powerful his knees buckled. What brought it on, he had no idea, but the image that formed in his mind was that of his hat, the red felt hat he'd worn as a boy.

Kamp's oldest brother had given it to him when Kamp was nine years old, at precisely the age when his adoration of his brother had reached its zenith. As such, the hat became a sacred object to Kamp, and he wore it through all the days of reckless gambols and imaginary wars fought on that mountainside. Like every other fragment of his shattered faith, the hat was now lost. Kamp couldn't recall what had become of it. Perhaps he didn't want to.

He wouldn't have had to think about it at all if the kid hadn't brought it up. How could the kid have known about it? The locomotive made of questions departed Kamp's consciousness. He swallowed his grief hard as he watched it go.

KAMP REMEMBERED what he'd left at home for his family to discover: the parts of a mother bear scattered around the house and the yard and the bear's cub mewling in the cellar.

He immediately recalled the admonitions of E. Wyles, "You have to take care of them. This is serious. You know that, Kamp. You have to take care. *Take care, take care, take care.*"

He worried, as always, what might have gone wrong while he wasn't at home, wasn't taking care. He imagined that the bear meat had spoiled and the hide along with it.

Or perhaps the bear cub had ingested his daughter. At the very least, Kamp imagined Shaw's fury for his having left her to cope with it all. But when he reached the path to his house, Kamp detected no trouble, and certainly no trauma. He saw the bear cub come running into the front yard with Autumn chasing in an uncertain stumble. Shaw watched from the porch, arms folded and smiling at Kamp as soon as she saw him. He jogged toward the bear cub, who scampered away and into the tree line.

Autumn said, "Daddy," and Kamp went to her, picked her up and kissed her on the forehead. He looked into her eyes, one brown and one blue and wondered by what right he should be allowed to hold a miracle in his arms. He walked up the stairs to Shaw.

She said, "We missed you."

"I thought you'd be angry."

Shaw looked into Kamp's eyes. "You never know what I'm thinking," and she kissed him on the lips.

"I have to finish working on that bear."

"Yes. You do."

Kamp went around the back yard, where he'd stashed the hide. He laid it out flat on the ground and inspected it. The kid had done a good job of peppering it to keep the flies off and salting it to keep it preserved. Kamp stretched the bear hide across two saw horses to let it dry. He knew he'd spend the entire next day scraping the hide until it was entirely free of flesh.

Night had fallen by the time he went back in, and Shaw had already put Autumn to bed. She'd also cooked Kamp a bear steak. He savored the first bite and washed it down with a long sip of water.

Shaw said, "Did you find what you wanted in town?"

"I found out that kid's name. Becket Hinsdale. Lives about a mile from here. His father is in charge of some coal mines." Kamp looked down at his plate while he said it.

Shaw's expression darkened.

He felt the shift in mood. "It's fine."

"No, Kamp."

"I don't really care about any of that anymore."

"Sure you don't."

"I also found out that Nyx Bauer is in jail, at least she was this morning. Don't worry. Emma Wyles told me she was going to bail her out." He looked back up at Shaw. "Emma sends her regards."

"Stay out of it. All of it."

"What about Nyx?"

Shaw took a deep breath. "None of this has anything to do with you."

Kamp rubbed his left temple. "I don't know that for certain."

He saw anger in her face, which was rare. "The last time you thought someone needed your help, look what it did to us."

Without letting the words sink in, Kamp reached across the table, took her hand and looked in her eyes.

He said, "When I was a boy, my brother gave me a red felt hat. I loved it. Wore it for years. I was wearing it the day my brother left. He walked away down the road, and when he turned around, just before he disappeared around the bend, he waved to me. And I took off the hat and waved it back at him. That was the last time I saw him."

"You never told me."

"Six months later, there I am splitting logs in the yard, wearing that goddamned hat, and here come two men in uniform. Told us what happened to him. I ran straight out of the yard and up the mountain. Got rid of the hat."

Shaw had tears in her eyes. "Where did you put it?"

"I don't remember. I put it all out of my mind."

"Why are you thinking about it now?"

"That kid brought it up. He said he used to see me wearing it all the time. Described exactly what it looked like."

"So?"

"That hat was long gone before that kid was even born."

KAMP ROSE WELL BEFORE DAWN, lit a candle and fixed a cup of coffee before pulling on his boots and returning to his work of preparing the mother bear's hide for tanning. He used the hiding knife to scrape the rest of the flesh away. The salt had done its work of drying the hide, but the job of cleaning it would still be long and tedious.

He liked to work before sun up partly because he knew he wouldn't be interrupted and mostly so that he could listen to the last solemn notes from the great horned owl that lived in the woods followed by the building chorus of day birds.

He cut and scraped by candlelight, face close to the pelt, fingers close to the blade. When the sun came up, Kamp stepped back and assessed his progress. Not much. In spite of the cold fall air, beads of sweat popped out on his face. He stood up, tilted his slouch hat back and wiped his forehead with the back of his hand. As he did it, he saw the now familiar form of the kid marching up the path. The kid took off his hat and gave Kamp a little wave, while Kamp settled back into his work.

The kid sidled up alongside Kamp and said in a low voice, "Iff'n I'm gonna help you out, you're gonna hafta get me started with a cup of that joe."

"Come back later."

"I'm here now."

"Yah, well, I don't have work for you to do. I don't have another hiding knife."

The kid smiled. "Well, son, you're in luck. I happened to bring my own." He fished a blade from his pocket and began working immediately in the same fashion as Kamp, only faster and with more skill.

Without looking up, the kid said, "Now, how 'bout that coffee?"

THEY WORKED FOR TWO HOURS STRAIGHT without talking. By the time they took a break, the hide was at least three quarters clean.

Kamp said, "You work fast."

The kid stood up straight, shoulders back, chest out. "Shit, where I come from, iff'n you don't eat what you kill, you go hungry. An' iff'n you don't skin what you kill, you go cold. At least in winter. Everything spoils faster where I come from, too."

"Where was that?"

The kid screwed up his face. "Say, you got a smoke?"

Before Kamp could say no, they heard a forlorn cry from the tree line, then another, and they realized the bear cub was back. It scurried straight for the bulkhead doors. As soon as Kamp opened them, the bear disappeared down the stairs into the dark cellar.

The kid laughed. "Looks like you got yourself a boarder."

Kamp studied the kid. He wore maroon velvet trousers with a jacket to match and a fine silk shirt. He had mud on both knees and bits of bear flesh on the cuffs of his shirt. He had a shock of blonde hair that had the texture of straw. On top of it, he wore a grey wool hat.

"You're lookin' at my hat. Some folks call it a mechanic's hat. I call it a forager's hat."

"It's a nice one."

"Nice one? Shee-*it*. It's a beaut." He took it off, held it at arm's length and inspected it proudly. "Margaret hates it. Says it's low class." The kid turned his attention back to Kamp. "Now, look here, son. Lamb of God says iff'n a man com-*peyls* you to walk a mile with him, you go with him in twain. An' I reckon I gone three with you already."

Kamp heard his stomach growl and felt himself losing patience. He said, "Thanks for your help, Becket, but I—"

"Don't call me that." Kamp saw the kid's fingers curl around the hat in his hands tight enough to drain the blood from his knuckles.

"That's your name. Becket Hinsdale."

The kid cocked his head to one side and parted his lips. "First off, like hell that's my name. And second, have you been performing researches on me? Some sort of detective work? I thought you got quit of that business. Who'd you talk to? Margaret?"

"The High Constable."

"Oh, that *eejit*." The kid spat on the ground and then looked at Kamp. "I don't like that, son, that you went around askin' after me. That disappoints me. It really does."

"Why?"

"Because, son, all you gotta do is ask."

Kamp took a deep breath and let it out slowly. "All right, if your name isn't Becket Hinsdale, what is it?"

The kid put his hat back on and said, "I'm about full up on your bullshit right about now. And seein' as this is the Lord's Day anyhow, I reckon it's time for a rest." And he turned on his heel and left.

As Kamp watched him turn off the path onto the road in front of the house, he thought about Shaw's warnings not to get involved with the kid and his family. Clearly they'd already attached themselves to him.

4

The next morning at sunrise, Kamp heard hoof beats on the road and half-expected to see the kid riding back up the path yet again. Instead, when Kamp parted the curtains in the front window, he saw a girl riding what he recognized as the Druggist E. Wyles' horse. The girl rode straight to the porch, jumped off the horse and strode up the steps. Kamp opened the door before she could knock, which didn't appear to surprise the girl.

She had pale blue eyes, porcelain skin, sharply angled cheekbones and long, fine hair with the color and texture of corn silk, and no hat. Her bangs were cropped close to her forehead, making her face fully visible and adding to the girl's otherworldly appearance. She stood straight, shoulders back and wore a grey pinafore dress but no jacket.

Kamp said, "Aren't you cold?"

The girl said nothing and didn't change her expression. She handed Kamp an envelope, and before he could open it, the girl turned to go. When she did, Kamp saw that the braid in her hair was tied with a red silk ribbon. Kamp watched her gallop back in the direction of town and then read the message.

It was written in Emma Wyles' precise hand, and it said, "Nyx still in jail. Require assistance."

Kamp pulled on his boots and put on his jacket. He went to the ice chest and removed what he thought was ten pounds of meat, give or take.

By this time, Shaw had partly awoken and had drifted into the kitchen. She picked up E. Wyles' note and read it. She pursed her lips, shook her head and put it back down.

Kamp said, "I know, I know."

She watched him wrap the bear meat in wax paper and put it in his canvas bag.

Kamp continued, "I promised Druckenmiller I'd give him some."

"Druckenmiller."

"Yah."

"The guy who abandoned you when those assholes tried to kill you?"

"Yah."

She raised her eyebrows at Kamp.

"I know what you're—well, I don't exactly know what you're thinking, but I can guess. And you're right."

Kamp picked up his bag, kissed Shaw once, and went out the front door.

He cut off the main road to get to Druckenmiller's house, figuring the High Constable might not have left for work yet and that he could just drop off the package. He tried the back door, which was unlocked, and let himself in.

"Sam? Sam? You there?"

He got no response and walked down to the cellar to find the ice chest. By the thin light coming through the small windows at ground level, Kamp slowly made out the contents of the room. Strings of garlic hung from a rafter above a jumble of wooden crates and garden implements. Along one wall, he spotted the old cold cabinet he knew Druckenmiller kept in the cellar. He went to it and put the package inside. When he turned to go back upstairs, he caught a glint of metal on the other side of the cellar.

It was an unusual firearm. Kamp held it up to the light and recognized it as a Henry, a brass-framed breech loader. He wondered where Druckenmiller could have come into possession of such a rarity. Kamp set it down and walked back up into the kitchen. He wrote a note— "Bear in basement"—set it on the counter and left the way he'd come.

That Nyx Bauer was still in jail meant at least a couple of things upon which Kamp could speculate as he walked to town. It meant that the police, or someone, must have found a reason to keep her longer. More troubling, though, was that E. Wyles couldn't get her out. And most troubling of all was that Wyles, by way of the message she'd had delivered to his doorstep, was asking for Kamp's assistance, something she was loath to do. And with respect to that message, who was that strange corn silk blonde-haired messenger, and from whence had she come?

He let himself feel the chill against his skin and the gravel crunching under his boots while the questions spun in his head. Every now and again a wagon or a carriage passed by, but mostly he walked alone and in silence. When he reached the outskirts of town, the noise of civilization reminded him of the business at hand. Kamp made his way to the police station, knowing that his presence would be unwelcome and expecting to have to pry answers out of Druckenmiller.

When he reached the station steps, though, he found the door locked. He peered in a side window and saw no one. He hustled three blocks to E. Wyles' pharmacy and found that she too was out. A message written in her precise hand had been affixed to the door.

"Kind apologies for the inconvenience. Closed. Shall return."

The note didn't say where she'd gone or when she'd be back. Kamp suspected that he might find answers at the courthouse, though he dreaded the thought of having to ask the Judge. He took a deep breath, set his jaw and marched for the courthouse steps.

Before he even made it across the street, however, he heard a now familiar voice.

"Where you been, son? I looked everywhere for you just about."

He didn't have to turn around to see it was the kid, and he continued across the street without acknowledging him.

"Here, let me get that for you." The kid ran ahead of him and held the courthouse door open. "You got official business here, or is you just soldierin'?"

Kamp blew past him.

"Okay, I'll catch you later then."

KAMP MADE HIS WAY through the narrow hallways to the imposing door with the brass sign at eye level that read, "Strictly No Admittance." He tried the doorknob. Locked. Then he rapped his knuckles on the door and listened.

It was possible that the Judge was in there, but not likely. He jogged to the lobby of the building, where he saw people streaming into a courtroom. When Kamp peeked inside the room himself, he saw all the people for whom he'd been searching. The High Constable Sam Druckenmiller sat next to the prisoner, Nyx Bauer, who wore handcuffs. She looked bedraggled but unbowed as she sat perched on the edge of her wooden chair, back straight, chin tilted back, eyes straight ahead.

Just behind her, Kamp saw the back of Emma Wyles' head, easily identifiable by her long braid, adorned with a feather. And sitting above them all was the heavy, the Big Judge Tate Cain. He hadn't seen the man for over a year, and though his long, pale beard appeared a shade or two whiter, he looked otherwise the same.

Kamp took a seat at the back of room, inadvertently sitting next to the kid.

In a low voice the kid said, "I love a good theatrical production. Don't you?" He smiled at Kamp, eyebrows bouncing up and down. Kamp looked for another seat and saw that the courtroom was already full.

He stared straight ahead, and the kid elbowed him in the ribs.

"Don't worry, I got popcorn here iff'n you get hungry."

The Judge said, "In the matter of the County of North-ampton versus Nadine Bauer, specifically the decision of whether to grant bail, the court will come to order."

Everything Tate Cain said sounded like a primordial croak and a last rite, as if emanating from the void and then returning to it.

The room, which had begun buzzing with excited chatter, immediately fell silent again, except for one persistent sound, the kid munching the popcorn. The Judge leaned back in his chair and slowly surveyed the room, searching for the source of the irritation. When he located the kid, the Judge fixed his gaze on him.

A moment later the uniformed officer appeared in the aisle next to them and gave the kid a stern look and said, "Knock it off."

"Right, right," the kid said and closed the bag.

In the meantime the Judge produced a black leather tobacco pouch and carefully packed the bowl of his briar wood pipe. When he struck the match, it echoed loudly. He inhaled sharply a few times forcing the flame to dance in the bowl, then took a long pull and let the smoke cascade from his mouth.

The Judge said, "Mr. Grigg."

A man in a smart, brown three-piece suit stood up, glanced briefly, if somewhat dramatically at the audience, and then addressed the bench.

"Your honor, and may it please the court, on behalf of the county, I request that you deny bail to the defendant, Nadine Bauer."

"On what grounds, Mr. Grigg?"

"Your honor, on the seriousness of the offense, felonious assault of a sworn officer."

The Judge sniffed, "Are you suggesting, Mr. Grigg, that this girl is some sort of threat to the police?"

"I am, your honor. I will add that when arrested, the defendant was in possession of a powerful narcotic."

"What narcotic?"

"Laudanum," Grigg said.

As soon as he said it, E. Wyles shot up from her seat and said in a steely voice, "She's done nothing wrong. This is ridiculous."

A gasp went through the courtroom. The Big Judge banged the gavel twice and said, "Madam, you'll remain silent."

E. Wyles fired back, "These charges are utterly contrived in the first place. She's a girl, for heaven's sake."

The Judge raised one eyebrow. "You're in contempt of court. Madam."

Wyles stood another moment and then sat back down. The Judge gestured to Grigg to continue.

The prosecutor said, "Your honor, lastly the defendant is most assuredly a flight risk."

The attention of the room shifted back to Nyx, who sat still, facing straight ahead.

The Big Judge Tate Cain leaned forward in his chair and looked down at Druckenmiller. "High Constable, remand the defendant. Bail denied."

Druckenmiller stood up and gestured for Nyx to stand. She glanced at the Big Judge, stood up and walked out with a uniformed officer in front of her and Drucken-miller behind. The only sound was the creaking of the floorboards under their feet.

Once they'd departed the courtroom, the Judge banged the gavel one more time. "Adjourned."

The room erupted into excited conversation.

"Ach, but she's a wild one."

"Didja see how she don't have no respect for *nussing?*"

"And such *hochmut!*"

"The hex is on her, say not?"

"She's a fiend."

"Yah, and a drug fiend too, sounds like."

Kamp hurried out of the courtroom before the kid could follow him and went straight back to the door of the Judge's chambers. He tried the doorknob again, and this time it was unlocked. He walked in, closed the door behind him and saw the Judge on the far side of the room, removing his robes to reveal a white cotton shirt and black bowtie with black wool pants and brogans.

Without turning to look at Kamp, the Judge said, "You're wondering why I'm dressed 'plain,' as they say."

In fact, Kamp was wondering, as the Judge typically wore a silk dress under his robes, always in the Victorian style. Kamp scanned the floor of the room for the high women's boots the Judge favored and didn't see them, either.

He said, "Why the change?"

The Judge turned to face Kamp. "Scotch, Wendell?" He produced a bottle and two tumblers and poured three fingers in each. He handed one glass to Kamp, raised his own and said, "To the law." The Judge drained half of it and sat down heavily behind his desk.

Kamp took a sip and set his glass down on a side table. "What's going on, Judge?"

The Judge pulled out his pipe, banged out the ashes on his desk, repacked the bowl and lit it.

"What's going on? Let's see. There's a war that just ended in Spain, and another one ended in New Zealand. And Ulysses S. Grant just said all the former Confederate soldiers have full rights again, to vote and so forth. All except five hundred officers. Grant said, in effect, fuck them. But it would appear that by and large the world is making peace." The Judge leveled his gaze at Kamp. "Maybe you should, too."

"You know what I mean, Judge."

"Do I?"

"What's going on with Nyx Bauer? What just happened?"

The Judge took a pull on his pipe and stared out the window. "In your studies at the college, did you ever come across the writings of an ancient Greek, a pre-Socratic, Empedocles?"

"I don't have time for this, Judge."

"Yes or no."

"No."

"Yes, well, Empedocles wondered, as some do, about the origins of life and how and why it develops as it does."

"Judge, this isn't—"

"He said there are two main forces, love and strife, that mix the elements and pull them apart. Love and strife, in other words, account for cause and effect, account for what you saw in the courtroom today."

Kamp looked at the floor and rubbed the bridge of his nose with his thumb and forefinger. "Okay, Judge, let me try it this way."

The Judge turned back to face him and finished his Scotch. "Go ahead, Wendell."

"What's your understanding of the crime Nyx Bauer committed and your rationale with respect to denying her bail?"

The Judge winced. "Did Emma Wyles send you?"

"No."

"Christ, she's a pill. Insufferable. Don't you think so? Be honest."

"I'm here because I care about what happens to Nyx Bauer."

"That's love."

"What's happening to her is unfair. You know it."

"And that's strife. See, Wendell, our man Empedocles was right."

"So, you're not going to help her?" He felt the fire starting at the base of his skull and realized he wouldn't be able to continue the conversation much longer.

The Judge unlaced his brogans, took them off and wiggled his toes. "So much better. It's not my job to help anyone. You know that. And as for Nyx Bauer, my god, Wendell, she's even more unstable than you are."

"That's not the point."

The Judge shifted restlessly in his chair, signaling that he wanted the conversation to end but realizing how hard it was to get rid of Kamp.

He said, "She committed a crime, a felonious crime, and in the eyes of the law, she's an adult. She must stand trial, and until then, she needs to be in custody."

"Why?"

The Judge stared at Kamp. "Wendell, has it occurred to you that Nyx Bauer is safer inside the jail at this point than outside?"

HE LEFT THE COURTHOUSE and went straight for E. Wyles' pharmacy. He found her back behind her counter, grinding ingredients with the mortar and pestle and with an intensity he'd never seen before.

Without acknowledging his presence, without even looking at him, she said, "The nerve of that goddamned judge." She jammed the pestle hard and twisted it.

He said, "I talked to him."

"And?" She stopped working and looked at Kamp.

"And he said he thinks Nyx is in danger."

"Let me guess, he made it sound as if she's in jail for her own good. All safe and sound."

"Something like that."

She gritted her teeth and went back to grinding. "That son of a bitch."

"Emma, what did she do? You never told me what Nyx did that caused them to arrest her."

"Yes, I did."

"No, you said you told the police she hadn't committed a crime, and then the police took her away. What did she do, Emma?"

Wyles looked up at Kamp and brushed a few strands of hair from her forehead with the back of her hand.

"The police officer put his hands on her, for no reason."

"And?"

"And she kicked him in the shins. She was only defending herself."

"What about the narcotic, Laudanum?"

"What about it?"

"Why did she have it?"

Wyles said, "It's not illegal to possess, or even take it."

"Emma, if you want me to help, you need to tell me all of the details."

She finished crushing the ingredients. "Nyx is a frightened girl. She's alone and confused, and we both want what's best for her. I thought perhaps if you talked to the Judge, it would help. I appreciate the fact that you tried."

"I love it," Kamp said.

"Love what?"

"When you get all worked up like this."

"Stop. This is serious. You know it is."

"Just like when we were kids."

"Don't goad me, Kamp. Don't."

HE KNEW IT WAS SERIOUS, and he knew that a sense of humor wasn't E. Wyles' strong suit, so Kamp listened to the growling of his stomach and headed outside to find lunch. He spied a pushcart on the corner only a half a block away, and his nostrils filled with a beloved aroma. Pierogies.

He made a beeline for the cart in spite of seeing the grey wool forager's cap and underneath it the kid, standing next to the vendor.

Kamp held up two fingers to the vendor.

The kid said, "Think you can fix me up as well?"

"I thought your parents were rich," he said, and then caught himself. "Oh, right, right, they're not your parents."

The kid said, "I'll thank you to curtail that sarcasm posthaste, first off. And second, you'll get paid back plenty, believe me."

Kamp held up four fingers to the vendor, then turned back to the kid and said, "If you're eating, I guess at least you won't be able to talk."

"Son, yer jus' full o' piss n' vinegar today."

The vendor doled out the pierogies, and Kamp headed for the road out of town. The kid walked alongside.

It felt good to get free of the town and to have a full stomach, and Kamp fell into a steady walking rhythm until he was lost to the outside world.

The kid said, "That was some clown show in there."

"Huh?"

"That business in the courthouse. You'da thought the circus came to town. An' all them *eejits* sittin' in there jus' to gawk at that girl an' watch her get squeezed through the wringer."

Kamp looked sideways at the kid. "What were *you* doing there?"

"Looking for you, son. Shit." He spat on the ground. "You know I love a smoke after a meal. You wouldn't happen to have one, wouldja?"

"I don't smoke."

"Really? Not no more? You used to. You an' yer brothers. Say how do you know that Nadine Bauer anyhow?"

"I thought you knew everything about me."

"No, son, nobody knows everything."

Since they had another forty-five minutes or so to walk, Kamp told him the story of how Nyx's parents were murdered, how the accused murderer Daniel Knecht was executed the following day and how Kamp found himself at the center of the vortex.

When he finished, the kid said, "Golly gosh damn, son, that's a helluva yarn. Explains a lot about the state that girl's in now."

"How so?"

The kid took a deep breath. "I can see a dark cloud's settled over her. Oh, but many's the time I seen her on that mountainside, back when she was a little girl, all bows in her hair an' flowers in her hand. Sweet, sweet girl."

"When was that?"

"Ten years ago. I remember one time I seen her over there on the other side, down from that big oak. Little Nyxie gathered up a big ol' bucket of raspberries, an' her little sister asked, 'Who's that for?' And that girl gave her a big ol' smile and said, 'Daddy.' She doted on her father, that Jonas Bauer."

"He was a good man," Kamp said.

"That he was. Makes me sad to hear how he met his end."

"A terrible shame."

The kid continued, "No, Nyx wasn't born with no killer instinct. And she ain't no stone killer, not sayin' that. But she may be goin' in that direction."

"Maybe."

"She needs to get outta that jail, first off, before she gets all turned around and twisted up in her own head."

"Agreed."

"Tell you what, though, I admire her grit, an' damned if she ain't ferocious. I'd put her up against Margaret any day, 'specially in a knife fight. And good lookin', too, fine figure of a young woman. A little too young for me, though." The kid pushed his cap back on his head and let out a belly laugh.

They pulled off the train tracks and crossed the iron truss bridge that put them on the road that brought Jonas Bauer's former house into view.

Kamp said, "It all happened right there." Immediately, he found himself flooded by memories of the event, Knecht's knock at the door in the middle of the night, the discovery of the bodies, the capture of the fugitive and his execution, which he failed to stop. He recalled the moment he'd first met Nyx Bauer, the horror and the crushing grief he'd seen on her face.

The kid snapped his fingers next to Kamp's face. "Son, son, where'd you go?"

Kamp tried to switch back into the present. "Who-wha?"

"Stay with me now."

"Right, right," Kamp said, fighting the noise and tumult gathering force in his psyche.

They walked closer to the house so that Kamp could see inside the front window, which had been replaced since he'd last been there.

The kid followed after him. "Now listen, I 'preciate goin' on nature walks with you, jerrycummumblin' 'round the countryside an' whatnot. An' I'm happy to lend a hand around the farm, seein' as how I'm better at real work than you. But we need to get down to brass tacks with this thing. I'm runnin' out of time."

Kamp walked to the front steps of Jonas Bauer's former house and sat down hard on the top step so that he was at eye level with the kid.

"What thing?" he said.

The kid stood directly in front of Kamp and took off his forager's cap. He spoke slowly.

"I need you to help me find the son-of-a-bitch who killed me."

Kamp looked at him with a flat expression. "You don't appear to be dead."

The color rose in the kid's face. "Ha, ha. Not funny. Yer not gonna get me worked up, son. Don't bother. Fact is, it don't matter whether you believe me or not." The kid's body language suggested it mattered a great deal.

Kamp stretched out his legs and then rolled his head from one side to the other. "All right, I'm listening."

The kid sniffed hard, cleared his throat, spat on the ground and began.

"Like I told you, I'm from West Virginia. Was born up in a holler to my mother an' father. Father was a preacher. Had three brothers an' a sister. I grew up there, worked for a living, breaker boy, and so on."

"When were you born?"

The kid screwed up his face. "Don't know, exactly. Wanna say, maybe, eighteen twenty-five, or thereabouts."

"You know what year it is now, right?"

The kid gave a look of disgust. "Course."

Kamp said, "That would make you forty-seven years old right now. You're not forty-seven. You're nine."

The kid looked at the ground and shook his head back and forth slowly. "I just tol' you, son, I got killed."

"When?"

"Eleven years ago."

Kamp tried not to sound patronizing. "Why does everyone else think you're a nine year-old boy from Pennsylvania?"

The kid gave him a hard stare.

"Sounds a little, you know, crazy."

The kid erupted, "Yer askin' me how the universe works? Kee-*rist*, how the hell should I know?"

"Settle down."

"Crazy? Me? Jesus, fella, I don't know the last time you looked in a mirror but...crazy? Shit, son, some folks think you got that market cornered."

"Think about how it sounds."

"God damn, son, I *know* how it sounds. How do ya think it *feels?*"

Kamp realized he'd made a mistake. "You told me before your name wasn't Becket Hinsdale, and I didn't believe you. But now I do. What's your real name?"

The kid was shaking, near tears. He resolutely put his forager's cap back on and said, "I took the lord's name in vain. I apologize for that."

Then he turned on his heel and marched out of the yard and down the road.

5

"Whoever the hell he is, he believes what he's saying."

Kamp curled his hand around his hot coffee mug and looked across the kitchen table at Shaw. The little girl was asleep upstairs, and calm had settled on the house.

Shaw gave him a wry smile. "What makes you say that?"

"At first I thought he was just making up stories about himself, and he probably is, but the way he talks—the conviction in his voice, the words he uses. He believes it."

Shaw leaned toward Kamp, closer to the flame of the candle in the center of the table. "Do you believe him?"

"Do I believe he's a thirty-six year old man from West Virginia? Not exactly."

"But you don't think he's lying."

"I don't think he thinks he's lying." Kamp looked up at the ceiling, rubbed his chin and shook his head.

"What is it?"

He looked back at her. "If it were just about the story he's telling about himself, I'd say it's all made up."

"But?"

"But he knows a lot of details about me. And other people, too, it would appear."

Shaw fixed herself a cup of coffee and settled back into her chair. "It's probably all things he heard from his parents. You said his mother knew who you were. He probably got it all from her."

"I told you about my red hat. He said he saw me get rid of it. I was alone that day. No one else was there. I'm certain."

"Okay, what else?"

"He said he saw me smoking cigarettes with my brothers."

"You never told me about that."

"Exactly. I never told anyone else, either."

"Okay, so he guessed right."

"Pretty specific guess."

"What do you think is really going on?"

Kamp gulped down the last of coffee. "Either there was someone there who saw me do all that and told the kid. Or told someone who told the kid."

"Or he's telling the truth." Shaw's eyes sparkled with curiosity.

Kamp said, "What do you think?"

She took a deep breath. "I think, whoever he is, he's a lonely person. He doesn't have friends and doesn't like his parents. He probably just wants you to be his friend."

"What about the rest of it?"

She shook her head gently back and forth. "There are more things in heaven and earth, Kamp, than are dreamt of in your philosophy."

"Is that a saying from your people?"

"No, yours. Shakespeare."

They heard their daughter crying upstairs, and Shaw went to investigate. When she came back down, Kamp said, "Is the bear still around?"

"She's been going out every night at sundown and coming back every morning."

"She?"

"Yes, girl bear. What's the news with Nyx?"

"Not good. She's stuck in jail until the trial, which she'll lose."

"Did you see her? How did she look?"

"Tired. Angry. You should've seen how many people were in that courtroom. My god. And it was only a five-minute hearing."

"People are fascinated by her."

"Or afraid of her. Or both."

"Did you talk to the Judge?"

"I visited him in his chambers afterwards. Appears he's going to let the process run its course. He seems to think she's better off in jail."

"Meaning what?"

"Don't know. He also wasn't wearing his usual outfit, you know, the dress. And he was drinking whiskey. I've never seen him do that before."

"Was anything else different?"

"Nope. Other than that, same old Judge."

Kamp looked at the floor and rubbed the sides of his head. Shaw went to him and pulled him against her chest.

"It's bedtime, Kamp, let's go."

Kamp breathed her in deeply, the soap she used and the scent of her skin.

"Later. I'm not going to be able to sleep." She kissed him on the top of his head and went upstairs.

KAMP COULDN'T ACCOUNT for much of what went on in his mind. He assumed his anguish was the after-effect of injuries suffered in the war, in particular a Minié ball that ricocheted off a tree and entered his head through the left temple. But Kamp also recalled on numerous occasions prior to that being told, in one way or another, that he was different. And it wasn't meant as a compliment.

Still, for all of the visions and phantasms, the imagined horrors and calamities—the madness—that appeared before his mind's eye on a regular basis, he never once had the feeling that he'd been alive before, that he'd had some kind of prior existence. And he couldn't recall anyone ever telling him such a thing about themselves or anyone else.

Kamp wanted to go to sleep, but he knew his mind wouldn't allow it. He found himself obsessively asking questions about the kid's story. If he'd died eleven years ago, and he was nine years old now, what was he doing for the two years he was dead? Where had he been? And if he's alive now but was a different person before, does that make him a ghost? A new facsimile of a previous person? Kamp knew that the longer he obsessed, the more ridiculous his speculations became.

The best he could do was change topics, and so he began ruminating about Nyx Bauer. Why would she be facing prison time for such a seemingly inconsequential offense? The police officer's pride must have been wounded when she kicked him, but prison? It didn't square with Kamp's firsthand understanding of the justice system. And he wondered to what extent Nyx's past, and the rumors about her, may have clouded people's thinking, including the Judge.

Kamp sat at the kitchen table and thought while he watched the candle burn down, then out. He stayed there motionless, eyes open, until dawn broke and the morning chorus began anew. Another lost night. He didn't move until he heard a low call in the front yard and a scratching at the bulkhead doors. Kamp poured a large bowl of milk and walked down to the cellar. He set down the bowl and opened the door and saw the bear's face looking down at him, head tilted to the side.

He made way for the bear who went straight down the stairs milk and lapped the milk noisily. As soon as she finished, the bear went to the preferred corner of the room, curled up and went to sleep. Kamp watched with a tinge of jealousy before walking out of the cellar and hitting the road.

He followed the trail alongside Shawnee Creek for a mile, his walk made easier by the fact that most of the leaves had fallen. The large stone house with the slate roof came into view, and Kamp started up the stairs that led from the bank of the creek to a patio at the back of the house. As he ascended, Kamp made out the form of a woman, standing and facing in the opposite direction. He saw a thin spiral of smoke curling above her head, and he smelled tobacco. The crunching of the leaves under his feet didn't alert her to his presence, so he cleared his throat.

Margaret Hinsdale whipped her head around, eyes wild, and stared at Kamp.

"I'm sorry to trouble you ma'am, especially this early in the morning—"

"He's not with you?"

"Who?"

"Becket."

Margaret Hinsdale's arms were crossed, her hair pulled back severely.

"No, ma'am, but I came here to talk about him with you."

She took a long drag on her cigarette and said, "So, you don't know where he is?" She tossed the cigarette butt on the ground and crushed it with her heel. She looked down at it and said, "It's a filthy habit, I know. Unwomanly."

"When was the last time you saw him?"

"Last night at supper," she said. "When was the last time *you* saw him?"

"Yesterday."

Her eyes blazed. "Yesterday."

"Please calm down, Mrs. Hinsdale."

"I *am* calm, Mr. Kamp."

"Kamp."

"If you'll excuse me." She turned and put her hand on the brass doorknob."

Kamp said, "Mrs. Hinsdale, why does your son think he's not your son?"

Her body went rigid, and she gripped the doorknob hard. She stood up straight and turned slowly.

Margaret Hinsdale said slowly, "This isn't the time. Kamp."

"Yes, it is."

"My son is missing. I'm going to look for him. You're being cruel."

"Where's your husband?"

"None of your concern."

Perhaps it had something to do with the rude treatment he'd received from this family or maybe the exhaustion he felt from not having slept the night before or for the past ten years. Or maybe it was because he thought it best to finish all important matters, once started. Regardless, Kamp wouldn't let it go.

He said, "Do you think your son is telling the truth, or do you think he's ill?"

She levelled her gaze at him. "Do you have children, Kamp?"

"Yes."

"Then you know what it means to worry, to suffer when something goes wrong, or worse, when you're convinced something will go wrong."

"I do."

"But you love them so much. They're yours. Now imagine if, every day, from the beginning, your child told you he didn't know you, didn't want to be in your home, that you weren't his father. How would you feel?"

"Tell me about how it started."

"I just did." Margaret Hinsdale lit another cigarette and sat down in a wooden chair. "The first words he ever strung together, the first sentence he uttered was, 'You're not my mother.'"

"Then what?"

"Then he began talking about the house, the house in West Virginia where he said he grew up, his brothers and sister, his *real* parents. The more he talked, the more he articulated his dissatisfaction with me and his father. He's quite a talker."

"I've noticed."

"Yes, well, as he got older he started talking about how he got here, to Pennsylvania, and about his death."

Kamp said, "What do you make of it?"

She looked at the ground and shook her head, "Why do you care?"

"He wants me to help him. He keeps looking for me. I need to understand his story if I'm going to be able to help him. Or you."

"We don't need your help."

"Mrs. Hinsdale, I can't imagine the sorrow you're feeling, but I need to know what you think is the truth about your son."

She looked up at the sky for a long moment and then sighed. "Either he's a very disturbed little boy, and always has been, or he's exactly who he says he is, whatever that means."

"Which do you think it is?"

Margaret Hinsdale stared into the distance across the creek.

"Four years ago, when Becket was five, he talked about his former home, incessantly begging me to take him there. 'Margaret, take me to see them. I miss my mama. I must go back there.' On and on and on."

"What did you do?"

"I took him. We boarded a train and went to West Virginia, the two of us, and looked for the place he'd described."

"What about your husband?"

"He wouldn't hear of it. He stayed."

"What happened when you got there?"

"Well, I'd researched enough to know which town it was, so we began there. And then I asked the local townsfolk if they knew of the people and places he'd described. One conversation led to the next, and soon enough, we'd found the trail to the right place."

Kamp said, "How did you know?"

"He jumped up and down, shouting, 'This is it! This is it! See, see! Just wait!' And he'd pulled me by my sleeve. I'd never seen him so animated, so blissful."

Kamp studied her face, sensing the how the story would end. "Was it the right house?"

"It was as he'd described it. There were a few small inconsistencies, objects and features of the landscape that didn't match his description. And there was one glaring problem."

"What was that?"

"All the people were gone. No one there at all. The house had been abandoned, and it was falling in on itself."

"How did he take it?"

Margaret Hinsdale pulled in a deep breath. "To say that that little boy was inconsolable would be a gross understatement. He fell to the ground and beat his fists. He wailed and wept. I thought he might die of grief on that very spot."

"Thank you for telling me," Kamp said, abashed.

"You're welcome."

"Did he ever tell you what he thought his real name was?"

She pretended not to hear the question. "Now if you'll excuse me, I must go inside."

"Mrs. Hinsdale, would you tell me where I might find your husband?"

Without looking at him, she said, "I will not." Then Margaret Hinsdale went back in the house and shut the door.

Kamp marched back down the stone stairs toward the creek and picked up the trail back toward his home. He quickened his pace, stepping over roots, between rocks and back onto the road. He thought he heard a commotion in the distance, the baying of hounds and the yelling of men. He broke into a run.

He saw horses, dogs and men swarming in his front yard. Kamp recognized Druckenmiller, but not any of the other men. He scanned the front porch and saw Shaw standing there, holding Autumn tightly to her chest.

A man shouted, "There he is!"

The group descended on him with the man Kamp had seen in the courtroom, the prosecutor Grigg, leading the way, pistol drawn. The man had sharp features and a muscular build.

Grigg said, "Where is she?"

"Who?"

"You know goddamned well."

"I don't."

Druckenmiller called from behind Grigg, "Ach, you *do*!"

Kamp felt his breathing slow and his focus narrow. He stared at Grigg and said, "Tell me what's going on."

"Nyx Bauer has escaped."

6

"Where are you coming from? You were away. What were you doing just now?" Grigg drew in a breath and waited for Kamp's answer. The men and the dogs behind him grew quiet.

Kamp studied Grigg's face. He imagined the cogs turning behind the man's eyes.

Kamp said, "Who are you?"

Grigg's jaw tightened. "Attorney, Commonwealth of Pennsylvania."

"Did you know Philander Crow?"

"I'm afraid we don't have time for a proper conversation about mutual acquaintances."

Druckenmiller unhooked the handcuffs from his belt.

Kamp felt his hands curling into fists. "What evidence do you have?"

"Evidence?"

"Yes, proof that I helped Nyx Bauer in some way."

Grigg motioned for Druckenmiller to handcuff Kamp and said, "Mr. Kamp, you were—"

"Kamp."

"Right. You visited Miss Bauer at the city jail, and you were seen in the courtroom yesterday."

"And?"

"And you are a known associate of Miss Bauer. That means you're contaminated by her illegality."

"Contaminated."

"Indeed. And the Commonwealth is aware of your history."

Druckenmiller said, "Put your hands behind your back. Go easy now."

Kamp looked at Druckenmiller. "Don't do it, Sam." Then he looked back at Grigg. "Did anyone see me help her escape? Is there anyone or anything at all that can show I'm involved in any way?"

A long moment passed as Grigg stared at Kamp, and Druckenmiller held up.

Kamp said, "If you'd like me to help you find her, I will. Otherwise, leave."

"You will be monitored," Grigg said. "Your movements will be closely tracked. If there is the slightest hint that you're rendering aid to the escapee, you will be arrested posthaste."

Kamp walked past Grigg and up the steps to the front porch. He put his arm around Shaw and guided her into the house.

SHAW SAID, "You know what they'll do to her if they find her."

"They won't find her." He placed logs and kindling into the brick fireplace in the front room of the house.

"Where can she go?" Shaw paced back and forth across the floor. "Where can *we* go?"

He struck a match and lit the kindling, and the wood began crackling right away. "We don't need to go anywhere," he said. "As for Nyx, that girl can take care of herself." He held his hands in front of the fire to warm them.

"I don't know that. You saw what she was like when she was here. How upset and confused. And then to be arrested and taken to jail. She's alone."

Kamp stood up and put on his jacket.

Shaw said, "Where are you going?"

"To talk to someone."

"Stay away from these people. All of them!"

When Shaw shouted, the little girl, who had been playing in the far corner of the room, began to wail. Kamp picked her up and rocked her back and forth until she stopped crying. He handed her back to Shaw and went out the front door.

He needed to get outside and to be alone and to work through the day's events. He also knew he needed to calm himself. He stuffed his hands in his pockets, put his head down and walked. Kamp replayed the scenes from the morning in his mind. He pictured the agony, barely concealed, on Margaret Hinsdale's face and the excitement and rage of the men looking for Nyx. He recalled Shaw's fear and anger and his daughter's distress. He saw himself at the center of all this swirling emotion but didn't know how he got there.

He'd learned through experience that the sole way to proceed, and the only way to keep from being overwhelmed by the intensity of others' feelings and by his own, was to feel the soles of his feet on the ground, feel the cold air in his lungs, feel his body moving. Once he did that, he could focus on one discrete question at a time. And the question that formed in his mind this time was how Shaw knew Shakespeare. Where had she learned that passage or seen *Hamlet*, a play he knew well but that they'd never discussed? Kamp allowed himself to travel back in memory to search for the moment he met her. The memory was gone, which didn't surprise him, considering the state he'd been in. He tried to remember what Shaw had told him about her life before they'd met. Apart from a few stories about her father, he knew nothing. Shaw wasn't one to volunteer information, though he realized now he never asked.

He kicked through layers of dry brown leaves, letting a carriage pass before stepping back on the road and fixing on the next question: who was Raymond Hinsdale? Each time he'd asked Margaret Hinsdale a question about the man, she'd brushed it aside or ignored it completely. Druckenmiller had told him that Raymond Hinsdale was in charge of the mining operation that took over after the death of the Silas Ownby. What did Hinsdale know of Ownby's death? What did he know about the murderous habits of the company for which he worked, Black Feather Consolidated? And what did Raymond Hinsdale think of his own son?

One question led to another and another, as he tromped through the last of the autumn leaves, making his way for the offices downtown. What he didn't question, though, was how Nyx Bauer had escaped from jail or where she'd gone. He'd already figured that out.

KAMP WALKED STRAIGHT INTO THE BUILDING that housed Black Feather Extraction, tipping his hat to the armed guard who stood outside the door. Margaret Hinsdale hadn't told him where her husband would be, but since Kamp knew he'd have to track the man down sooner or later anyway, he decided he'd simply go to the man's place of business. He planned to walk up the stairs to the top floor and then work his way through the building until he found Hinsdale.

It had been easier when he was a detective, a sworn officer of the law. People typically acquiesced to his demands without thinking. By affecting the manner as a police detective now, he assumed that people would let him pass. And they did. He marched straight to the highest floor of the building and entered the executive hallway. The wood paneling on the walls was finely crafted, as were the windows. The floors, however, were bare. Kamp passed several smaller offices on his way to the double doors that would lead to the office of Raymond Hinsdale. When he reached them, he tried the handle and found it locked.

He took off his hat and knocked gently on the door, expecting to talk his way past Hinsdale's secretary. But no one answered. He continued down the hallway until he came to another set of double doors, also closed and locked. He heard men's voices inside and smelled tobacco smoke. It sounded to Kamp as if the meeting inside were ending. Both doors swung open, and half a dozen men emerged. Several wore three-piece suits with watch chains, but two of the men wore work clothes, canvas jackets and pants and white shirts. Rough but clean. He studied their faces as they filed past him. They all appeared red-faced and angry.

Kamp didn't know what Raymond Hinsdale looked like, but he didn't think Hinsdale was among the men who'd left the room. When he peered inside, he saw a tall man with black hair facing out the window.

Without turning to facing him, the man said, "I would address you as Mr. Kamp, but I already know what you'd say."

The man turned around and approached him, hand extended, "Raymond Hinsdale. Pleasure to meet you."

Kamp assessed the man's features. Wavy, black hair, brown eyes and a square jaw. Hinsdale stood a good six inches taller than Kamp and appeared every bit the match for his wife, both in his physical appearance and in his bearing.

"Would you like to sit down?"

Kamp sat in an ornate leather chair at the table, while Hinsdale walked back to the row of windows. Hinsdale loosened his silk necktie and sat on the windowsill, keeping his feet on the floor. He let out a sigh.

Kamp said, "Long day?"

"The meeting that just took place. The labor force and the management. Negotiations. The workers want higher pay for less work. They want to bargain. They want concessions."

"What did you give them?"

Hinsdale raised his eyebrows a flicker. "I didn't give them anything. That's the function of the managers."

"What did the managers give them?"

"Nothing." Hinsdale rubbed his jaw. "Everything is manageable, even if it's not negotiable."

"I came to talk about your son, Mr. Hinsdale."

"I know."

"According to your wife, he's missing."

"Thank you for your concern," Hinsdale said, "but he's been found. Or rather, he's been returned home."

"Who by?"

"I'm afraid that's a family matter." Hinsdale walked to a side table, opened a drawer, and produced a pipe. He packed the bowl with blended tobacco and lit it. Hinsdale opened the window a crack to let out the smoke. "You understand."

"How's business?"

Hinsdale smiled for the first time. "Booming." He took a pull on his pipe. "We're growing even faster than we thought we would. We've had to move up to bigger offices twice already."

"Twice?"

Hinsdale gestured out the window. "We started on the South Side."

"Silas Ownby's old place. Confederated Coal."

"Correct. Then we moved across the river to Market, and now we're on Main."

"Impressive. Why is there an armed guard outside the front door?"

Hinsdale crossed his feet at the ankles. "Very impressive. Breathtaking, really. Is there anything else I might help you with? Might you also be here to inquire about employment? If so, I can direct you to our person."

"Mr. Hinsdale, what do you make of your son's story?"

"His story." Hinsdale crossed his arms in exactly the way his wife had earlier that day.

"Yes, his belief that he's a man from West Virginia who was murdered. That he's not really your son. What do you make of that?"

"None of us can invent our origins, much as we might wish to."

"So you believe he's just making it up."

"He is a very willful boy. And extraordinarily imaginative. You've met him. Tell him what to do and he does the opposite with twice the vigor."

He looked intently at Hinsdale. "Is that how you were as a boy?"

"I was not." Kamp could tell the question caught him sideways or perhaps touched a place the man had forgotten.

Hinsdale regained his composure while he relit his pipe. "Are you familiar with the Bible passage where Jesus talks about kicking against the pricks?"

"Yah."

"That's what young Becket loves. Kicking against the pricks. But he does it to his own detriment. The way of the unfaithful is hard." Hinsdale looked squarely at Kamp when he said it.

"Are you saying he's unmanageable?"

Hinsdale gave him a wan smile, set down his pipe on the windowsill and stood up, indicating his intention to end the conversation.

Kamp didn't move. He said, "Mr. Hinsdale, how much do you know about Silas Ownby?"

"Another time, perhaps." Hinsdale gestured for Kamp to leave.

"You know he was murdered. How much do you know about your superiors, about Black Feather Consolidated?"

"How much do I know? More than you, I'm afraid."

For the first time in the conversation, Kamp saw irritation flash across the man's face. Hinsdale went to the side table, opened a drawer and pulled out a folder that contained a sheaf of papers that Kamp recognized.

"This is a report, a sad little tale full of sound and fury I believe you wrote." Hinsdale picked up a few pages and leafed through them. "I've read it in its entirety."

"Where'd you get it?"

"The principals of Black Feather Consolidated shared it with me soon after I was hired. They insisted I read it, insisted I see the kind of scurrilous rubbish that people will dream up, the lies people tell in order to tear down their betters."

"Betters."

"Do you know how your service to the city, how your work is regarded? As a joke, albeit a sick and tragic one. We've all had a good laugh about it, though. I admit."

The guard appeared in the doorway and put his hand on his holster.

"Charles," Hinsdale said, "would you show Mr. Kamp out of the building?"

"HE'S GOADING YOU, KAMP. You ruffled his feathers, that's all." E. Wyles washed her hands at the sink in the back room of the pharmacy.

"He had the report I wrote. I gave one copy to the county and the other one to the commonwealth. So how did Black Feather get it?"

E. Wyles looked at him with an arched eyebrow. "They all work for Black Feather, including the police. That was your whole point, wasn't it?"

"Can I change the subject?"

She rolled her eyes. "Please do." Wyles dried her hands and opened a crate full of colored glass bottles, one of many stacked in the back room. "And help me with these." She handed him a bottle and then another, and he set them on the counter.

He said, "Emma, have you ever heard someone say they were someone else?"

"Heard them say what?"

"Has a person every told you they had a life before this one?"

She shook her head with frustration. "Just say what you mean, Kamp."

While they worked to unpack all of the crates and sort the bottles, he told E. Wyles about the kid, about everything he and his parents had said. When he'd explained it all, he said, "What do you think?"

She stood up and wiped beads of perspiration from her brow. "I've helped deliver hundreds of babies, and I've talked with all the parents about them. Germans, Hungarians, Lenapé, British. I've assisted in the birth of children of families of every ethnicity in the valley."

"And?"

"I've heard stories now and again."

"About what?"

"About what you're describing. When the child is old enough to talk, he or she claims to have been born to the wrong family. Begs to be taken to their real mother, and so on."

Kamp removed the last of the bottles from the last crate and set them on the floor.

He said, "Have you seen it more in one group of people than another?"

"No," Wyles said, "I've seen and heard about cases from every group, every religion. But some are much more open to talking about it. And some people prefer strongly that it never be spoken about at all. It goes by a number of names, usually 'reincarnation.'"

"Is there any proof?"

She said, "You mean verifiable evidence that one person died—typically a sudden death—and was reborn as a new person? Not exactly."

"Meaning what?"

"Well, the child himself or herself is convinced, of course. And in many instances they can identify people and things from what they say is their past. Revered objects and so forth. In a number of cases, the person has birthmarks they say correspond to events, usually violent, in the previous person's life."

"Why do you think it keeps happening?"

"I have no idea."

"But you think it's real?"

E. Wyles leveled her gaze at him. "Why does it matter?"

KAMP SPENT A GOOD PART of the walk home asking himself why it mattered. Why did it matter if the kid thought he was someone he wasn't? Why did it matter if he and his parents suffered because of it? Why did it matter that most everyone, at one point or another, felt lost and alien to his or her own self?

With these and other problems of the universe revolving in his consciousness, he let his feet guide him toward home. He didn't look up until he felt a tug at his sleeve and heard the Appalachian drawl. It was the kid.

"You sure ain't hard to find, son. All's I need to do is go out perambulatin', and I'm sure to find you out here wanderin', too."

He looked down at the kid, who wore his typical outfit, a velvet jacket and trousers that looked new, and the grey wool forager's cap.

Kamp said, "Your father told me you'd been returned home."

The kid took off his cap and shook his head angrily. "First off, Ray isn't my father. My real father was a preacher who died. I was there. I seen it. An' second, yeah, I was returned back to the house this morning, but I lit out again straightaway."

Kamp kept walking, letting his arms swing freely at his sides. He said, "How'd you do it?"

"Do what?"

"How'd you break Nyx Bauer out of jail?"

The kid's scowl transformed into a toothy grin. "I knew you was a sly one. I knew it! How'd you figure me for it?"

"Lucky guess."

"Ha, sure. Well, it was one of my more heroic capers, I'll admit. An' you can bet ol' Nyx was outta there like jackrabbit lightnin' when I sprung her. Didn't wait around for no chitty-chat, didn't thank me or nothin'. Just gone!"

The kid kicked a rock down the road for emphasis.

"How'd you do it?"

"Oh, well," the kid said, beaming and hooking his thumbs into his belt loops, "I jus' went an' told that overnight fella, Obie, to let her out."

"I thought they had extra police guarding the station."

"Shee-*it.*" He spat on the ground. "Everybody gets bored eventually and goes home."

"So you waited for them to leave."

"That's right. Jus' before sunup, them boys they had standin' out front with scatter guns called it quits. An' I know that sorry-ass Drecken-whatever don't show up 'til at least nine. So as soon as the others was gone, I crept up and banged knuckles on the door. That poor Obie opened the door, soused to his gills. So drunk he had to lean against the doorframe. So I says to Obie, I says, 'Obie, I need you to fetch me that girl Nyx Bauer, and don't say nothin' to nobody.' "

Kamp kept walking and looking ahead at the horizon. "And what did Obie say?"

The kid laughed, "That's the best part. Obie said, 'Sure thing,' jus' like that, and then went an' got her."

"That simple."

"Course. 'Cept for three things. First, I was wearin' a disguise. I took that bearskin you an' me worked on. I took that an' draped it over myself, so I looked like the creature itself. An' number two, I put the cold barrel of a .45 to his forehead, an' thirdly, I asked nice."

"So you dressed up as a bear and pulled a gun?"

"Now, don't get sore, son. I already put that skin back where I found it."

They rounded the bend on the road where Kamp's house came into view. He expected to see the posse back in his yard, but it was empty. They continued on to the turn-off that led to the house.

The kid said, "I done you another favor, son. They's startin' to pile up."

"How do you figure?"

"Well, you know if we'd left her in that cell, that would'a been it for her. They'da strung her up or throw'd her down a hole for sure. And before they sent her to that last dark an' lonely, they would'a done even worse to her. You know that."

Kamp nodded.

"An', hell, you couldn't jus' go in there and crack her out, guns blazin', bodies fallin'. You can't be doin' that, not with a family to worry about. I'm craftier n' you, anyhow."

Kamp turned on his heel, looked at the kid and said, "Who are you?"

"You really wanna know? No more a' this Becket Hinsdale garbage?" He stared at Kamp, dead earnest.

"Tell me."

The kid raised his eyebrows and studied Kamp. "Iff'n I tell you, it's in for a penny, in for a pound, if you get my meaning. You're gonna help me find that son-of-a-bitch who killed me, starting tomorrow. You got that?"

He nodded, and the kid thrust out his hand, "My name is Truax, Abel Truax. Born 1825, died 1861. Folks used to call me A.T. Pleased to meet you."

7

"Abel Truax?"

"That's what he said." Kamp talked between bites of supper.

Shaw said, "Does that name sound familiar to you?"

He tilted his head back. "Nope."

He'd begun telling Shaw the story after getting home and checking to see if the bearskin was where he'd last left it, stretched between the saw horses in the back yard. It was there, and if the kid hadn't told him he'd moved it, Kamp wouldn't have known.

Shaw sat across the table opposite from him and said, "Do you think he's telling the truth?"

"As soon as they said Nyx escaped, I assumed he had something to do with it. But I have no idea."

"Well, if he did do it," she said, "he has some brass balls."

"Tell me about it."

89

"What about that Raymond Hinsdale? You talked to him, too, right?"

Kamp finished his meal, wiped his mouth and tossed his napkin on the table. "Not a nice person."

"Anything else?"

He took her hands in his and looked in her eyes. "I want to hear some of your secrets. Tell me how you know about Shakespeare." He rarely saw her blush but now saw color in her cheeks.

"Kamp, do you know where Nyx is?"

"Don't change the subject. Shakespeare. Hamlet."

"He was a white man," Shaw said, "more like a boy, though. A missionary." Her hair wasn't braided and fell across her face. Shaw brushed it back with her first two fingers, focused on him and smiled. "He wanted to save us Lenapé."

"How'd that go?"

She made a wry face. "I'm not sure his heart was in it, the saving part."

"Didn't work, huh?"

"No, he was more of what I guess you'd call a theater person. He talked more about Shakespeare than he talked about Jesus. A lot more. Seemed like it got him in trouble with his people."

"What about your people?"

"He didn't matter much to them. They just called him *gakpitschehellat.*"

"What's that?"

"It means fool, or madman."

"What about you? What did you call him?" He leaned in and studied her eyes and the three freckles across the bridge of her nose.

She let her gaze drift to the ceiling. "His name was Daniel J-something. I called him Jay. Like the bird."

Kamp leaned back in his chair. "What did you think of him?"

Shaw smiled. "Well, yes, I thought he was mad. But you know how I feel about madmen."

"But what did you think about what he was doing?"

"I thought he was harmless, but I loved what he taught us. He told us about Hamlet. He called me Ophelia."

"Oh, did he now?"

She nodded, blushing again.

"What happened to him?"

Shaw's brow furrowed, and they heard a loud thud in the cellar. Kamp rushed down the stairs to find the bear cub whimpering at the bottom of the steps to the bulkhead doors. The bear had grown significantly and now weighed sixty pounds or more. He pushed one of the bulkhead doors open, the bear scampered out, and he shut it again.

He tromped back up the stairs to the kitchen and said to her, "When are we going to send that bear on its way?"

"We don't know," Shaw said, "spring?"

"We?"

"Autumn adores Nush."

"Nush?"

Shaw smiled. "Yes. Short for *nushèàxkw*. Our word for bear."

"Really." He let out a sigh.

"Don't worry, Kamp. She'll be hibernating soon. In the cellar."

"How will we get what we need down there?"

"Very quietly."

HE THREW THE LAST LOG on the fire and stretched out on the floor in front of it. He lay on his back and watched the light from the flames as it flickered on the ceiling. He soon became drowsy and slipped into a dream state, where he walked alongside the bear. They followed the trail up the mountain behind the house to the small clearing where Shaw's father conducted the naming ceremony for Autumn.

As Joe had raised the baby in his hands, they'd heard the report of a rifle. After a moment, the ceremony resumed with Joe speaking the baby's true name. Kamp heard the echoes of the hunter's shot as he and the bear continued up the mountainside. In his dream he felt warm and weightless. He and the bear continued up the trail to the large mountain oak tree near the top, the tree where Kamp played war with his brothers as a small boy.

If you made it to the base of the tree, it meant you won the war. You were safe. Kamp stood there now, gazing up through the broad, spreading canopy, discerning the outlines of the leaves lit by an orange glow that grew brighter. A sound accompanied the light, music, soft at first and then gathering force to a mighty brass fanfare.

By the time Kamp snapped awake to the howl of a coyote, the coal that had bounced out of the fire had burned a dime-sized hole in his pants. He brushed away the ember and sat up sharply, checking his body to see if anything else was alight.

Kamp tried to hang onto the vision he'd seen moments before, but the dream was gone. He rubbed his eyes with both hands, stood up and went to the kitchen to fix himself a cup of coffee. As he waited for the water to boil, he stared into the silent darkness outside. The bear was out there somewhere, and so was Nyx. And somewhere, scattered underground across the blood-soaked country, each of his brothers.

He thought about Shaw's story about the missionary. As soon as she'd begun, Kamp had wondered whether she'd loved the man and then wondered whether he should have started asking questions after all. He let his mind drift off the topic and then onto the matter at hand. Since he had a name, Abel Truax, he had somewhere to start, and he resolved to begin his investigation in earnest the next morning.

AT FIRST LIGHT Kamp pulled on his boots, put on his canvas work jacket and headed out the back door. He pulled two warm eggs from the hen house, tilted his head back and cracked the first one so that the contents dropped into his mouth. He was repeating the process with the second egg when he heard footfalls approaching.

He knew the kid would reappear soon enough, but he'd hoped to slip out this particular morning before he showed up.

The kid said, "Got any for me?"

Kamp heard the shriek of the Black Diamond Unlimited in the distance, and he broke into a run, calling over his shoulder, "Get some yourself."

He hustled down to the road that ran parallel to the railroad tracks, cutting onto the narrow trail that twisted its way to the bank of Shawnee Creek. The whistle grew louder, and now the headlight of the 2-8-0 locomotive came into view. He knew he'd have to hurry. The kid kept pace with him but only with difficulty.

He said, "Jesus, son, where's the fire?"

Kamp focused on the ground in front of him. If he tripped now, he was sure to miss the train. He picked his way across the round stones in the creek. Behind him, he heard a loud splash and then cursing, but he didn't slow down. By the time he reached the gravel beside the tracks, the Unlimited had already passed, except for the last few boxcars and the caboose. Kamp ran hard alongside an open car, timing his leap. He caught the iron door latch, and in a single motion swung into the car in a kind of pirouette. He heard the shouts of the kid and was surprised to see him keeping pace with the train.

It appeared, though, that the kid wouldn't make it. He ran fast but not fast enough to get in the right position to jump. The kid kept running anyway, putting his head down, balling his fists and pumping his arms and legs.

Kamp looked ahead and saw the railroad trestle just ahead. If the kid kept running and didn't see it, he'd slam into the abutment.

Kamp said, "Don't jump. Don't do it! Stop!"

The kid kept running anyway and leapt, catching the latch with both hands. But he didn't have any momentum to swing his body into the boxcar and instead dangled with his feet inches from the train wheels.

Kamp said, "Lift up your foot, your left foot. Reach for that step."

The kid scanned the outside of the car and saw the iron stirrup, and he lifted his left leg as high as he could and stretched. He came within a few inches of the stirrup but could not touch it. Kamp lay down on the floor of the boxcar and extended his arm toward the kid.

He said, "I want you to let go of the latch and reach for my hand."

The kid focused on Kamp's outstretched arm. He let go of the latch with his right hand and tried to keep hold with his left. He immediately lost his balance and tipped sideways, hanging on only by a few fingers.

Kamp lunged, nearly flying out of the car himself, and caught a handful of the kid's jacket and shirt. The kid then let go of the latch entirely and grabbed Kamp's arm, and Kamp slowly hauled him into the boxcar. Kamp rolled onto his back, breathing hard and letting the tension wash out of him. The kid caught his breath on hands and knees before sitting with his back against the wall.

He tipped the forager's cap back on his head and started to sing, "Now lis-ten to the jin-gle, and the rum-ble, and the roar'...you know that one, son? Ever heard that ol' song? You're trav-lin' through the jun-gle..."

Kamp shook his head.

The kid said, "I know."

"Know what?"

"I know what you're wonderin'. And I don't blame you a bit. I'd wonder the same myself."

Still lying on his back, Kamp said, "What's that?"

"You're wonderin', with a name like Abel Truax, how could this boy possibly be from West Virginia?"

"What do you mean?"

"The name Truax is French. You're thinkin', there ain't no Frenchmen from West Virginia, right?"

"Not really."

"Well, that's a fair point, an' you're right. Mostly. Hardly any French to speak of down that way. But my father moved there before we was all born. Said the Lord told him to. So there's that."

The kid untied each of his shoes and removed them. Then he peeled off his wool socks as well and laid them on the floor of the boxcar to dry. "You're right to wonder, though. A Frenchman from West Virginia." He shook his head at the thought of it.

Kamp propped himself on one elbow and said, "That wasn't what I was wondering."

"What, then?"

"If you are, or were, actually a man from West Virginia, why do you live with people who aren't your parents, people who aren't your family? Why live under their roof, wear their clothes?"

The kid gave him a grin. "I love the way I think you's gonna come at me with a straight ahead question an' then here you come from the sideway. I'm starting to take a shine to you, son. I really am."

"Answer the question."

"Well, first off, we grew up in the holler with hardly nothing by way of worldly possessions. My father didn't believe in no filthy lucre, and we wouldn'ta had no cash to pay for it even if he did. But livin' at Ray an' Margaret's, that fine house, that hot food."

"You're saying that once—"

"I'm sayin' that, yes, once you start farting through a silk sheet, you learn to like it. That's the first thing. And second, an' I can tell I'm gonna hafta keep repeating this one. Second, I'm here to find the son-of-a-bitch who killed me. Don't matter where I live, or how. One place is as good as another 'til I finish what I came for. Besides, this rich kid get-up is the perfect disguise. It's magic."

"Then why do you need my help?"

"Well, son, you know people, an' you see things I don't and can get into places they won't let no kid go. An' you been hardened by war, but you ain't hard-hearted. That'll help. And besides, you's a wild bastard, just like me."

The kid stretched out on his back and placed the forager's cap over his face and wiggled his toes.

Kamp said, "Do you realize what would have happened if I hadn't caught you?"

"Yeah, yeah," the kid said from under his hat, "you did me a good turn. 'Preciate that."

"Train would've cut you in half, and you'd have been killed."

The kid lifted the cap a couple inches off his face, turned to Kamp and said, "Son, when it comes down to it, dyin' is nothin'. Livin' is harder." He stared for a moment out the side of the boxcar. "I sure could use a cigarette, though."

8

Nyx Bauer smelled the smoke from Kamp's fireplace before she saw the sparks spilling from the chimney. She'd spent the night in the woods on the mountainside behind his house. When she'd bolted from the police station, she'd had the presence of mind to take a heavy wool blanket which had guarded her, to a point, against the approach of winter.

But much as she wanted to seek shelter, to be taken in by Kamp and Shaw, to get warm and be fed, Nyx wouldn't risk exposing them to the wrath of the law, not to mention the local citizenry. So she camped outside, shivered, and plotted where to go next.

Nyx didn't regret leaving the jail. During the days she'd spent there, she'd realized that no one intended to let her go free. At first, the men—the jailers and her fellow prisoners—had been respectful, deferential, perhaps even afraid. But as hours passed and then days, Nyx could tell that whatever special status, whatever magic powers had been ascribed to her, had vanished. The men began leering, and not even the druggist Emma Wyles, who came every day to boost her morale and to rail against the jailers, could protect her.

On the night she escaped, an hour or so before she'd heard the insistent knock at the door, the drunken jailkeeper, Obie, had been ogling her. There'd been no other prisoners or police officers in the station, which was unusual, and she sensed that Obie saw it as an opportunity. He'd stood up from his desk, ring of keys jangling at his hip and slowly crossed the room.

He'd focused on Nyx, who avoided his gaze. Obie only looked away to find the right key and turn it in the lock.

He said, "Don't talk" and then made his way into the cell. She smelled the whiskey strongly on his breath. Nyx had previously sized him up. He looked clumsy but still physically imposing with a powerful frame and large hands. She knew that only a well-placed kick to the testicles would bring him down, and she readied herself to deliver it.

At that moment they both heard a knock at the station door, and Obie paused to listen.

Under his breath he said, "*Gott in himmel,*" then turned back to Nyx.

The knocking turned to pounding, and then they heard a voice through the door. "Obie, it's me."

Obie had stood up straight and clenched his fists but didn't go to the door.

"Obie, open up."

He cursed again, then said to Nyx, "Just wait once." He crossed the floor, weaving drunkenly.

Obie turned the lock on the door, swung the door open and said, "Ach, this better be—" and saw a black bear's face at eye level. Nyx could see that the person wearing the bear skin was standing on a chair, but apparently Obie couldn't.

Nyx heard the click of a revolver being cocked and then the kid's voice, "Sir, I'll be taking that young lady, and then we'll be on our way."

By this point, she was already out of the cell and in the back room of the jail. She found the wool blanket and then went straight for the door, passing Obie and the bear, who stood motionless in the moment they were having. She slipped past them and into the night.

What Nyx Bauer hadn't taken from the police station that night was a gun. She knew Druckenmiller kept all of the weapons in a locked cabinet but thought she might not have time to get the key off Obie's ring. Besides, Nyx figured she'd just recover the Sharps from its hiding place, the tool shed behind the house where she used to live.

But by the time she got there the next morning, some of the neighbors and a few men she didn't recognize had already congregated in the yard. They must have learned of her escape, and perhaps they'd already found the Sharps. Either way, Nyx couldn't risk trying to retrieve it. And so, she'd hunkered down in the woods behind Kamp's house, wrapped in the grey blanket, watching and waiting.

She watched as Kamp lit the morning fire in the fireplace and emerged at dawn, as usual. She fought the impulse to run to him, knowing that if she did, he and Shaw and their daughter would be imperiled. Nyx also felt certain he would come looking for her regardless, and knowing Kamp, he'd find her.

So she watched as he picked the eggs from the hen house and ran for the train with the kid chasing him. When the sun rose higher, Shaw and the girl left the house as well. They walked in the little yard, Autumn stopping every other step to bend close to the ground to marvel at a dead leaf or a caterpillar.

While the little girl played, Shaw began to sing, "*Kommt ein Vo-gel ge-flo-gen.*" Nyx knew the song by heart, because her mother often sang it to her and her sisters. She felt a stab of grief and fought the urge to cry. Nyx also wondered how Shaw knew the song. She'd never heard her speak German.

And then Nyx Bauer heard the first dog, heard its long, high, wild howl in the distance and another and another until she could discern the baying of a pack of hounds. Shaw heard it, too, and scooped up the girl and hustled into the house.

Nyx stood up and ran, hurrying back into the woods and swinging wide of Kamp's house by a few hundred yards. She knew that the High Constable's house was close by and that he probably wouldn't be home. Nyx smashed a window at the back of the house and climbed through. She scrambled down to Druckenmiller's cellar where she found a potato sack that she filled with everything she could carry: dried vegetables, a ring wurst, jars of preserves. In the ice box she found a package marked "bear meat," and she threw that in the sack as well.

Even from the cellar, Nyx could hear the barking of the dogs approaching. She was ready to bound up the steps and out of the house when she caught a glint of brass on the other side of the room. She went to the rifle and picked it up, noticing that it was unlike any she'd seen before. It looked sturdy and mean, so she took that, too.

Bursting out through the back door, she heard the hounds close now, and the clatter of hooves. Nyx sprinted into the tree line, toward Shawnee Creek until the baying began to recede. But since the dogs had her scent, she knew they'd find her as soon as they realized she'd left Druckenmiller's house.

Nyx clambered down the bank of the creek. She clutched the potato sack in one hand and the rifle in the other, and with both hands full, she couldn't lift the hem of her dress above the water line. Not that it would have mattered. Most places were ankle- to knee-deep, but in some spots the creek reached a depth of a couple of feet. So powerful was her need to get away, though, that Nyx hardly noticed she was soon soaked in nearly freezing water up to her chest. She knew that to escape the hounds, she'd have to travel a good distance in the creek. After a quarter mile or so, Nyx climbed onto the opposite bank.

She didn't have time to think about the powerful shivering that already shook her body, didn't have a moment to think about what it would mean in an hour or two. Nyx Bauer only had time to run, and so she lit out for the mountains, real mountains and the safe place she hoped to find there.

THE SCREECH OF THE TRAIN BRAKES roused the kid from his slumber, and he put on his socks.

He motioned to his feet and smiled at Kamp. "Already dry."

Kamp winced as he climbed down from the boxcar.

"What's the matter, son? You hurt?"

He didn't bother telling the kid about the time he landed all wrong on his leap from a moving train, the leap that nearly destroyed his right elbow and hip. Instead, he scanned the train yard, looking for anyone who might take exception to his presence, or to the kid's. Seeing no one, he walked straight across the yard and onto Third

Street. The kid buckled his shoes, hopped down from the car and ran to catch up.

Before the kid could say anything, Kamp said, "Go do whatever you need to do. Although you might want to stay out of sight."

"Why would I do that?"

"You held a gun to the jailkeeper's head and let a prisoner escape."

"Aw hell, son, no one's gonna figure me for that. I guarantee it."

Kamp said, "Think about it," and he headed off down the street, mixing with the rest of the souls on Bethlehem's South Side. He pulled his slouch hat low and walked toward the county courthouse. Once inside, he went straight to the part of the building that housed the county records. He knew that in addition to official notices, he could also find newspapers stored in chronological order.

Kamp tiptoed into the room where the newspapers were kept and softly closed the door behind him. Since the kid was nine years old now, Kamp began with the year 1861, the year the kid said he'd died. He sifted through broadsheets filled with stories of death, destruction, mayhem as well as the occasional heart-warmer about the lost dog who, after a prolonged absence, found his way home. He scanned for news of a murder, which would have gotten a headline, even in Bethlehem. He also worked through the years 1860 and 1862 for the sake of being thorough, and he found numerous reports of killings. He also came across stories of deaths that, while not ruled to be murders, certainly could have been. For instance, he found an item regarding the demise of a certain Rudiger Schwenk who, according to the paper, was discovered dead in his kitchen. The paper said he'd died of "blunt force from an object" and that a cast iron skillet had been found next to him. Still, the death had been categorized as an accident.

What Kamp didn't find was the name Truax. He pilfered every broadsheet that contained a story involving a murder or suspicious death, two hundred and seventeen in all. He placed them in his haversack and buckled it.

He moved to the room where he knew the birth and death certificates were kept, locking the door behind him. He heard the courthouse murmuring and sputtering to life around him, the creaking of the floorboards above and the clanking of radiators all around.

He went to the cabinet marked "H," and looked for the year 1861. If Abel Truax had died in 1861, Kamp assumed, the kid would have been born as Becket Hinsdale that same year.

But he didn't find a birth certificate for Becket Hinsdale in 1861. Presumably the kid couldn't have been born before Abel Truax died, if the ridiculous logic held. He'd have to have been born in a later year. Kamp went through all the birth certificates for 1862 and again came up empty. He moved onto the next year before hearing a knock at the door.

Through the door he heard a woman's stern voice. "Excuse me. Is there someone in there?" He heard her trying the doorknob. "Excuse me. Who's in there?"

He said, "It's me," hoping that would suffice.

"And who is me, please?"

"Kamp."

"Who?"

"Kamp."

"Well, whoever you are, sir, you need to come out of there."

"In a minute."

"Sir, I'm afraid you'll have to come out now."

"Go talk to the Judge." He kept thumbing through birth certificates as he talked. "Tell the Judge, it's Kamp."

"I will not disturb his honor."

"Just tell him I just need to find something."

The woman said, "Oh, for heaven's sake."

He heard her footfalls recede and focused back on the birth certificates. Finally he found the right one:

Hinsdale, Becket.
Time / Date of Birth: 11:57P.M., October 30, 1863.
18 Sainter's Mill Road
City of Bethlehem

County of Northampton
Commonwealth of Pennsylvania
Signed, Wyles, E., Midwife

Kamp recognized the address as the Hinsdale residence he'd visited. And he noticed Emma Wyles' signature beneath her typed name and next to the official county seal.

He heard footsteps approaching again and then the woman's voice. "I spoke to the Judge. He said, and I quote, 'Be gone, Wendell.' You'll need to leave this instant."

He put the birth certificate back in its place and closed the cabinet. He unlocked the door and walked out of the room.

Tipping his cap to the woman, Kamp said, "Ma'am," and he left by the side door.

FOR THE FIRST TIME THAT DAY, Kamp felt angry, and by the time he reached the door of the pharmacy, he realized he'd have to struggle to keep his temper in check. He found E.Wyles at her typical station, mixing ingredients at the counter.

She looked up at him and said, "Oh, hello—"

"How come you lied?"

"I did no—"

"You said you didn't know the Hinsdales."

"No, I didn't."

He felt the fire at the base of his skull erupt. "The kid and his mother. You said—"

"Settle down!"

He could see hurt in her eyes and behind that, fear. He took as deep a breath as he could, lowered his voice, and said, "You told me you didn't know them, but your name is on the kid's birth certificate."

E. Wyles drew a breath through her nostrils and touched her hair gently. "I said information regarding people whom I may or may not treat is private and confidential. I don't tell you anything simply if you ask, and certainly not if you demand."

"I'm trying to help these people, Emma."

"So am I."

They heard someone come through the back door and looked to see who it was. The girl with corn silk hair, porcelain skin and wide-set blue eyes appeared in the doorway. The girl saw the tension and the color in their faces, Kamp's aggressive posture, and Wyles' stiffened shoulders.

She said, "I'll come back later," and she left.

Kamp turned back to Wyles and said, "Who is that?"

"Is there anything I can help you with, Kamp?"

By that, Wyles meant he should leave.

"One more thing. Is there anything you can tell me about that kid's birth that was unusual?"

"Unusual?" She rolled her eyes and exhaled.

"Just tell me, Emma, and I'll leave."

She turned back to face him. "It was a very difficult delivery. Margaret Hinsdale lost a great deal of blood. And the baby had the umbilical cord wrapped around his neck, twice. When he was born, that boy had been choked by the cord. He wasn't breathing. No breath, no heartbeat. I didn't want to tell Margaret Hinsdale for fear she'd die as well."

Wyles paused and looked at the floor.

"Then what happened?"

"Then the baby's body jerked one time. He started breathing, his eyes opened and he began to cry. He was fine after that."

"Anything else?"

Without looking at him, she said, "Kamp?"

"Yes."

"Get the hell out of here."

HE HEADED FROM WYLES' SHOP straight to the New Street Bridge, paid the one-cent toll and started walking across. Kamp heard a commotion behind him at the toll booth.

He heard the kid say, "I'll borry one from you today an' pay you back two t'morrow, but right now I need to catch up with that fella up yonder."

Kamp couldn't hear what the toll collector said, but the kid's reply was louder, almost belligerent.

The kid said, "Mister, I didn't have no time to grab my coin purse when I left the house this morning. Let me cross, an' I'll catch you tomorrow."

Kamp hustled back to the toll booth, flipped a penny to the collector and took the kid by the shoulder. The kid muttered under his breath, "*Eejit*" and walked alongside Kamp. He stopped when they got halfway across and stared at the smokestacks of Native Iron.

Still angry, the kid said, "You know, the first day I rode into this town, it wasn't half-bad, almost even kinda pretty." He pointed to the iron-making plant. "That abomination there, it was jus' a wee bitty l'il factory. Friendly-lookin'. But shee-*it*, it's whallopers now, a regular leviathan. Ugly beast breathin' fire an' filth into the air." He let out a long breath, shook his head, and started walking again.

"When was that?"

"What?"

"When you first got here."

"I got here in the spring. I remember that. Cherry blossoms and whatnot. An' I recall the first newspaper I seen said war's on. So that was sixty-one." He tipped his cap back and looked up through the trusses while he walked.

Kamp said, "What brought you to town?"

"Jesus, but yer full of questions."

"Why did you leave West Virginia?"

"Came here to help a fella. Two, actually. One that was locked up, an' the other who wanted him free."

"How'd it go?"

The kid said, "I got myself locked up straight away. Imagine that, me comin' to try t' spring a fella an' gettin' throw'd in jail myself. Disturbin' the peace. Course, I was wild-ass back then. You were, too."

A man walked past them, going in the opposite direction. The man wore a three-piece suit, a stylish frock coat and a fine Bollman hat.

The kid said to him, "Say, friend, you wouldn't happen t' have a smoke, wouldja?"

The man looked down at the kid, sizing him up, sniffed, "Certainly not" and kept walking.

The kid turned to Kamp, "See, that's another thing right there. Weren't none like that when I got here. Puffed up an' pompous sons-a-bitches." He spat on the ground and started walking again.

Kamp said, "You got here in 1861."

"That's right."

"And Becket Hinsdale's birth certificate said you were born in 1863."

"What of it?"

"Well, if you died in 1861 and were born again in 1863, where were you for two years?"

The kid glared at him. "Here an' there."

"The two years in between. Where were you?"

"I see where yer goin' with this."

As they stepped off the New Street Bridge and onto New Street, Kamp said, "If you weren't alive for those two years, where were you?"

The kid stared up at the clouds and said, "Folks are really starting to piss me off around here, they really are." He looked at Kamp with a flat expression. "Present company excluded, of course."

They walked in silence for a while, taking a left on Lehigh and heading toward Main Street. Kamp wanted to hit Druckenmiller with a few more questions, and if the kid didn't want to be careful about showing his face around town, well, that was his business.

Main Street was packed with wagons, horses and people, the course of commerce. In among the clamor, Kamp saw Druckenmiller's crook bobbing.

He sidled up to the High Constable and said, "Morning, Sam. How's business?"

Druckenmiller glanced sideways at him and hissed, "Jee-zis *Christ*."

Kamp said, "Good to see you. Say, I heard you had a bit of *troovel* at the station."

The High Constable hunched his shoulders, looked at the ground, and kept walking.

"How'd it happen? How did Nyx Bauer escape?"

"Stop goading me, Kamp."

"Your man Obie screwed up."

"You told me you'd leave me alone." He turned onto Market and picked up his pace.

"How was that bear meat I gave you?"

Druckenmiller wheeled on Kamp, eyes hard. "Ach, she stole it."

"Who?"

"Nyx Bauer! Took it right outta my own cellar."

"How could—"

His cheeks turned bright red. "You know she put the hex on poor Obie, too."

"A hex."

"Yah, put the hex on him, seduced him. Then she called upon a dark spirit, a demon, to come help her. Demon broke in and let her out. Damn near killed Obie."

Kamp raised his eyebrows. "You're shitting me."

"Ach, it's *true*. She took flight with that demon. Hounds picked up her scent, though. She broke into my house and picked it clean. Took all my food. I didn't do *nussing* to that girl. *Nussing!* Except try to help her."

"What about that *bix*?"

"That what?"

"The rifle in the cellar, Sam. Did she take that, too?"

"What do you think?"

"Where do they think she is now?"

The High Constable tilted his head to the side and studied Kamp. "You really think I'd tell you? Ach, it don't matter no how. She'll get what she deserves soon enough."

Kamp said, "Well, *machs gute*, Sam."

Druckenmiller turned and trudged up the street toward the police station and said something under his breath that sounded like, "Screw you, too."

The kid, who'd been leaning against a store window and listening to the conversation approached Kamp.

He breathed a large sigh. "What was that bit about a rifle?"

"When I was in Druckenmiller's house the other day, I saw a rifle, a rare one."

"Rare how."

"A special kind. A .44 rimfire. Repeater."

The kid said, "Sounds like a Henry. Some folks call it a sixteen. I call it a seventeen. Sixteen plus the one in the chamber."

"How do you know about it?"

The kid leveled his gaze at Kamp. "Well, son, that fine rifle you saw in that fool's cellar. It belongs to me."

"That so."

"Must be the one. One helluva whimmy-diddle, I tell you. Mr. Bell give it to me 'fore I come up this way. Said I'd need it. Yer own personal war machine. Ever seen one before?"

"Yes."

Kamp bought two pierogies from a street vendor who wrapped them in wax paper, put them in a bag and handed it to Kamp.

The kid's eyes twinkled from under his blonde hair.

He said, "You know, I thought this whole day was goin' in the slop jar, you know, right down the ol' shithole 'til I heard that moron open his trap. An' then, first off, looks like I found my gun. That's good." He started to giggle. "And second, did I hear right? That girl seduced Obie? An' a demon come an' fetched her?" The kid started shaking with laughter. "A demon come an' sprung her an' they flew away?" He was laughing so hard he could barely talk. "You can't make *up* this garbage!" The kid doubled over and held his belly.

When he finally stopped laughing, he said, "I tol' you these *eejits* are too dumb t' figure out squat."

Just then, a carriage pulled up next to them. Two men in wool uniforms jumped out. One of the men grabbed the kid by the shoulders, and the other stood in Kamp's way.

Kamp said, "You can't do this." Neither of the uniformed men said a word.

As they loaded him in, the kid yelled, "Raymond Hinsdale will have your heads for this. Tell 'em, Kamp! Tell 'em it's so!"

Before Kamp could say or do anything, they'd shut the door, and the carriage started to roll. Another carriage started off right behind it. As it passed by, he saw a man staring at him through the carriage window. Raymond Hinsdale tipped his hat gently to Kamp and was gone.

9

Kamp sprinted back over the New Street Bridge, straight to the courthouse and pounded on the door of the Big Judge Tate Cain's chambers.

"Open the door."

No answer. He bounded up the stairs to the main level of the building and peered into the courtroom. He saw the Judge sitting at the bench, and he appeared to be alone. Kamp burst into the room, but as he entered, a large, uniformed bailiff blocked his path. He slammed into the man's chest.

The bailiff grabbed him by both shoulders, held him in place and said, "No admittance."

The Judge craned his neck and saw that it was Kamp.

He said, "Edward, please inspect him."

The bailiff jabbed his hands into Kamp's armpits and then ran them down his ribcage, around his waist and up and down each leg. He even reached into Kamp's boots.

He called over his shoulder, "Nix."

The Judge said, "Approach."

Kamp walked to the bar. "Checking for weapons?"

"How may I help you, Wendell?"

"What's going on with the kid?"

"The kid?"

"Come on, Judge. The Hinsdale kid. He got picked off the street half an hour ago. What's going on?"

"It was described to me as a medical matter or possibly a religious one."

"Meaning what?" He heard the emotion rising in his own voice.

The Judge sat back in his black, leather upholstered chair. "Meaning that he's not well and must be held for the time being, and examined."

"Examined?"

"Indeed. And held for the time being."

"Where?"

The Judge leaned forward, stared down at Kamp and said, "It's far better for the boy than what they wanted."

"Who?"

"He committed a very serious crime, Wendell. He orchestrated a prison break."

Kamp's body went rigid, and he had to fight to keep himself in the moment. He felt the bailiff lean toward him.

Kamp said, "Ach, it's bullshit she was in jail in the first place. You know it is."

"I adjudicate the matters that come before the bench, including the matter regarding young master Hinsdale. I signed the commitment order. As for Nyx Bauer, unless she stands trial, justice can't be done."

"Last time we talked you said she was safer in jail. What did you mean? Who's after her?"

The Judge gestured slightly with his right hand, and the bailiff took Kamp by the shoulders again.

As the bailiff guided him forcefully out of the courtroom, Kamp said, "You seem a little *fergelshtered* yourself, Judge. Who's after you?"

As the bailiff shoved him out, he heard the Judge say, "Love and strife, Wendell. Love and strife."

KAMP HURRIED TO THE HOSPITAL, where he suspected the kid had been taken. Two men stood in front of the doors. Neither wore a uniform, but each held a shotgun. He didn't recognize either man.

He approached them slowly, taking off his hat and holding it in both hands.

"Afternoon, fellas."

One of the men focused on Kamp. The other one didn't, and neither man said a word.

Kamp looked at the shotguns and said, "Expecting a war?"

The man on the left tightened his grip on the gun and said, "Not as such."

"Well, if you don't mind, I'd like to get through."

The man on the right said, "No visitors."

Kamp looked at the ground. "Well, that's too bad. He's in a lot of pain." He twisted his hat in his hands.

The man on the left said, "Who is?"

"My brother. Accident in the mines."

"Accident?"

"Yah. Explosion blew his leg clean off."

"Oh."

"Balls, too."

"*Gott in himmel.*"

"Yah, yah." Kamp shook his head and kept looking at the ground. "I come from the druggist just now. She give me this medicine to ease his pain. Morphine." Kamp pulled the bag of pierogies from his pocket and held it up.

"Morphine, huh?"

"Yah, well, I see you boys have a job to do," Kamp said, and he turned as if to go.

The man on the right said, "What's your brother's name?"

Kamp looked at the man. "Abel."

"Well, you tell Abel we hope he feels better soon." The two men stepped aside.

Kamp said, "God bless you," and walked into the hospital.

Kamp knew that by virtue of having passed by the men at the door, he was safe, to an extent. Most people inside would think he belonged there, or at least that he wasn't a threat. Then again, he'd caused trouble at the hospital more than once before.

He took off his jacket, slung it over his arm and tried to appear casual as he searched the men and boys' ward for the kid. The ward was very crowded. Some of the patients' heads were wrapped with bandages, some were moaning, some were asleep, but Kamp saw none that looked like the kid. He realized that if the kid were at the hospital, they'd keep him off the ward, lest he pester, wheedle, goad or otherwise foment unrest among his fellow patients.

Kamp left the ward and looked for a cellar door but found none. He walked quietly to the back of the building to what appeared to be a maintenance wing made up of a supply area and a repair shop. No sign of the kid or anyone else. Just before he turned to go, he saw a wooden door that didn't appear to lead to the outside. Perhaps a storage closet.

Outside the door, Kamp noticed a stack of boxes and a row of bottles, as if the items had been removed from the closet. He crossed the room and tried the knob. Locked.

He considered breaking down the door with his shoulder and thought better of it. He scanned the counter across the room, looking for the right tool and saw nothing that would help. Above the counter, though, was a pegboard that held an assortment of implements. He picked out a large hammer and chisel and went back to the doorknob. Kamp listened to hear if anyone was coming and satisfied that no one was, he raised the hammer and gave the chisel one mighty whack that sheared off the doorknob.

Kamp swung the door open and saw a dark, narrow room, empty except for a single wooden bed. He made out the figure of the kid, who wasn't moving. More troubling, he wasn't talking. He leaned in close to the kid's face and saw that he'd been gagged. They'd stuck a wool sock in his mouth and secured it with a kerchief. Kamp untied the kerchief and pulled out the sock.

The kid took a gulp of air and then another. He turned to face Kamp and said, "Son, they ain't whupped us. An' they never will. Remember that."

"We need to move. Fast."

The kid said, "You ain't gettin' me out, not now anyhow. Look how they got me done up. Makes me feel honored in a strange kind of way."

Kamp pulled back the blanket. The kid had been shackled to the bed by both hands and both feet.

"Guess they thought with Nyx Bauer lurkin' out there an' me with my proclivity for bustin' out, they din't wanna take no chances."

Kamp ran to the workbench to look for a tool that could break the chains. He found none and went back to the kid, who said, "Son, son, slow down. Listen."

"We don't have much time."

"That's why I need to tell you a few things now."

"Talk."

The kid licked his lips and began. "First off, I tol' you I come here originally to help a friend, Mr. Jacob Bell. He sent me to protect another friend of mine, fella by the name of Tucks, Onesimus Tucks. Me an' Tucks was breaker boys together when we was kids. An' Mr. Bell owned him."

"Owned."

"Exactly. Tucks was a slave, in West Virginia. But Mr. Bell didn't want him to be a slave no more. So he set him free. Decided there shouldn't be no such thing as slaves in the first place, but there it is."

Kamp stepped out of the room to listen for footsteps again, then came back in and said, "Hurry up."

"Okay, so that's first off. Second, another fella laid claim to Tucks, said he wasn't Mr. Bell's to begin with. Wanted him back."

"That's why you had to protect him."

"Exactly. So, it wasn't easy to find Tucks, on account of he had to hide ever'where he went. But I tracked him up this way an' stayed in a seven-cent flop underneath a whorehouse whilst I looked for him, but that's neither here nor there."

Kamp heard a commotion through the wall of the closet. "Anything else?"

"No, 'cept that just when I found my ol' friend Tucks, just when I was fixin' to spirit him away, that's when it happened, when they got me. Hit me at the back of my neck. Lights went out. I was dead."

The commotion grew louder, and Kamp could tell people were looking for him.

He said, "Who hit you?"

"God *damn*, son, that's what I been askin' you to help me with! Now, go figure it out. Git."

Kamp sprang out of the room and across the repair shop floor. He hit the back door at a dead run, tumbling onto the lawn of the hospital. He heard shouting behind him, but he made it to the tree line and saw that no one chased him.

BY THE TIME THE MOUNTAINS CAME INTO VIEW, Nyx Bauer was beginning to lose feeling in her hands and feet. She'd left the dogs far behind, and it had been hours since she'd heard their baying grow faint and then vanish. In order to make better time, Nyx dropped the potato sack full of food. The rifle she kept.

But she still needed to make considerable distance between herself and her pursuers, and even then, she knew she needed to avoid anyone she didn't know. In other words, Nyx Bauer intended to be invisible as she fled, and she succeeded. She crossed the landscape via forest, stepping onto the road only in the most secluded stretches. And now, as the sun slid behind the trees, she saw smoke curling from a chimney from a cabin way back in the woods. Nyx had reached her destination.

She stepped heavily up the steps and onto the porch. The front door swung open, and the form of a man holding a shotgun appeared in the doorway.

He scanned the woods and said, "Anyone else behind?"

Nyx shook her head, and he put his arm around her, guided her into the cabin and locked the door.

KAMP RAN BY WAY OF RAILROAD TRACKS. He ran because he wanted to lay eyes on his family and because he needed to feel the safety of home. He pushed down a fear that when his home came into view, it would be on fire. It wasn't. When he saw the candle burning in the front window, he slowed to a walk and breathed a sigh. His family would be there, and he'd be able to relax.

When he went in, however, he saw neither Shaw nor Autumn. Instead, the first person he saw was Margaret Hinsdale, standing arms crossed, eyes blazing.

As soon as she saw Kamp, she said, "You must *do* something?"

"Where are they?"

"Who?"

"My family."

"They're upstairs. You know what's happened, don't you?"

"What."

"They've taken him!" She produced a case and removed a cigarette with trembling hands. Kamp struck a match and lit her cigarette. He heard a door close on the second floor, and when Shaw came down the stairs a moment later, he looked at her with raised eyebrows. Her expression gave away nothing.

Margaret Hinsdale inhaled deeply and focused back on Kamp. "Tell me what you know."

Shaw said, "I'm making tea. May I offer you a cup, Mrs. Hinsdale?"

"Yes, please. Thank you. Margaret."

Kamp removed his hat and massaged his forehead. "Margaret, what did your husband say?"

"My husband?"

"Yes, what did he tell you about what happened to your son?"

"He said Becket's under observation. At the hospital."

Shaw returned from the kitchen with a cup of tea and motioned for Margaret Hinsdale to sit down.

Kamp said, "What else did he say?"

"He said Becket's in trouble and that he's not well." She took a sip from the cup. "But I don't believe him."

Shaw said, "Why not?"

Margaret Hinsdale took another sip and then a long drag on her cigarette. She stared out the window as she exhaled the smoke. "Raymond's been acting strangely. Nervous. Secretive."

Kamp said, "Did Becket ever say anything to you about a Jacob Bell or an Onesimus Tucks?"

Margaret Hinsdale erupted, "Oh, for heaven's sake. Let's focus on the present, the real world, shall we?" She looked unhinged, even to Kamp.

"I visited your boy at the hospital. If you want to help him, I suggest going there immediately."

The color drained from her face. "They're going to hurt him, aren't they?"

KAMP AND SHAW WATCHED Margaret Hinsdale walk down the path toward the road and turn back in the direction of her home.

He said, "She didn't ride here?"

"Nope. She said she spent the afternoon searching in the woods for that boy. When her husband came home, he told her the story about the hospital. And then she ran here." Shaw turned to him. "What does any of this have to do with you?"

Kamp paused for a moment and then said, "How's Autumn? How was her day?"

"Her day was fine. She's fine. Don't change the subject."

"What about the bear?"

"The bear looks tired, ready to hibernate."

Kamp went to her, put his arms around her waist. "You're beautiful."

She laughed. "Answer my question."

"Question?"

"Yes."

He looked in her eyes and then searched her face. He brushed the crescent-shaped scar above her eyebrow and then kissed it gently. "Tell me about how you got this. What happened?"

Shaw looked him in the eye. "You really want to know?"

"I do."

"Then answer my question. What does any of this, these people and their problems, have to do with you?"

"You really want to know?"

"I do."

"Honestly?"

She grabbed his ear and twisted it hard. "*Yes.*"

"They need help."

"You can't save them. You can't save that boy."

"I know."

10

Angus led Nyx Bauer to the bedroom, helped her lie down and covered her with a heavy blanket. He drew a pot of water from the well behind the cabin, put it on the stove and went back into the bedroom, unlaced Nyx's boots and slid them off as gently as he could. He did the same with her socks. He saw that all of her toes were badly frostbitten. Angus checked her hands as well. Same thing.

Nyx said, "Is it bad?"

"Naw, just a little frostnip. Rest now."

"I can't feel anything."

"You will, girl, you will."

Angus gently massaged Nyx's right foot and then her left. He pulled out a metal bathtub and set it in the middle of the bedroom floor and filled it with hot water.

He said, "This will do the trick." He took off the rest of her clothes and helped her into the tub.

Nyx screamed, "It's too hot! It's too hot!"

"It just feels that way on account of you're so cold. Give it time."

Angus took a washcloth and washed the dirt from Nyx's face. "Now tilt your head back." He rubbed a bar of soap with both hands and then started working the lather into her hair.

Nyx said, "I didn't know anywhere else to go. Kamp told me I could always come here."

"He's right. Now just relax once. You're safe."

Nyx let herself slide deeper into the steaming water. "It's good to see you again," she said.

The bath complete, Nyx stepped unsteadily from the tub. Angus toweled her off and handed her the bedclothes he'd worn in a previous life.

He fed her the stew he'd made himself for dinner and put her to bed. After a few restless moments, Nyx grew quiet. When he was sure that she was fully asleep, Angus took another look at Nyx's frostbitten toes, which had all turned an angry purple-black color. Maybe, he thought, a few can be saved.

KAMP DIDN'T FALL ASLEEP until the first faint grey of dawn appeared on the horizon. It took him that long to convince himself that there was nothing he could do to save either the kid or Nyx Bauer from their respective fates. But when he awoke to the gold morning light an hour later, he found himself somehow resolved again to do just that.

He went to the courthouse to find the Judge and wring as many details out of him regarding the kid as he could. But the Judge wasn't there. He checked the courtroom as well as the rest of the building and couldn't find the man. He pulled the brim of his slouch hat low, held his jacket closed and leaned into a cold gale as he left the court-house.

Before he even reached the top step, a man blocked his path and pressed two fingers into Kamp's sternum to stop him. Kamp noticed the man's expensive black leather shoes, polished to a bright shine and his grey wool three-piece suit, complete with watch and chain. He looked at the man's face and recognized the prosecutor, Grigg.

Kamp felt the fire sparking to life at the base of his skull. "Stop touching me."

Grigg pulled his hand back and said, "Good morning, Kamp."

"Where's the Judge?"

"I haven't seen him, but perhaps I can answer your questions."

Kamp sized him up. "I doubt it."

Grigg pulled in a breath. "In any case we need to talk.'"

"Then talk."

The prosecutor scanned the sidewalk, the street and the windows of neighboring buildings. "In my office."

Kamp set his jaw. "Say it here."

Grigg lowered his voice. "I have information regarding the child, Becket Hinsdale. And Nyx Bauer. Now, if you'll follow me."

The two men walked back into the courthouse and up a flight of stairs to the office previously inhabited by the late district attorney, Philander Crow. Kamp had often met with Crow in this office during his short tenure, and at the time Kamp had noted the lack of decoration or personal effects of any kind. The same was true now, as the room had bare walls and no pictures, no indication of any kind that an individual worked there.

Grigg took a seat behind the large, oaken desk and gestured for Kamp to sit. He remained standing and kept an eye on the door.

"If you think you're under surveillance or in danger of any kind," Grigg said, "let me assure you that's not the case."

Kamp watched the door for another moment and then looked back at Grigg. "Say what you're going to say."

Grigg picked up a pencil and spun it between his fingers. "People are afraid of Nyx Bauer. They're nervous about when she'll appear again, and about what she intends to do."

Kamp said, "You know what happened to her parents."

"Of course."

"And maybe you can imagine the consequences for Nyx and her sisters. It changed her, is changing her."

Grigg shook his head slightly. "That's not the point." He set the pencil down.

Kamp felt heat spreading across his forehead. "Since her parents were murdered, very few people have demonstrated kindness or compassion to that girl. Many believe she's cursed."

The prosecutor stiffened his gaze. "There are rumors about her. Rumors that she killed a man with a rifle."

"When?"

"Last autumn."

"But you're not certain."

"It's a rumor."

"Did someone find the victim?"

"No."

"Do you know what her motive may have been?"

"I do not." While he spoke, Grigg stared calmly at Kamp.

"No victim, no facts. Just rumor. What's your point?"

"I believe you wrote that the murders of Jonas and Rachel Bauer weren't committed by the fellow who was executed for the crimes but that they were killed by another man, called Hugh Arndt, in the service of a larger plan."

"That's right," Kamp said.

"And then Miss Bauer killed Mr. Arndt, right?"

"I don't know, but if she did, do you blame her?"

Grigg set down the report on the desk. "Of course not. But there's another rumor as well."

Kamp let out a long sigh.

Grigg continued, "The rumor is that she's not done, that she intends to punish all of them."

"That's her business."

"They won't leave her alone. That's why the police were following her, why she was arrested on phony charges and why she would have been in prison for a long time."

Kamp inhaled slowly through his nostrils. "Mr. Grigg, the last time I saw you, you were in my front yard, threatening me, frightening my family."

Grigg, who'd been leaning forward, sat straight up in his chair. "That was for your protection, of course, for the public good. Please do extend my apologies to your family."

Kamp raised his eyebrows. "You're the prosecutor. If she'd been put away, you'd have been the one to put her there."

"She's a secondary concern, although you're right." The prosecutor pulled the watch from his pocket and looked at it. "I bring it up because I know she's a primary concern of yours. And you also want to help the boy, Becket Hinsdale."

Kamp rubbed his left temple and looked at the floor. Grigg stood up and went to the window. He looked out at the stacks of Native Iron, blasting smoke high into the clouds and then at the crowded street below.

He said, "My sense, Kamp, is that you envision yourself as something of a countervailing force against the harmful influences in the community. A moral agent."

"Not exactly."

The prosecutor turned away from the window to look at Kamp. "Since you're not employed by the city anymore, you can act with relative impunity. You have the freedom to do things I can't."

"I don't follow."

Grigg sharpened his focus. "We want the same thing."

"What's that?"

"To expose the Fraternal Order of the Raven. And to destroy it."

"It's in the past."

The prosecutor sat on the edge of the desk in front of Kamp.

He said, "You're highly intelligent and courageous. But in everything you're doing, you're acting alone. A man alone, attempting what you're trying to do, cannot succeed."

Grigg walked behind the desk, opened a drawer and pulled out the copy of the report that Kamp had submitted to the Pennsylvania Attorney General's office a year before.

He said, "It's a masterpiece, produced at dire risk of life and limb, as I understand it. Scandalous and powerful, but ultimately meaningless."

Kamp stared over the prosecutor's shoulder and out the window.

Grigg continued, "I believe that we can work together and bring justice."

"That's what your predecessor thought."

Grigg tilted his head to one side. "Philander Crow wasn't my predecessor, per se. He was a county district attorney, and a disgraced one, at that. I work for the commonwealth. We're committed to smashing the Order of the Raven, starting with Black Feather Consolidated, which is nothing more than a murderous cabal."

Kamp breathed a sigh. "I don't believe you."

The prosecutor held up a silver eight-sided coin that gleamed in the mid-morning sun that slanted in through the window. "Remember this? I know all about it. I know more than you even."

"I said I don't believe you, and I don't trust you. Goodbye." Kamp turned to leave and grabbed the doorknob.

"Becket Hinsdale will be transported to Grace Lutheran Church later this morning. His mother is attempting to have the boy's troubles characterized as a religious matter. You might want to stop by, if you intend to help him."

Kamp said, "All right, I have a request."

"Go ahead."

"I need to see police files for every murder going back twelve years. Can you get them?"

"Of course. And one more item. Apparently, after Miss Bauer killed the man, Hugh Arndt, she buried the body and the head she kept."

"Kept?"

"Indeed. It's been said that she preserved the skull. Although I'm sure you've heard these rumors."

KAMP HADN'T HEARD ANY OF THE RUMORS. He'd avoided the ceaseless stream of community gossip during the past year, and Nyx herself had never mentioned going after Arndt. Made sense, though.

As he hustled from the south side of Bethlehem to the north, Kamp reflected on the day Shaw's father, Joe, had conducted the naming ceremony for their daughter on the mountainside. As Joe held the baby aloft, a single shot had rung out, the source of which he'd never discerned. Perhaps now he knew.

He heard the hammering first, an insistent pounding on metal. And when Kamp crested the hill that brought Grace Lutheran Church into view, he saw a man dangling in a harness from a large wooden crane next to the church building. At first glance, Kamp wondered if perhaps the Reverend A.R. Eberstark had invented a novel form of punishment for his congregants but soon realized the man was doing work of some kind. Thus the hammering. Kamp cut through the cemetery, picking his way among rows of headstones and passing the graves of Jonas and Rachel Bauer. He noticed that Jonas's stone bore the epitaph, "*Wer bis zum Ende ausharrt, wird gerettet werden.*"

Looking toward the church, Kamp also noticed two horse-drawn carriages, the same two that he'd seen when the kid was spirited from the sidewalk on Market Street. The first belonged to the hospital, the second to Raymond Hinsdale.

He scanned the building and the grounds for guards and spotted a man at the far corner and another in a second floor window of the church. Kamp caught the gleam of a rifle barrel as well. He opened his jacket and held his hands wide to show he wasn't armed. As he walked toward the front door of the church, he called out over the hammering, "Friend of the family" and walked in.

The pounding somehow resounded even louder inside the church, echoing powerfully off all the hard surfaces. Kamp strained to listen for voices in the narthex and the nave, heard none, and then went through a door to the left of the pulpit.

He knew it led to the back rooms of the church, because he'd been there before, at the funeral for the Bauers. Kamp heard low voices behind a closed door and knocked softly. The talking stopped.

He said, "It's Kamp."

The door opened, and he saw the frowning, tear-stained face of Margaret Hinsdale. She said nothing and let him enter the room, the office of the Reverend A.R. Eberstark. Raymond Hinsdale was there, along with the High Constable Sam Druckenmiller, the Reverend himself and seated in a chair in the center of the room, the kid. The hammering outside, which had been continuous, stopped. Everyone but the kid stared at Kamp.

Raymond Hinsdale broke the silence by saying, "Nice to see you, Kamp. But with all due respect, this is a family matter."

Without looking at her husband, Margaret Hinsdale said, "He's staying," and the meeting proceeded.

Druckenmiller stared straight ahead and said without warmth, "Morning."

"Morning, Sam."

The Reverend A.R. Eberstark wore his vestments, including a silk, purple chasuble. He cleared his throat and said, "We find ourselves in a most harrowing situation. We're here to—"

At that moment, the hammering started anew, drowning out the Reverend's words. He waited for it to stop, then began again, "Today, we must—"

The pounding started up again. The Reverend's face turned red, and he said to Druckenmiller, "Tell that man to stop!" The High Constable left, and momentarily the banging ceased.

Kamp said, "What are they doing out there anyway?"

"Cloaking the steeple," Eberstark said.

"Beg your pardon?"

"Cloaking the steeple. Encasing it in copper."

Druckenmiller returned and closed the door behind him. "He says he'll take a break once. There's more on the way, though."

The Reverend said, "Thank you, son, that'll be—what do you mean 'more on the way?'"

"Wagons, carriages, men on foot. People comin'. Lots."

Eberstark's eyes grew wide. "Coming for what?"

"Don't know," Druckenmiller said, "mebbe they heard about this here." He gestured to the kid, who sat motionless in the chair, looking at the floor.

Holding his arms wide, the Reverend A.R. Eberstark collected himself, took a deep breath and said, "Yes, well, just as Jesus cast out unclean spirits and so, too, did Martin Luther. Today a foul demon, by the power and grace of the almighty one, will be cast out of this—"

A loud knock came at the window behind Eberstark.

Through the glass a man shouted, "Reverend! Reverend! Open up!"

The color brightened in Eberstark's face as he spun on his heel to face the man. "Not now!"

The importunate man continued, "Reverend, we want to see!"

Eberstark looked over the man's shoulder and saw a crowd forming behind him. "See what?"

"*Ach*, the exorcism!"

They heard a commotion at the front of the church, voices and footfalls that grew louder and then a knock at the office door and another man's voice.

"We heard that boy is demon-possessed. Open up!"

Raymond Hinsdale said, "This is a private matter!"

Through the door, the voice said, "Not no more."

The Reverend A.R. Eberstark collected himself, looked at Margaret and Raymond Hinsdale and said calmly, "Dear ones, this is a sign."

Margaret Hinsdale said, "A sign of what?"

"A sign of the power of the living and almighty god who intends to pour out his grace on this little one. And all those lambs assembled outside must be allowed to witness this miracle, and be blessed thereby. We shall move the solemn ceremony to the front lawn of the church forthwith."

Raymond Hinsdale said, "Are you insane?"

"You're putting the boy in great danger," Kamp said. "You don't know what those people will do once they've turned—"

Eberstark boomed, "God shall not be mocked!"

In a small voice the kid said, "It's all right, son. It's the proper thing to do."

11

By the time the guards had tied the kid to the chair and transported him to a hastily assembled platform on the front lawn, the crowd had created its own center of gravity, pulling in scores of people from every direction. The Reverend A.R. Eberstark took his position on a small wooden pedestal atop the platform. He spread his arms wide, the chasuble giving him the appearance of wings, as if he were a magnificent purple bat.

Eberstark said, "May God's grace be upon all of you as we participate in this sacred ritual."

Kamp studied the Reverend's face and saw a combination of excitement, anticipation and arousal. He looked at the crowd and saw the same expression reflected there. He scanned the scene for Raymond and Margaret Hinsdale. They stood near the door of the church, arms crossed and looking helpless. Margaret Hinsdale smoked a cigarette that bobbed crazily between her lips.

Eberstark spoke again, "We are gathered here today to defend this young one, Becket Hinsdale, from a most foul fiend, who's taken up residence in this boy's very being."

A woman said, "Help that poor boy!" A shudder rippled through the crowd, low murmurs of assent and deeply furrowed brows.

Eberstark said, "With grace and thanks to the most high God, the evidence is clear. We know this demon's nature by the way it evidences itself: secret knowledge, speaking in a way the boy never learned, disrespect for the parents and all manner of rambunctiousness. The demon also transformed this boy into a beast of the field and abetted in the commission of a most nefarious and egregious crime."

The woman in the crowd shouted, "Heaven help that child!"

Another woman said, "May Jesus save him."

The Reverend looked lovingly at each woman in turn. "Let us pray." All bowed their heads, except for Kamp, Raymond and Margaret Hinsdale, and the armed guards. "Dear and merciful Lord, bless us now, give us wisdom and discernment. And help us to gird our loins against the foul fiend. Amen."

Kamp made his way through the throng to Margaret Hinsdale and took a place beside her.

Under her breath she said, "*Do* something."

"How did this happen?"

She said, "I went to the hospital, and they were getting ready to take him away."

"Where?"

"I don't know. But I pleaded with them not to, of course. They said it was ordered by the Judge and that the only exception would be religious one."

"Meaning what?"

"I had to say that I thought he was possessed by a demon."

"Unbelievable."

"In any case they said that if the demon could be exorcised, if they could tell it was really gone, Becket would be able to go free."

"Did you talk to Becket?"

"Yes, I told him all he needed to do was play along and everything would be fine."

"Oh, Jesus."

A hush fell over the restive crowd as an attendant carrying a large bowl of water took his place next to the Reverend.

Eberstark said, "We'll perform with the ritual blowing, beginning with the insufflation."

He bent slowly over the bowl.

"I breathe above the water of this font."

As he inhaled, the Reverend moved his head in the form of the cross. Then he stood up and looked out over the crowd.

"And now the exsufflation." He turned to the kid, bent down and breathed on his face three times in the form of the cross, saying, "Be gone, unclean spirit! Make way for the spirit, the paraclete!"

As Eberstark said it, the kid shook forcefully in his chair, gnashed his teeth, threw his head back, arched violently and then slumped forward.

The crowd fell silent again and leaned in, all eyes fixed on the kid, who stopped moving.

Then a man in the crowd shouted, "The demon has flown!"

"May God bless you, Reverend," a woman said.

Margaret Hinsdale whispered, "Oh please, oh please, Becket." She clasped her hands in front of her.

The Reverend A.R. Eberstark took a step back, and said, "My child, hast thou been healed?"

The kid raised his head, looked out over the crowd, blinking slowly as if he'd just awoken.

He said, "Healed? There wasn't nothing anything with me to start with."

The crowd let out a collective sigh, and the Reverend smiled and said, "This house is clean!" He focused back on the kid and said, "How do you feel, my child?"

The kid said, "Good. I feel good. Loose these cords, please."

"Of course, of course."

Laughter and relief spread through the crowd as the attendant untied the ropes binding the kid's hands and feet.

"Arise, my child."

The kid stood up and smiled, and the crowd cheered. Margaret Hinsdale hugged Kamp.

The Reverend put his hand on the kid's shoulder and said, "Just a few questions so that we know the healing is complete."

"Go ahead."

"My child, what is your name? Where were you born? And who are your parents?"

The kid puffed out his chest and tilted his chin back. He looked over at Kamp and the Hinsdales and gave them a wink.

Margaret Hinsdale pulled in a sharp breath and said, "Oh, no."

In a loud, clear voice the kid said, "My name is Abel Truax. I was born in a low-down holler in West Virginia in the year 1825 to my mother Louisa Truax and my father Martin Truax, may God rest their souls."

Eberstark pulled back in horror, and the crowd erupted.

The kid motioned for everyone to be quiet, then said, "An' iffn' you wanna know somethin' else, one night I heard a swellin' o' trumpets an' then I was killed in this very churchyard, right over there." He pointed toward the side of the building. "Maybe one of y'all standin' here is the one that done it."

The faces in the crowd wore stunned expressions, and no one spoke, except the Reverend, who said, "Demon, from whence hast thou traveled?"

The kid said, "Well, truth be told, after I was murdered, I lived in a tree for two years atop that hillock over yonder." He pointed to the mountain above Kamp's house.

Eberstark said, "You came from the pit!"

"No, no, preacher, I lived in a tree up there, where for two years I saw all manner of things, some beautiful. Some not."

The Reverend hardened his gaze. "And what did you see, foul fiend?"

"Well, I seen you up there more than once."

The crowd gasped.

"*Me?*"

"Yeah, many times I seen you up there in congress with a fine young woman or two."

"What?" The Reverend tried to act shocked.

The kid laughed. "Talk about cloaking the steeple!"

"Enough!" The Reverend went apoplectic, and the people surged toward the platform. Kamp knew that in the people's eyes the kid could transform from victim to sacrifice as quickly as a crowd of ordinary citizens could turn into a mob.

The kid said, "I'm sure you done even worse than that, ain't that right, preacher? Tell these here fine folks what you done in secret. Maybe you's the one with the demon. Maybe we oughta just go ahead an' instuffalate you!"

Eberstark pointed his finger and bellowed, "It's the father of lies himself!"

He clutched his breast with both hands and stumbled backward. The men in the front row of people lunged for the kid who deftly jumped backward, as the mob broke into its frenzy.

The kid pulled the forager's cap from his pocket, put it on his head and jumped down into the swirl, zigzagging sharply amidst the tangle of limbs. Many caught a handful of his shirt or jacket, but none could hold onto him. And eventually they lost track of him altogether. He burst from the back of the crowd and sprinted into the cemetery, escaping the notice of all but one.

The hammering, which had stopped entirely for the proceedings now started again in earnest, and the confused people searched to find its source.

The workman, floating above the scene like some ersatz angel, pointed in the direction of the cemetery and said, "He's there!"

Kamp's eyes went to the guard at the corner of the building. The man was raising his rifle, locating the kid in his sights. Kamp burst into a run and from a distance of a few yards dove at the man with the gun. He led with his elbow, connecting with the shooter's jaw an instant before the gun went off. Both men went hard to the ground.

Kamp scrambled to his knees in time to see the other guard and a uniformed policeman run the kid down amidst the headstones, tackling him and dragging him back into the mob. Some of the people resisted the urge to spit on him. Some didn't. Margaret Hinsdale ran to him and shielded him from the jeering and the scorn.

Kamp scanned the scene for Raymond Hinsdale and saw him rooted to the same spot where he'd been the whole time. He appeared dazed, face ashen.

From the direction of the city, a fast-moving carriage came into view. The driver pulled the horses to a stop in the churchyard. The carriage door popped open, and the prosecutor Grigg bounded out, holding a folded sheet of paper. He located the High Constable and went straight for him.

The sight of Grigg roused Raymond Hinsdale from his stupor. He walked to where Grigg and Druckenmiller conferred. Kamp noticed that the Reverend A.R. Eberstark tried several times to join the conversation but was rebuffed. Kamp himself made his way toward the group of men, as well. He saw Druckenmiller telling the story of what had just happened and Grigg nodding. Raymond Hinsdale listened but did not say anything.

Some of the spectators, meanwhile, had gone to the vegetable garden behind the church, because they needed something rotten to throw. The guard and the policeman pulled the kid away from Margaret Hinsdale and marched him back to the platform, and Grigg stepped up and stood next to him.

The prosecutor cleared his throat. "By order of the Honorable Tate Cain, Judge, Northampton County—"

A tomato soared out of the crowd and barely missed Grigg's head.

"Stop that!" he shouted. "Settle down. Effective this day, November twenty-three, in the year of our lord, eighteen hundred and seventy-two and by order of the Honorable Tate Cain, this boy, Becket Hinsdale, is hereby remanded to the Pennsylvania Hospital for the Insane."

The announcement brought a volley of rancid vegetables from the mob. A fetid head of cabbage hit Raymond Hinsdale in the chest.

The men with guns cleared a path through the mob for Druckenmiller to lead the kid to the hospital carriage.

Margaret Hinsdale shrieked, "Why, Becket?"

The kid looked at her and then found Kamp.

He said, "I had t' do it, son. I had t' try an' draw out the killer. I know you understand. It's up to you to figure it out from here."

Druckenmiller ducked the kid's head as he loaded him into the carriage. The driver snapped the reins, the horses bolted forward, and the carriage was gone.

A pair of women from the church consoled the Reverend A.R. Eberstark, each taking an elbow, cooing and walking him gently back into the church. The armed guards saddled up and rode away. A stone-faced Raymond Hinsdale guided his sobbing wife to their fine carriage and departed, too. One by one or in pairs, the mob diffused back into the landscape until the only people left outside were Kamp and the workman, still suspended in mid-air, who finished pounding the last copper panel into place.

The man holstered his hammer and via the rope and pulley lowered himself softly to the ground. He stepped out of his harness and stared up at the steeple, scratching the whiskers on his chin.

With a look of satisfaction, he turned to Kamp, tipped his hat and said, "All in a day's work."

12

Over the years Shaw had grown accustomed to seeing Kamp walk home looking tired and dirty. It wasn't uncommon to see him come through the door splattered head-to-toe in mud from the fields or covered in sawdust. But rarely, if ever, had she stood at the window and watched Kamp trudge the path to their front door with his head hanging low. He did so now. She also noticed a hitch in his step.

The little girl noticed nothing amiss with her father's bearing, or if she did, she sought to correct it immediately. Autumn ran out onto the porch as soon as Shaw said, "Daddy's here."

Kamp, who'd been lost in a forlorn reverie, looked up to see his daughter's face and looked into her luminous eyes, one brown, one blue. Her joy at seeing him put a lump in his throat. He scooped her up in his arms and held her high as she giggled.

155

In a very earnest voice she said, "Where *were* you?"

For the first time that day, Kamp smiled and said, "At church."

He set her down, and Shaw took her turn, putting her arms around Kamp. He pulled her to him, and she laid her head against his chest. Shaw inhaled deeply and caught a variety of scents, including dirt, sweat and gunpowder.

"You don't smell like church," she said.

OVER THE STEW Shaw prepared, Kamp told her the story of the failed exorcism. After the meal, Kamp made a fire and played with Autumn until she grew tired. By the light of the fire, he read her a story as she fell asleep in a nest of blankets on the floor. Kamp felt a powerful relaxation overtaking him as well. He unlaced his boots, took them off and stretched out on the floor next to his daughter.

He said, "Shaw, tell me a story."

From the kitchen, she said, "What story?"

"Tell me what happened to that missionary. The Shakespeare one."

He felt the dream machine starting, throwing pictures onto the back of his eyelids. He blinked his eyes hard and opened them to stay awake as Shaw walked back into the room and sat down next to him cross-legged. She twirled a forelock of his hair.

"You don't look long for this world."

"I saw their gravestones."

"Whose?"

"Jonas and Rachel Bauer."

"Oh, my love." She stroked his forehead with the back of her hand.

He looked up at her. "Tell me what happened to the missionary."

"I think you already know what happened."

"The details. I need to hear the details."

She cradled his head and rubbed the star-shaped scar at his left temple. "Now cracks a noble heart."

Kamp fought sleep. "Do you want to know what it said? Jonas Bauer's stone?"

"Of course."

It said, "*Wer bis zum Ende ausharrt, wird gerettet werden.*"

"What does that mean?"

His eyes were closed now. "He that shall endure unto the end will be saved. Shaw?"

"Yes?"

"Is that true?"

The words trailed off as he said them, and he became quiet. She watched the heavy, even rise and fall of his chest.

"And flights of angels sing thee to thy rest," she said.

KAMP WOKE UP ALONE ON THE FLOOR. Red and orange embers in the fireplace warmed his feet, and the blanket Shaw had placed on him before going to bed warmed the rest of him. He lay on the floor for a few minutes, tensing various parts of his body to see where it hurt most.

He began with his left arm, the one that had taken a bullet the year before, flexing the bicep and then the tricep. No pain there. Kamp then bent his right elbow, which had been broken in a leap from a moving train. The elbow was stiff and sore but not as sore as Kamp's right hip, a casualty of the same unfortunate fall from the train. The old injuries, Kamp knew, had been aggravated when he'd tackled the man with the rifle and landed on his right side. He exercised his muscles gently, feeling life come back into them.

He reflected on the dream he'd been having just before he awoke. He'd been an observer in the Garden of Eden, the moment of expulsion. In the dream Adam was Raymond Hinsdale and Eve the shame-faced Margaret. A snake with a million geometrical patterns and a multitude of colors on its skin slithered around their ankles. He couldn't see its face.

Kamp rubbed his eyes with his thumb and forefinger, banished the dream and stood up when he heard the familiar cries of the bear outside. He laced up his boots and went out to find the bear pacing back and forth by the bulkhead doors. Even in the pre-dawn black, he could tell the animal had grown considerably since he'd seen her last and figured she must be approaching seventy or eighty pounds. He swung one of the doors open as quietly as the hinge would allow.

He said, "Good morning, girl," as the bear vanished down the stairs.

He knew he had hours until his family woke up and even longer until he could find anyone he needed to talk to in town. Kamp went to the back room of the house, where the mother bear's hide remained salted and stretched between the two saw horses. By the light of a lantern, he removed the last bits of flesh and moved onto preparing the solution for pickling the hide. He drew water from the well behind the house into a barrel and added the chemicals in the correct amounts before placing the hide in the barrel to soak.

By this time the dawn chorus was going full-throat, and he saw the first purple glow of morning. He put on a clean shirt and then his canvas work jacket, headed out the backdoor and up the mountain trail behind his house.

Kamp passed the clearing where he'd heard the rifle's crack just before Shaw's father held the baby aloft and spoke her true name for the first time. Kamp continued on to the oak tree close to the top, where he and his brothers played war, where he'd run when the word came that his oldest brother was dead.

He knew that this was the tree the kid said he'd lived in for two years after he was killed. The kid said he'd seen the Reverend's trysts here. How many people had met here and for what secret purposes, Kamp would never know. He tilted his head back, gazed up into the branches and back down at the ground. Nothing grew on the ground at the base of the tree. No flowers, no grass. He thought about the kid again. Why would anyone, even a ghost, live in a tree for two years?

The scream of the Black Diamond Unlimited pulled him from his reflections. His muscles and joints felt warm and probably as good as they'd feel all day. By the sound of the train whistle, he calculated he had ten minutes to get to the tracks and catch out. And it would take him just about that long to get there. So Kamp broke into a run.

THE ROOSTER STOOD ON THE FENCE beside the henhouse, arched his neck and let fly with the first cock-a-doodle-do of the morning, though Angus was already awake. In truth he'd barely slept since the girl trudged to his front door, clutching the rifle with her blue fingers. He'd fallen asleep easily enough but didn't dream and soon awoke. Angus had gotten out of bed, lit the lantern, and with great care disassembled the gun Nyx brought with her.

He could tell the gun had seen a great deal of use and had been expertly maintained. The Henry only needed a cleaning and some oil, and it was already up to Angus's high standards. His hands moved quickly, no motion wasted, and the gun was back together by sunup.

Nyx had brought no bullets, though. Angus would fix that soon, but not now. The rooster, meanwhile, had reached the height of his crowing. Angus figured the bird had to have woken up Nyx, but when he checked in on her, she wasn't moving, save for the easy rise and fall of her ribcage. He peeled back the blankets where they covered her feet. Nyx's toes appeared even blacker than the night before.

He went to the kitchen, cooked oatmeal and biscuits and set them on a tray next to Nyx's bed. He doused the cooking fire, closed the heavy wooden shutters on every window and locked them.

Angus wriggled into the girdle he wore whenever he left his cabin. It covered his torso, flattening his breasts entirely. Over that, he put on a heavy flannel shirt. From a canister on the windowsill, Angus took a handful of bear fat and rubbed it in his hair. He combed it straight back, except the long forelock, which he combed upward. Angus laced up his heavy boots and put on his winter coat. He wrote a note and set it on the table next to Nyx's breakfast. It read, "Back later."

He picked up the rifle he always kept by the front door and left, locking the front door behind him. Angus went to the fence where the rooster continued crowing.

Angus said, "*Kumm mitt mich*, Charles," and picked up the bird under his arm. He put the greatly discomfited rooster into the henhouse and locked that door, too. Angus studied his cabin's chimney for a long moment to see if any smoke still issued from it. None there.

AS SOON AS THE TRAIN pulled into the South Side station, Kamp jumped down out of the boxcar and went searching for answers to the mounting number of questions. He went to Grigg's office first to retrieve the files that the prosecutor had said he'd provide. But the man wasn't there, and his office door was locked. Through the office window, Kamp saw a stack of files and thought perhaps they were the ones he wanted. He wrapped his jacket around his fist and cocked it back, preparing to smash the window.

"Oh, don't go to all that trouble." Grigg called to him from the end of the hall. "I have the key."

Once inside the office, Grigg spread the files across the top of the otherwise empty desk.

"What you asked for. It's all here. Every scrap of paper related to each murder committed by one or more of the upstanding human beings in this fine city."

"For the past twelve years."

Grigg nodded slowly. "For the past twelve years. May I inquire as to the purpose of your researches?"

Kamp ignored the question and began leafing through the first few files.

Grigg said, "There's none named Truax. I already checked."

"What about Tucks?"

"Who?"

"Onesimus Tucks."

"Not that I recall."

Kamp looked at Grigg for the first time. "Do you know anything about a murder of a runaway slave?"

"I'm new in town. And slavery's over, remember? If such a crime had been committed, it would have to have been a long time ago."

"I realize that."

"And if it were the killing of a runaway slave, it likely wouldn't have even been considered a crime. Alas."

Grigg noticed the tension in his Kamp's jaw, the dirt on his elbows, the furrow in his brow. "You're frantic, disheveled. You're hunting ghosts. They don't exist."

Kamp rubbed his left temple with the first two fingers of his left hand. "What do you want, Grigg?"

"What do *I* want?"

"Yes, as payment."

Grigg closed the office door. "Information."

"Like what?"

Grigg let the question hang until Kamp looked up from the files to face him. "Where's Nyx Bauer?"

"Don't know."

"You're lying."

"You told me you wanted to expose the Order of the Raven. Dismantle it."

"That's right, Black Feather as well," Grigg said.

"What does Nyx have to do with that?"

"Two things. First, they think she's plotting revenge against them for ordering the killing of her parents. And second, they believe she has more, or has access to more, information that could harm them."

"She doesn't."

"In any case I've learned that they've sent a hunter to find her. A professional."

"Who?"

"They wouldn't tell me."

13

The crowing of the rooster didn't wake Nyx Bauer, and neither did the sound of Angus cooking breakfast or locking the door, saddling up and riding away. All these sounds she expected and allowed to soothe her while she slept. But in the way that someone can listen to the outside world even while sleeping and never entirely rest, she remained vigilant.

The sound that woke her was a soft prying sound, more of a request to enter than a demand. Nyx heard it at a window in the front room, the sound of a quiet visitor gently tugging on the shutter to see if it was unlocked. As soon as she located the source of the sound, Nyx's heart began to thud. Someone was trying to get in, to break in. That the person was working so quietly troubled Nyx even more. Precise and persistent, she could tell.

Nyx heard heels knocking on the porch as the person shifted from window to window. Her eyes went to the doorway of the bedroom and to the back of the cabin's main room where a rack of gleaming rifles stood ready. Silently, Nyx pulled back the blankets and swung her feet over the side of the bed. And without thinking, she tried to stand up. Nyx bit down hard on her bottom lip to stifle the scream that started when her ruined feet hit the floor.

Tears streamed down her face as she waited for the wave of pain to pass. She lowered herself to the floor and began crawling on hands and knees. Nyx heard nothing outside now but a raven's slow croak.

She focused on the gun rack, sizing up each weapon. She preferred rifles but assumed they were all unloaded, and she didn't see any cartridges. She zeroed in on a 12-gauge shotgun, action open, on Angus's work counter. Beside it lay two shells.

Nyx heard a noise at the back door and saw the brass doorknob jiggling. If the lock gave way or if the person simply forced open the door, Nyx knew she'd be a goner. She considered lunging for the shotgun and taking her chances in a firefight. She felt certain that the noise of making a move would give her away, though. And she didn't trust her frostbitten fingers to do what she wanted.

She decided to wait. The knob stopped moving. Nyx counted a breath, then another. If the person were coming, she thought, they were coming now. She tensed to spring, but the moment never arrived. She heard boot heels on the porch outside once more, and again, then nothing. Nyx crawled to the window in the front room. Rising to her knees, she unlatched the shutter and pulled it open a sliver.

She saw a lone figure crossing the clearing, moving toward the creek. The figure wore a grey hunting cloak, hood up, and a rifle on a shoulder strap with brass fittings that reflected sunlight. She could see that a scope sat atop the rifle. Even though Nyx hadn't made a sound and even though the shutter was barely open, at the moment she looked outside, the figure turned to look back at the cabin. Due to the hood, Nyx couldn't see a face, and after a moment, the figure disappeared into the woods.

KAMP SAT HUNCHED over his stack of files in the library of the college where he'd studied when he returned from the war. At the time, he'd needed to find silence and solitude to let the slow healing commence. He'd always gone up to this particular desk by way of a spiral staircase at the back corner on the building's third floor, a spot walled in by stacks of ancient tomes and with a view all the way to Native Iron and beyond that, the river. Often times, he'd sit back in his chair and let the conflicts of men play before his mind's eye, those he'd taken part in, those he'd observed and those he couldn't stop imagining.

He fought to focus on the task at hand, though Grigg's words spun in his mind, the part about how he was chasing ghosts of Abel Truax; of Nyx Bauer, the girl who'd died the moment a madman invaded her sleep; and of himself, the boy he was before men in blue wool uniforms appeared to deliver the news, the boy who'd buried his red hat. Sitting, staring at the stacks, Kamp tumbled backward in his memory, through years of empty searches, lost causes, fresh graves.

But at this desk he'd begun to try to live a life in the present, and here, apparently, he was trying to do it again. Each file before him was written up in the same way, more or less. Name, cause of death, and a few brief comments. Kamp had asked for twelve years' worth of murder files, and Grigg had said he'd given him all of them. He counted them now and found there were nine files in all.

Kamp himself had killed several men and knew of at least eight more killings, including the murders of Jonas and Rachel Bauer. Yet none of the homicides he'd committed or knew about appeared in the official records. Nothing about Roy Kunkle or the others blown to pieces in the coal mine. Nothing about the shotgun murder of the district attorney Philander Crow or the assassination of the coal boss Silas Ownby. All invisible to the public, all officially lost.

From what he could tell, all the files in front of him, the cases officially ruled as homicides, could easily have been suicides. There were three deaths by hanging, five single gunshot wounds and a drowning. None of the cases had been solved, no arrests made. Kamp reflected on his year as Bethlehem's first-ever police detective. He recalled that whenever he'd attempted to investigate an incident as murder, he was quickly and persistently dissuaded from doing so.

Nevertheless, he was certain that none of the cases before him could have been a West Virginian named Abel Truax or a freed slave named Onesimus Tucks, because all of the murder victims in the official files were women.

Kamp knew the police files could offer him nothing, fragmented and misleading as they were. But he knew of another source of information, a much more detailed, comprehensive accounting of the dead. He stuffed the murder files into his haversack and departed his former sanctuary. As he left the library, he reflected once more on the topic of chasing ghosts, wondering if, since he returned from war, he'd been capable of doing anything else.

Kamp hurried down South Mountain to the mayhem of Fourth Street at midday and angled across town to the building that housed the morgue.

In his time as detective, he'd learned that there was no process, no event more dependable than death, and no official more consistent or efficient in cataloguing death than the coroner, A.J. Oehler. Kamp relied on the cool quiet of Oehler's morgue, and the sound of the coroner's pencil scratching out the corporeal details but never noting the dreams of the dead.

He saw Oehler there now, inspecting a body, taking notes. Oehler had a wispy fringe of grey hair around an otherwise hairless, pink head, giving him an appearance not unlike a Teutonic vulture.

Kamp cleared his throat.

Without looking up, Oehler said, "Oh, I know it's you. I'm just not paying attention."

"Nice to see you, too."

"What do you want?"

"How long you been in this job, A.J.?"

"I'm busy, Kamp."

"Were you already on the job back in, say, sixty-one?"

"Your point, please."

The coroner covered one body and moved to the next, pulling back the sheet to reveal an old man with a caved-in skull. Oehler resumed the note-taking.

"I have to find someone who died, probably eleven years ago. It was a man in his thirties. Died from a blow to the back of his head, or the back of his neck. Let me look at your files."

Oehler said, "I don't remember."

"There was another man. A runaway slave. Around the same time. Maybe even in the same place. Lutheran Church. Both murdered, maybe."

"Then talk to the police. You remember the police? All those fellows who tried to help you and despise you now."

"I already did."

Oehler stopped writing and looked at him. "Well, I don't remember, I don't care, and, no, you may not look at the files under any circumstances."

Kamp felt flames of anger tickling the base of his skull.

He said, "I know you don't care about doing the right thing, either. You make your living writing things down, but none of them, none of these people matter to you, do they? Everyone of us is just like the rest. You just run 'em through, like a factory. Is that it?" Kamp gestured to the roomful of corpses.

The coroner removed his wireframe glasses, looked him in the eye, and said, "You're insulting me, insulting the integrity of the work I do, of which you know nothing and understand even less. You have no regard for anyone, living or dead, but yourself. You are a fool, and you have no business here."

Kamp pulled in a deep breath. "The white man was murdered outside the Lutheran church eleven years ago. Possibly the black man as well. Their names were Abel Truax and Onesimus Tucks, respectively. If you had anything to do with it—and by that I mean, if you performed the postmortems—I'm sure you'd remember it."

"Kamp?"

"Yes."

"Get the hell out of here."

THE MORE PEOPLE DISAVOWED KNOWLEDGE of a murder or said they didn't remember it, the more certain Kamp became that it had happened. He realized that this logic was unsound. But in practical experience, he'd found that often the pattern held true. And, of course, the more forceful and obstreperous the denials, the greater the likelihood of any person's involvement. In war it was the opposite. Everyone wanted credit for the kill. Moral inversion.

Kamp shuffled back over the bridge, staring over the railing and comparing the river's turbid swirls to his ruminations. The less people told him, the greater his compulsion to reveal the invisible, the narrow road to madness. His boot heels scuffed on the wooden bridge as he fixed his sights on the police station.

An armed guard stood at the door, and when the man noticed him approaching, Kamp saw his shoulders tense and his grip on the shotgun tighten. Kamp relaxed and took a deep breath.

Kamp said, "*Wie gehts?*"

"What?"

"How goes it?"

"It goes."

Kamp saw the blood drain from the man's knuckles as he squeezed the stock of the gun, though his finger wasn't on the trigger.

The guard said, "Show me."

"Show you what?"

An emotion passed across the man's brow. It may have been annoyance, or malice. "That you don't have no gun, nor no knife."

Kamp held his jacket open, lifted his hat above his head and then showed the man the contents of the haversack.

"Boots, too." The man sniffed, cleared his throat and spat on the ground, while Kamp took off one boot, then the other and turned them upside down. The man motioned for Kamp to go inside.

The High Constable Sam Druckenmiller sat back in his chair, feet up and boots off, reading a broadsheet. When he saw Kamp, he winced.

Kamp said, "You look comfortable."

"Yah, well, why wouldn't I be?" Druckenmiller set down the paper and planted his feet on the floor.

"I guess if I had a guy with a shotgun protecting me, I'd feel comfortable, too."

"I don't have no time for your horseshit today. And that guy out there, not my idea."

"Whose was it?"

"What do you want now?"

"Answer one question."

Druckenmiller's face went purple. "*Ach*, one question, then another and another and another! It don't quit with you. You promise to shut up, and then you don't. You promise to go away, and then you come back."

"The rifle, Sam. The Henry I saw in your cellar."

"Ach, *leave!*"

The front door opened, and the guard leaned his head in. Druckenmiller said, "It's all right, it's okay." The guard shut the door again.

"Eleven years ago, a man who came here from West Virginia, looking for a runaway slave. He brought that rifle with him, and he was murdered. And the rifle ended up in your cellar. That means there's a direct line between you and a murder. My question, Sam."

"Yah."

"How did you get that gun?"

The High Constable scratched his head and rubbed his eyes, focused on Kamp and said, "Years ago, my pappy had a farm. Vegetable farm, a big, beautiful garden, ya know. Acres and acres. My pappy loved it. But there was one problem."

"What was that?"

"Ach, the *grundsow*. *Grundsow* diggin' his holes and tunnels hither and yon. Pappy goes to plow the field, workhorse steps in one of them holes and snap, there goes a leg. All Pappy wanted to do was farm the field. All the horse wanted to do was plow that furrow. They was just minding their own business. And now Pappy has to put the horse down just because of a worthless god-damned groundhog."

"Answer my question, Sam."

"That's what you are, Kamp. A *grundsow* that keeps diggin' holes and poppin' up here and there. But Pappy had a solution for his problem, same one as for you, someday."

Kamp reached across the desk and slapped Drucken-miller hard on his face and grabbed a handful of his shirt. Through gritted teeth, he said, "Where'd you get the Henry?"

Druckenmiller said, "Someone seen your cousin in town today. Your cousin, Agnes. Remember her? Except they said she looks more like a man now. Like she wants people to think she's a man."

"The gun, Sam. Where'd you get it?"

"Agnes is a good girl, I'm sure. But folks don't like to see something disgusting like that. Makes 'em nervous and *boseheit*, ya know, very angry. You should talk to your cousin before something bad happens to her, too."

The fire erupted at the base of Kamp's skull, and he closed his free hand around Druckenmiller's throat. Before Kamp could cut off his breath completely, Drucken-miller let out a loud croak. The guard burst through the door, gun raised, finger on the trigger. Kamp relaxed his grip.

Druckenmiller said, "Show this man the door."

KAMP KNEW HIS COUSIN would never risk going to town unless the situation were urgent. And he knew there was only one person in Bethlehem Angus trusted. When he reached the door of the pharmacy, Kamp saw a hand-written sign that read, "Gone for the day." He sprinted around the back of the building, where he saw E. Wyles standing next to her horse and cinching the saddlebag that clinked with the sound of metal implements. She put a foot in the stirrup.

"Emma."

"Not now."

"I have to go with you."

"It's private business." E. Wyles swung her leg over the horse's back, snapped the reins and was gone.

14

Kamp reached the train yard as the wheels of the Black Diamond Unlimited started turning. He knew the locomotive was headed back up the line and that if he caught it, he had a decent chance of getting to Angus's cabin before E. Wyles. He tossed his canvas haversack in an empty boxcar, climbed in after it and situated himself in a dark corner. Getting on this train was easy enough, he thought. Getting off would be harder.

He watched landscape fall away through the open door, the last yellow blades of autumn and brown branches under an iron sky. The train chugged past homesteads with sturdy clapboards and fresh paint, and farms with grain silos that soon gave way to hills thick with trees and bare outcroppings of rock with just enough space for the river to slither through with the Black Diamond Unlimited alongside it.

The back-and-forth sway of car put Kamp in a lucid trance that slowed his thinking. He replayed the conversation with Druckenmiller. He hadn't expected the High Constable to share information with him, especially information linking him to a murder. Druckenmiller's refusal to answer the question didn't mean the man knew precisely how or why he had the rifle. People often preferred not to know the origin or history of a gun in their possession. But knowing Druckenmiller, if there had been a simple story, he would have told it. And the High Constable had never threatened him before. Something must have emboldened him. Kamp reflected on the moment the guard came through the door, shotgun raised, first finger on the trigger. He knew the man wouldn't shoot. Why did he feel certain of this?

THE UNLIMITED BLASTED ITS WHISTLE as it rounded the bend for Lehighton. He remembered that sometimes the train stopped there, and sometimes it didn't. He'd know soon enough, though, because if it were stopping, he'd feel the train begin to slow. And he had to get off, regardless. His cousin's cabin was a few miles due east of the town. It became clear that the train wasn't stopping. A few more shrieks of the whistle, and the Unlimited reached the rusty truss bridge over the river.

The last time Kamp jumped from a moving train, it hadn't gone well. Instead of landing in a fluffy snow drift, he'd crashed into a submerged railroad tie. His prospects for a safe landing looked even worse now. The rocky riverbank dropped sharply to the water, and the river itself looked far too shallow. Still, he had to get off, now.

Kamp stood up, cinched the strap of his haversack around his wrist and prepared to make his leap. He saw that three-quarters of the way down the bank, fifteen feet or so, jagged rocks gave way to loose gravel. Kamp took two steps back. The Unlimited let loose one more wild shriek, and he launched himself out of the boxcar. He sailed over the rocks and down the steep bank, heels digging squarely into soft gravel before momentum and gravity conspired to take him tumbling head over feet to the river's edge.

He stood up, brushed himself off and tested his limbs. Definitely nothing broken. Apart from muddy knees and a new tear in the elbow of his jacket, he was no worse for the wear. Kamp picked his way across the dry tops of rocks in the river and hopped onto the far bank. In an hour he'd be at the cabin.

"WELL, WHEREVER THE HELL I AM, it's better than the last place they had me. Better by a damn sight," the kid said.

"And where was that?" the nurse said. She wore a spotless, white linen dress with a plain, matching mob cap.

"Hospital in Bethlehem. Had me rolled up tight in a closet."

Without smiling, the nurse said, "No one's going to do that to you here."

The kid said, "Well, if that's so, would you go ahead an' loose these binds?"

The nurse ignored the question.

"How'd I get here anyways? I don't remember no journey, not at all."

"Well, you're here now." While she talked, the nurse poured liquid from a colored glass bottle into a table spoon.

"Where's here?"

"Open your mouth."

The nurse approached him with the tablespoon.

She said, "This is the Pennsylvania Asylum for the Insane."

With a little more force than necessary, the nurse shoved the spoon in the kid's mouth. He gagged and then swallowed.

A smile spread across the kid's face. He said, "Nurse?"

"Yes."

"No matter what anyone says, you don't seem insane to me. Not at all."

"Becket, you're safe here. Our mission is to restore you to health, and I assure you we will be unflagging in our efforts until you're all better again."

"Unflagging, huh."

"Yes."

"Nurse?"

"Yes, Becket."

"Two things. First off, I greatly appreciate what you just said. I can see I'm better off here than anywheres else. And second, I'd love a smoke right about now. You wouldn't happen to have a cigarette, wouldja?"

"Of course not."

AS SOON AS KAMP got within fifty yards of the cabin, Angus appeared on the front porch, holding a rifle across his chest.

He called out, "Normally I shoot first."

When Kamp reached the porch, Angus hugged him a little harder and a moment longer than usual and then took a step back.

Angus said, "Let me look at you. Jesus but you look a little rough."

"Nice to see you, too."

He waited for Angus to invite him inside, and when he didn't, Kamp said, "How's she doing?"

Angus made a wry face. "She's better now, or she will be soon enough."

He took a long look at his cousin. "I heard you went to Bethlehem."

"Yah."

"Are you all right?"

Angus met his gaze. He said, "This ain't about me" and led him into the cabin.

It didn't surprise Kamp that E. Wyles had gotten there first, after all. What did surprise him was how much work she'd already accomplished. Water boiled on the stove, and an assortment of bandages and medicines were arrayed on the dining room table.

He knocked softly on the bedroom door and then cracked the door open. He saw E. Wyles drawing liquid into a syringe from a small medicine bottle. She looked at him over her shoulder, then shook her head.

Kamp entered the room and saw Nyx lying on her back. Her hair was fever-sweat matted to her forehead, and her eyes rolled in their sockets.

When she focused on Kamp, she said, "It's me this time."

Wyles inserted the needle into Nyx's arm and depressed the plunger.

Kamp gently brushed the hair from Nyx's forehead and said, "Everything is all right."

Nyx stared into his eyes until the drug took hold. She said, "No, it's not" and slid into semi-consciousness.

Wyles put the stopper in the medicine bottle and turned to Kamp. "Since you're here, you might as well do something useful."

Angus stood in the doorway, and Wyles said to him, "Keep lookout." She turned back to Kamp and looked him up and down. "Change your clothes, scrub your arms and hands. Get as clean as possible."

As she said it, Wyles set the wooden case on the bed next to Nyx and opened it. Kamp saw an assortment of surgical tools. She pulled back the blankets to reveal Nyx's frostbitten toes. He immediately recognized the sight and smell of gangrene.

"Kamp, get ready. And hurry up."

WHEN KAMP RETURNED he saw that Wyles had scrubbed both of Nyx's feet, and under them, she'd placed a metal pan. He noticed, too, that she'd strapped Nyx's lower body to the bed. From the wooden surgical case, Wyles selected a metacarpal saw with a fine ivory handle.

She said to him, "You'll her down at first. Then, you'll help me control the bleeding while I tie off the blood vessels. Understand? This will go fast."

He placed his palms on Nyx's shoulders, and faced away from Wyles. Nyx didn't stir. He heard Wyles draw a deep breath, and then she said, "Here goes."

An instant later, Nyx's eyes opened wide and she thrashed under Kamp's hands. Nyx wailed, "Daddy! Daddy! Make them stop." Then she shut her eyes.

Kamp looked back over his shoulder and saw that Wyles was working with great speed and precision. In seconds, she'd sliced off two toes. He turned back to face the wall and heard another toe land in the metal pan.

Wyles said, "All right, one more thing."

Nyx opened her eyes and looked at Kamp, "No more, no more! Don't let them do it."

Kamp said, "Why don't you—"

He turned around to see Wyles holding Nyx's left wrist tight. In one deft motion, she sliced off the little finger.

Nyx's body went slack, as the blood sprayed.

Wyles said, "That's it. Stanch the bleeding there, while I tend to her feet."

Kamp followed her instructions, and within minutes, Wyles had sutured and dressed all of Nyx's wounds. She put all of the blood-soaked gauze and linens in the metal pan and handed it to Kamp. Lastly, she removed the straps from Nyx, who now lay motionless. Wyles wiped the sweat from Nyx's forehead and then motioned for Kamp to leave the room. She closed the door behind him.

Through the back window of the cabin, he could see that Angus had started a fire outside. When the bedroom door opened again, E. Wyles emerged wearing a clean white dress, and she handed the clothes she'd been wearing to Kamp.

"Burn everything," she said.

He set Wyles' clothes atop the metal pan and carried it all out the back door to the fire. He tossed it into the blaze, including the pan and the severed digits. He looked at his own clothes, covered with splotches of blood. Kamp unlaced his boots and took off all of his clothes and threw them in the fire, too. He carried his boots back into the cabin. When Wyles saw his naked body, she turned, scoffing.

"You said, 'everything.' "

Angus followed Kamp in the door and gave a laugh. "Don't worry, cousin. Nothing I haven't seen before. I got some clothes you can wear. Clean. Follow me."

Angus gave him a union suit, canvas pants, a flannel shirt and a pair of wool socks. After he got dressed, Angus said, "Good as new."

When Kamp returned to the main room of the cabin, E. Wyles was packing up the medical case and cinching the bag she'd brought. She put on her coat and scarf.

Without looking at him, she said, "I need to go."

"Where?"

"There are a number of expectant mothers who require my assistance."

"Ach, you can't just—"

"And I must return to the store tomorrow."

Wyles disappeared into the bedroom. She turned out the lantern next to Nyx's bed and left the room, closing the door behind her.

He said, "Is she going to be all right?"

"I don't know. She's hypovolemic. In shock."

"And you're just going to leave her here?"

Wyles approached Kamp and stood directly in front of him. "I removed all of the gangrenous tissue. But there's little else to do, except for keeping the wounds clean and making sure that she's properly nourished. Angus can do that. And when she comes to, be certain to keep her off her feet. Understand?"

"At least stay here tonight."

For all the years Kamp had known E. Wyles, he'd rarely ever seen her angry. Now, she appeared enraged.

"Do you realize that each minute I stay here is a grave risk to all of us?"

"How so?"

"People will realize, if they haven't already, that I'm gone and that I left shortly after Angus visited me. They'll deduce that Nyx is here. And you coming here is even worse. If we're found here, we'll be slaughtered."

"Then we need to move."

"She can't travel yet. She has to be much more stable."

"How long will that take?"

E. Wyles stood up straight and pulled in a breath. "The best thing for you to do is to leave. Go home to your family. And keep away from Nyx."

Wyles slung her bag over her shoulder, picked up the medical case and headed for the back door.

As she left, Kamp called after her, "Tell Shaw I'll be home as soon as I'm certain Nyx is all right. She'll understand."

KAMP AND ANGUS DIDN'T TALK as the long night passed, but neither did they sleep. Instead, they listened, Kamp at the kitchen table and Angus in a chair by an upstairs window. They listened for sounds of distress in Nyx's bedroom, for barking dogs in the distance or for the crunch of footsteps on fallen leaves close by. They listened to the voices in their own minds, voices from far back in their shared past, voices that preached shame and foretold doom.

In the first charcoal light of dawn, Angus came quietly down the stairs and pulled on his boots.

He said, "Morning, cousin," and went out the door.

Kamp went to the window and watched Angus douse the fire in the back yard with a bucket of water that sent up one great grey plume of smoke. Angus inspected the ground, sifting through the cinders and picking up pieces here and there. He found the metal pan and tossed the handful of pieces into it.

When he came back into the house, Angus went to his workbench, lit a lantern and dumped out the contents of the pan. The bones from Nyx's toes and first finger clattered onto the wooden bench.

"All that's left," Angus said.

15

Shards of morning light slanted across the kid's face, and he squinted hard against them. His hands were still strapped fast to the bedframe. The door opened, and the nurse from the day before reappeared.

"Mornin', sunshine," he said.

"Hello, Becket. How are you?"

"You wanna know?"

"Yes."

"You really wanna know?"

"Yes, I do."

"Shee-*it*, I'm amazin'. I'm right as rain on this fine blue sky sunny day."

"Please refrain from using foul language, Becket."

"Right. Shit. Of course. Say, would you loose these binds? I'd like to shake the dew off the lily of my own accord, iff'n it's all right by you."

"Becket, today you're going to meet a man." As she spoke, the nurse unbuckled the straps at his wrists and ankles. "A very important man would like to speak with you."

"Got a name, has he?"

"The man who runs this hospital. Does that sound good?"

"Sure. Say, where's the toilet? I feel like maybe I'm gonna need to pinch one."

"I'd like you to get dressed now, Becket." He looked down and saw that he wore only a pair of undershorts. The nurse handed him a white cotton shirt and pants.

"What's this?"

"This is what you'll wear here. This is what everyone wears."

"It's not what you're wearin'."

"I'm not a patient, Becket." Her voice shifted to a slightly higher pitch.

"Yah, well, if it's all the same to you, I'll wear what I wore when they drug me in."

"That won't be possible."

"Then jus' lemme wear my hat. It's a grey wool type deal—"

"We don't allow the—"

"Some folks call it a mechanic's cap. I call it a—"

"The answer is no. Now, if you'll get dressed, we can go outside. And later today you'll meet our founder, the man who runs this institution."

"Outside?"

"That's right. Wouldn't you like that?"

The kid took the clothes from her and dressed as quickly as he could.

THE KID FOLLOWED THE NURSE through three sets of locked double doors before they reached the yard. He saw dozens of people, some walking in pairs, some sitting alone on benches, all of them wearing the official garb. He noticed an oval-shaped wooden track, perhaps six feet wide in the center of the yard. Several of the patients rode bicycles on the track, pedaling slowly and unsteadily. The kid scanned the perimeter of the yard. A stone wall encircled the property. Ten feet high or so.

He said to the nurse, "You know, these fine folks out here don't seem crazy, not to me. A little dazed, maybe."

"That's kind of you, Becket."

"Say, iff'n it's all right with you, ma'am, I'd like to set awhile on that bench over yonder."

"Of course, you're free to go wherever you like."

He walked to a bench under the bare canopy of a large chestnut tree, the bench closest to the wall. The kid sat down and looked right and then left. He jumped up, ran for the wall and started scaling it. Orderlies came sprinting, peeled him off the wall and hauled him back into the building.

They took the kid in the back door, up two narrow flights of stairs and then down a finely carpeted hallway with wood paneling that gleamed. The first orderly turned the brass doorknob, and the second ushered the kid into a large office with wide windows that overlooked the grounds. They ordered him to sit on a leather couch and handcuffed him to a nearby radiator.

A man strode into the room. He had flowing hair, wireframe glasses and a beard in the Van Dyke style. He wore a three-piece suit and shiny, black brogans.

The man looked at the kid and then focused on the first orderly.

"Remove those binds. Now."

The orderly took off the handcuffs, and then left with the second orderly following. The man turned his attention to the kid.

"Good day, Becket. I'm Doctor Alastair MacBride. How do you do?"

The kid looked up, "I done better, truth be told."

"We're just happy you're here, Becket."

"I didn't mean t' seem ungrateful, what with tryin' t' go over the wall and whatnot."

The doctor gave him a warm smile. "Fear not, son. We favor moral treatments here. Compassion. And discomfort is quite understandable. You're in a new setting. Strangers. That would give anyone the jitters."

"And then some."

"But let me assure you, you're in the perfect place, young man. That's certain."

"Is that why you brung me in here? To tell me that?"

"I was told you have a delightful personality. And an extraordinary imagination."

"Who tol' you *that*?"

MacBride carried a chair across the room and sat down facing the kid. "Becket, your father has asked me to take special care of you while you're here."

"Who? Ray?"

"That's right. Raymond Hinsdale. Your father."

"He ain't my father, no. Let's clear that up. My father's name was Truax. Pastor Martin L. Truax. That man had the fire o' *God* in him. Passionate. You can believe that. Upstandin', too, 'specially for a preacher. Ray's not all bad, but nowheres near Martin L. Truax for a father."

The doctor shifted uncomfortably in his chair. "Becket, if you'll permit me—"

"Name's Abel. Wanna know how my father died?"

"No, I—"

"Well, fine, I'll tell ya. He died handlin' on serpents. That's right. He took up them reptiles as a faith demonstration. But one o' them ol' snakes bit 'im, got 'im right between the thumb and first finger. I was there. I seen it. They played a long and lonesome trumpet song at his funeral. Beatifullest melody you ever heard."

The kid tilted his head back and closed his eyes. When he opened them again, he focused on MacBride. "Okay, doc, what did you want to talk about?"

The doctor spoke in a professional tone, firm and gentle. "As part of your treatment, your father Raymond Hinsdale has asked me to ask you some questions."

"For what?"

"To help you find your way out of your delusion." MacBride produced a tablet. He held it out so that the kid could see the writing on it. "I'm just going to ask you each question, and I ask you to provide me with a detailed answer."

"Go 'head."

"First question, when you helped Nadine Bauer escape from jail, where did she say she was going?"

The kid shook his head slowly. "She didn't say nothing."

"Think hard."

"She was outta there too fast."

The doctor took off his glasses and leaned toward the kid. "Let's talk about the night you say you were murdered. In the churchyard, correct?"

"That's right. I was hiding in the dark."

"Why were you there?"

"I was there to save a good man. I was waitin' for 'em to bring 'im outta the cellar."

"Save him from what?"

"Folks who wanted to put him back into the bondage."

"He was a slave."

The kid grew more animated. "Not no more. He was free. Legally free. And he deserved to be."

"Do you know why, if he'd been freed, someone sought to return him?"

"Don't know. Some folks is just crooked. Evil. Maybe they was insane."

"Do you remember who they were? What they looked like."

"No."

"If you were hiding, how did they find you?"

"God *damn*, if I knew that, I sure as hell wouldn't be here."

"Where would you be?"

"Look, doc, I'm sure you's a bona fide expert on lunatics an' all, but what's this got to do with helping me?"

The doctor sat back. "I've upset you. I apologize."

"It's all right."

"Next question, why is Wendell Kamp helping you?"

The kid looked up with raised eyebrows. "Wendell? That's his first name? Wendell?"

"Why is he helping you?"

"'Cause I asked him to."

"Why?"

"So's he could help me find the son-of-a-bitch who killed me."

"Do you find it odd that you, a nine-year old boy, believe you were once an entirely different man?"

The kid winced. "No odder'n sittin' in this here bug house, shootin' the shit with the likes of you."

"You know, your friend Kamp was a patient here once."

"Bullshit."

MacBride stood up and went to his desk. He pulled out a beige folder marked "Kamp, W. W., Capt. US Army", and began reading.

"Patient admitted January two, eighteen sixty-three. Madness, insomnia, delusional suspicion, disobedience. Rumination in the extreme."

"Yeah, that sounds like him. What's your point?"

"Simply that there's no shame in being here."

"Never said there was."

The doctor stood up, signaling the end of the conversation. "Additionally, we'd like to make sure that Kamp doesn't have to come back here."

"Meaning what?"

"Becket, it's most important that I tell patients the truth. And the truth is, you haven't done a very good job of answering my questions. Your father will not be pleased to hear of your lack of progress."

"Jee-zis *Christ.* Ain't you heard—"

"The better you behave, Becket, and the more honestly and correctly you answer our questions, the less likely we'll have to punish Kamp."

"He didn't do nothin' to you."

"That's immaterial. If you've gotten him ensnared in your delusion, he'll certainly need additional treatment as well."

MacBride opened the office door, and the orderlies reappeared. The doctor said, "Take good care of him, gentlemen."

The orderlies led the kid back down the finely carpeted hallway and down the two flights of narrow stairs. They walked him in the direction of the room where he'd spent the night. But they didn't even slow down and went right past it.

"I think you fellas missed our stop. It's right back there."

The men said nothing and turned down another staircase and then another until the dampness and the darkness made it clear they'd reached the cellar.

The first orderly lit a match, and the trio shuffled into the blackness. The second orderly pushed open a heavy metal door, and the kid could see a single object in the room. It looked like a baby's crib, only larger, with no mattress. The second orderly placed the kid in the crib, and the first closed the lid that locked into place.

The kid said, "I think you got it fastened too tight. I can't even bend my legs."

The first orderly said, "This is for trying to run away from people who want to help you. It's for your own good."

The kid said, "Yeah, well, if this here is one of them moral treatments, I'd hate like hell to see the immoral ones."

"Sweet dreams," the second orderly said, and they left, closing the metal door behind them.

16

"You can't do that girl no good by pacing back and forth on this floor."

Kamp stopped and looked at Angus, who was seated at his workbench.

"We have to do something."

"Ach, there's nothing to do right now. Why, it's already starting to make you *narrish*, you know."

"Yah, yah."

"A little nuts."

Kamp said, "We have to make sure she's safe," and he went back to pacing.

"Cousin, listen. She's as safe here as she can be. It's going to take time. And we can't move her anyhow. I'll take care of her. Emma's right. You need to go back. Go back and take care of your own family."

"Yah." Kamp rubbed his temples. "You're right." He put on his canvas jacket and slouch hat.

"Let me get you something to eat."

Angus wrapped up some biscuits and half a ring wurst and handed the package to Kamp, who put it in his haversack and then walked to the bedroom door where Nyx was sleeping. He cracked the door, looked in on her, then closed it again.

He turned back to Angus. "They're coming for her. Today or tomorrow, who knows."

Angus took a pause, then said, "Oh, I'll be ready."

He took Angus gently by the shoulders and kissed his forehead. "*Machs gut,* cousin."

"Yah, you as well." Angus offered him a rifle. "It's loaded."

"No."

"Ach, take it."

"Not this time."

KAMP WALKED OUT OF THE WOODS and onto Long Run Road. He knew that if he were spotted, they'd be at Angus's cabin within minutes, but he had to make time. He planned to catch the passenger train out of Lehighton, and he knew he would have had to ditch the rifle before getting aboard.

Pulling his hat brim low, he hustled into the station, bought a ticket and climbed the steps in to the car. He sat down and opened his haversack. He wanted to read the murder files Grigg had given him, but first he needed to eat. Kamp polished off a biscuit and a length of ring wurst and then began reading the first file. As soon as he settled into the cushioned seat and the train wheels began to turn, though, sleep began to overtake him. He fought to keep his eyes open, focusing on the clothes he wore, the shirt and pants Angus had given him.

Soon, his eyes closed, and images began to flash against his eyelids. He saw fragments from his last ride on a passenger train when they sent him from the front to Philadelphia, to the hospital. He pictured the straps they used, the straitjacket. Most of all, as Kamp tumbled down into slumber, he heard the screaming mixed with the croaking of ravens outside his window. The dream scene shifted to the Judge's chambers, the clothes the Judge had worn, what they'd talked about. A trumpet blast accompanied a flash of insight, and the dream went dark.

"Hey, buddy."

"Yah, yah."

Even before the conductor tapped Kamp's shoulder, he snapped awake. He focused on the man's brass buttons and leather belt.

"You're here," the conductor said.

"Where?"

"Ach, *Bess'lum.* Third Street."

Kamp knew he had to get home, had to make sure everything was all right there. He also didn't want to linger in town, lest any of his adversaries see him and seek to block his way. But he had to find the Judge first.

HE POUNDED ON THE DOOR of the Judge's chambers.

"Judge, open up. It's me."

No answer. He waited another minute, listening. At first, there was silence. And then, Kamp heard the sound of the Judge banging his pipe on his desk.

"Judge, I can hear you. Let me in."

He heard the floorboards creaking, and a moment later, the door opened. The Judge leaned out and looked both ways down the hall.

Once inside, Kamp said, "Something wrong, Judge?"

"What do you need, Wendell? You want to know about the medical order I signed for the Hinsdale kid?"

"No."

"Involuntary commitment. Textbook case. Aberrant behavior, criminality. Inciting a riot."

The Judge went to the coat rack and threw on his robes.

"Empedocles?" Kamp said.

"What?"

"Last time I was here, you brought up a philosopher named Empedocles. You were trying to make a point."

"Wendell, I don't have time."

"I know why you're scared. I know why you put the kid away."

"That child is ill, Wendell. Deranged. I can't say that I'm surprised you've taken up with him."

"One of Empedocles' better-known writings had to do with the transmigration of souls. I know you know that. Reincarnation. The idea that a person could die and be born with memories of their previous life."

"So what?"

"You believe that's what happened with that kid. That's what made you think of Empedocles. You think that's how the kid knows people's secrets. You knew Abel Truax, and he knows about you—your habits and your past. And he could tell other people, couldn't he? That's why you're nervous, why you changed the way you dress, even in private."

"Nonsense."

"That's why you got rid of him."

"As usual, Wendell, you're seeing through the glass darkly. Very, very darkly."

"By putting that kid in that hospital, you signed his death warrant."

"When people know your secrets, they kill. Not just mine or yours or your cousin's or Nadine Bauer's. All of ours. It works the same for all of us, Wendell. Why can't you see that? If that child weren't locked in a hospital, the mob would have ripped him to pieces."

"How did you meet Abel Truax? And did you know a freed slave named Onesimus Tucks?"

"Wendell, *stop!*"

The Judge's voice rattled the window frames. "These are all figments of the boy's imagination. You're losing your footing. I urge you to see all of this for what it is, madness. Please."

KAMP TRUDGED THE MILES back from Bethlehem, trying and failing to concentrate on his feet hitting the road, the air filling and leaving his lungs. For all the distance he'd traveled in the past two days, for all the inquiries he'd made and assistance he'd attempted to render, he'd made no progress.

And if his going to Angus's cabin alerted Nyx's pursuers to her whereabouts, he may have even sealed her fate in the process. He'd done nothing to help the kid and learned nothing about the man Abel Truax or the fugitive Onesimus Tucks. Nothing to show for any of it but the bruised heels he'd earned when he vaulted himself from the train and down the riverbank.

At the very least, Kamp thought, when he turned onto the path that would bring his house into view, Shaw and his daughter would be waiting for him. He'd feel their love, eat a hot meal and have a good sleep. He closed his eyes and breathed a deep, relieved sigh, imagining it.

When his house came into view, however, there was no candle in the window, no one moving inside. The orange afternoon sun had started its slide below the horizon. Kamp's heart began hammering in his chest. He ran to the front porch and into the house.

"Shaw. Shaw!" No sound, save for the creaking of floorboards under his own steps. A toy bear lay at his feet, button eyes staring up at him.

"Autumn."

Kamp went upstairs and found no one. He hustled back down to the kitchen and found a note written in Shaw's hand—"*At Hinsdales.*"

He went straight back out the front door, down the path and onto the road. In the failing light, Kamp scrambled on the trail beside the creek. He caught a bramble across the face and pushed through it, reaching the base of the stone stairs and taking them two at a time until he made it to the house.

Through the patio window, he saw that the crystal chandelier above the dining room table was lit and that Shaw sat across the table from Margaret Hinsdale. Kamp knocked on the back door, and when it opened, Margaret Hinsdale appeared, her face drawn.

"I'll get a towel," she said and gestured for him to come inside.

"For what?"

She called back over her shoulder, "You're bleeding."

He went to Shaw and held her to him. She reached up and wiped the blood from his cheek.

Shaw said, "What happened, love?"

"Nothing."

She looked him up and down. "Whose clothes are those?"

"Long story. Where is she?"

Shaw leaned down and looked under the table. "Look who's here."

Kamp looked under, too, and saw his daughter, playing with wooden blocks.

The little girl turned her face to him. "Daddy!"

She crawled out and held her arms out to him so that he could pick her up.

Margaret Hinsdale returned, talking while she cleaned Kamp's face.

"Becket used to play with those blocks for hours. He was quite good at making buildings. And even better at knocking them down."

Shaw stood up and said, "Thank you, Margaret, for your hospitality."

"You're leaving?" Margaret Hinsdale's eyes showed fear.

"Yes, the girl needs to sleep."

They heard a clatter of hooves coming to a stop in front of the house.

Margaret Hinsdale collected herself. "Yes, well, thank you ever so much for coming. And, Kamp, you'll be coming with us tomorrow, correct?"

"Where?"

"The hospital. To see Becket."

He looked at Shaw, who nodded slightly. He said, "Why, I don't know that I can—"

The front door of the house swung opened and was slammed shut.

"Margaret!" Raymond Hinsdale's voice boomed through the house.

"We're in here."

Raymond Hinsdale burst in, enraged, and sized up the scene. For an instant Kamp thought the man might attack. He handed his daughter to Shaw and felt the fire starting at the base of his skull.

Hinsdale focused on him and said, "What are you doing here?"

Kamp saw the fibers working in Hinsdale's clenched jaw.

Margaret Hinsdale said, "I invited them. They're helping me."

"What?"

"I've asked Kamp to come with us tomorrow to visit with Becket."

He ignored his wife and took a step closer to Kamp. "I said, what are you doing here? What do you want?

Money?" He pulled a billfold from the vest pocket of his Chesterfield coat and removed two twenties.

Margaret Hinsdale gasped and reached for the money.

"How dare you, Ray—"

He caught her with the back of his left hand, knuckles to her chin, twenties fluttering to the hard wood floor. A rope of saliva and blood stretched down from the corner of Margaret Hinsdale's mouth, and Autumn began to wail.

Kamp launched himself at Raymond Hinsdale, colliding squarely with the man's torso and knocking him backward over the dining room table. He pinned him down and put him in a tight chokehold.

Kamp said, "Don't ever do that again."

"Who are you to tell me anything? You're a flea. You're nothing. Get out of my house. Take your dirty family with you."

Kamp squeezed Hinsdale's throat until the man's eyes closed and his lips turned purple. Shaw grabbed his arm.

"Don't," she said.

Kamp adjusted his grip and added pressure. A trickle of drool issued from Hinsdale's mouth, and he let out a gurgle.

Shaw thumped Kamp hard between the shoulder blades with her fist and shouted, "Stop!"

Kamp relaxed his grip, and Hinsdale slumped forward, taking ragged gulps of air. Kamp put his arm around

Shaw, who was holding Autumn. Together, they made their way to the door. As they left, he looked back over his shoulder and saw Margaret Hinsdale, kneeling at her husband's side, talking softly and consoling him.

17

"She came to our door. She was very upset, crying. She said you had to go with her to the hospital, and she didn't say why."

Kamp listened as he placed logs on top of the kindling he'd started in the fireplace. "Did she say anything about him?"

"Who?"

"Her husband."

Shaw propped her elbows on the kitchen table and put her hands under her chin. "No, not really."

"Meaning what?"

"She kept saying it's his fault."

"What is?" Kamp struck a match and set fire to the kindling.

"She didn't say."

"What about the kid? Did she say anything about him?"

"Just that she's worried."

"She should be."

Shaw paused and then said, "*I'm* worried. About you."

Kamp stood up from the fireplace and faced her. "Don't," he said.

"You were getting better. You were feeling better. And sleeping."

Kamp rubbed his eyes with his thumb and forefinger. "I have to figure this out. Once I do, things will settle down."

"No, they won't!" Shaw slammed her fist down on the table. "They won't, Kamp. These people just want to tangle you up in their problems and then shove you down under them."

"Why?"

"Because that's how they are! That's how *òpinkòk* are. All of you."

"Who?"

"*Òpinkòk.*"

What's that?

"Possums. White people."

Kamp said, "So I shouldn't help them?"

"No."

"What about Nyx?"

"No. There's nothing you can do for her."

"Why did you walk Margaret Hinsdale back to her house if you didn't want to help her?"

"To get her out of our house. Kamp, you would have killed that man if I hadn't stopped you."

"Yah, well, I couldn't just let—"

"You do that, and it's the end. For the three of us. Don't you see that?"

Kamp hung his head. He took off his hat, unlaced his boots and set them by the fire. "What happened to the bear?"

"She's hibernating. Maybe you should, too."

ANGUS FELT CERTAIN he could nurse Nyx Bauer back to health. Emma Wyles had given him detailed instructions regarding the care of the girl's wounds. She'd told him how to clean and dress Nyx's feet and hand and how to identify and fight any new infection. Angus brought the same level of precision and diligence to nursing that he brought to gunsmithing.

The only thing Wyles hadn't adequately explained was the intensity of the pain and grief Nyx would have to endure as part of her convalescence. Nor could Angus have prepared for the toll the girl's suffering would take on him.

Nyx had regained consciousness the day after the surgery, not long after Kamp left the cabin to catch his train back to Bethlehem. She woke up screaming and didn't stop for the better part of an hour. She then demanded that Angus show her the extent of her injuries. When

Angus removed the bandages and she saw the stumps, Nyx had said, "They're gone."

Angus cleaned and dressed the wounds again and then administered laudanum in the way Wyles had taught him. He put the syringe in Nyx's arm, pressed the plunger, and minutes later the girl's eyes grew heavy.

Nyx said, "Where did you put them?" And then she'd drifted back to sleep.

Nyx's anguish touched off a storm of feeling within Angus, sparking emotions he hadn't allowed himself to feel since long before he'd escaped to the cabin. Angus pushed them down as far as he could and channeled the sadness and fear into his work, namely the construction of shotgun shells. Along with the buckshot he poured into each shell, Angus added fragments of bone. In this way, his own grief was quelled, somewhat.

Angus kept a number of guns loaded at all times, a rifle by the back door, scatter gun at the front. He packed a pistol in a boot holster. He thought it likely that within a day or two, a gang of men would ride up to the cabin and that he'd open fire without delay. After all, he wouldn't allow them to take her, and would never be taken himself.

But it didn't happen. Days passed and then a week. He watched the tree boughs fill with snow, the creek freeze over and a grey fox pass through. But no visitors, except for Emma Wyles, who returned exactly one month after the surgery, on the exact day and at the time she said she would.

A blizzard started that morning, and as he sipped his morning coffee, Angus was surprised to see the figure of Wyles, head down and tilting into the great gales and walking her horse to the front door of the cabin.

Once inside, Wyles took off her coat and went straight to the room where Nyx lay in bed. Tears filled the girl's eyes when she saw Wyles, who inspected her feet.

"It all looks better. Much better."

"I can still feel them," Nyx said. "All the time."

"Ghost pain. It's normal. It will go away." Wyles held Nyx's left hand and rubbed the stump where her little finger had been with her thumb. "It's much healthier now."

"Easy for you to say."

"Without the surgery, you would have died. In any case, you're ready to start walking again."

A look passed between Nyx and Angus.

"What is it?"

Nyx swung her legs over the side of the bed and stood up. She wobbled at first and then adjusted her balance, wincing with each step. She walked to the bedroom door and back to the bed.

"Extraordinary, Nyx. Well done."

"So I can leave now?"

"No."

"Why? I'm ready." The color began to rise in her face.

Wyles remained unperturbed. "A few reasons. First and most important, your body needs rest."

"But I can—"

"And you're a fugitive. They're looking for you."

She shook her head. "I doubt it. Everyone's probably forgotten about me by now, I bet."

"They haven't, and they won't. They're scared of you, Nyx."

"Scared of *me*? They're the ones who—"

"Believe me, I know. The rumor, though, is that not only did you escape but that you're coming back for revenge."

"On who?"

"On all of the people you think were involved in hurting your parents."

Nyx paused and took in a breath. She looked out the window and said, "I already took care of that."

"Yes, well, the problem is that those who fear you—the police, the captains of industry, so-called—they think you're out to get them. They know you can hurt them."

"I'm flattered."

Wyles leveled her gaze at the girl. "Is that your intention?"

Nyx bit her lip and raised her eyebrows. "There must be some kind of deal you can make for me."

"Deal?"

"Yah, just go back and tell them I'll mind my own business. I won't hurt anyone as long as they stay away from me."

"Nyx, that's not how it—"

"This, all of this," she gestured to her feet and hand, "it all started because the police wouldn't leave me alone. And if that shit heel Obie hadn't come after me, I wouldn't have—"

"I understand."

"No, you don't. Of course you don't! It's not happening to you."

E. Wyles pulled in a deep breath. "I'm afraid it is."

"What do you mean?"

"I've lost business. They've begun harassing me as well. Someone threw a brick through the front window of the pharmacy."

"Why?"

"Well, at your hearing I spoke on your behalf. And I suppose now people assume that I'm aiding and abetting a fugitive, which of course, I am."

Nyx sat up straight and hardened her gaze. "Are you saying I should go back and let them arrest me?"

"Absolutely not. I'm saying that you should stay here a while longer, remain invisible. Do not leave this cabin. Remember that as long as you're here, Angus is in grave danger as well. If anyone knows you're here, they'll punish him, too.

"Got it."

"And once you're fully healed, you must never go back to Bethlehem."

"Ha. That shouldn't be too hard."

NYX WATCHED WYLES leading her horse back into the storm and then disappearing in the tree line.

As soon as she was gone, Nyx turned to Angus and said, "I need you to make me some special boots."

"Ach, I'm not no cobbler."

"So what? I need you to put something in there to fill the space where my toes would've have been."

"A prosthetic."

"Exactly. And I need you to do it right away. I have to get going."

"You heard what the druggist said. She said—"

"She doesn't understand."

Angus waited until the girl turned to face him. He said, "What Emma said, about the rumor, about you taking revenge on them that hurt your parents. That's what you intend to do, say not?"

Nyx smiled at the corner of her mouth.

"Ach, Nyx, it don't solve nothing if—"

"They'll get what they deserve. That's all. I mean, Christ, Angus, look what they've done to you."

"I made my—"

"Just help me with the boots, and I'm gone."

THE METAL DOOR SWUNG OPEN, and the kid saw a candle flame approaching. When the flame appeared directly over the box where the kid was trapped, he saw the face of the nurse.

She said, "It's time for you to come out of there, Becket."

The nurse unlatched the spring-loaded lid, and it popped open. Then she helped the kid to a seated position.

"Are you all right? You must have been frightened."

The kid bent one leg and then the other. He blinked a few times, paused, then said, "Hell, I warn't born in the woods to be afeard of no owls. But what in blazes did y'all stick me in there for?"

"Jesus said, 'Spare the rod, spoil the child.' "

The kid scratched his scalp with both hands and said, "First off, Jesus didn't say that. Second, I reckon the rod woulda been a far sight friendlier than this here torture box. Lastly, Jesus said we oughta take care of rats an' pigeons, too, but I don't see y'all worryin' about them, not at all."

"Well, let's get you out of there."

The nurse put her arm around the kid and walked him back up to the ground floor of the hospital. The blizzard had relented, and the noonday sun glinted off the polished wood floors. She walked him to a white porcelain-tiled bathroom. In the center of the room stood a steaming tub of water.

The nurse said, "You can take off those filthy rags. Take as long as you'd like in the bath. And here are some clean clothes to wear when you're finished. I'll be just outside the door."

"Shit, what's the occasion?"

WHENEVER HE ALLOWED his mind to slow, Kamp was able to see Shaw's logic, and he knew she was right. He reflected on the moment he'd first heard of the murders of Jonas and Rachel Bauer. He'd been gripped with the urge to protect their children and capture their killer. Finding the alleged fiend Daniel Knecht and bringing him back to the Bauer house seemed to be the first step in getting justice.

But when the mob outside the house turned murderous, Kamp bumbled into the first set of unintended consequences. And his subsequent investigation of the crimes led to an escalation of violence that resulted in a clearer understanding of the matter, perhaps, but not resolution. And certainly not justice.

He knew Wyles was right, as well. For the sake of Nyx's safety, he needed to stay away. Same for Angus, same for the kid. Kamp's intention was always to help people and to put things right, but inevitably and without trying, he provoked conflict and destruction.

By sunup, he'd resolved to leave the rest of the world, such as it was, in peace. And he set about working on projects he'd previously laid aside, beginning with the bear hide. He tanned it with a mixture of the bear's brain and hot water, then hung it in the back yard. And by the time the first golden rays of morning hit Kamp's face, the hide had begun to dry. He dug a hole in the backyard and built a simple tripod above it. Kamp filled the hole with wood and lit a fire. After softening the hide, he draped it over the tripod and bathed it in smoke thereby. Half an hour later, it was finished.

He carried the hide into the house, spread it on the floor in the front room and admired it. Kamp started a fire in the fireplace and took off his boots. He went to the front window and saw Raymond Hinsdale's fine carriage gliding by on the road. He heard Shaw and Autumn come down the stairs, and soon his daughter stood at his side.

She said, "What are you doing, daddy?"

"Learning how to mind my own business."

18

The carriage came to a stop in the drive that coiled in front of the impressive marble steps leading to the portico and underneath it, the front doors of the Pennsylvania Hospital for the Insane. Margaret Hinsdale emerged from the carriage first, carrying a box wrapped with a red ribbon. Raymond Hinsdale then stepped out as well, and the two were met at the top of the stairs by a man in a three-piece suit and white laboratory coat. The man wore a beard in the Van Dyke style and wireframe glasses.

He smiled broadly when he greeted them. "Good day to you, Mr. and Mrs. Hinsdale, I'm Dr. MacBride."

Raymond Hinsdale shook hands with MacBride. "Pleased to meet you, doctor. Impressive building you have here."

"Thank you. Indeed. Greek revival. Won't you come with me?"

With purposeful steps, he led the couple down the wide main hall. Patients sat quietly in wooden chairs on either side of the hallway. They read books or gazed out the window, as if perhaps lost in the contemplation of a tree or cloud.

Margaret Hinsdale said, "Doctor, this place, this hospital, it doesn't seem as if it's a, a…" She paused, searching for the right word.

"A lunatic asylum?" MacBride said. "Of course not, that's our approach, the new model. Moral treatment."

He stopped walking and turned to face her. "I assure you, though, madam, no matter how docile they appear, every one of these patients"—he made a sweeping gesture— "is utterly insane."

MacBride began walking again, guiding them into a sitting room filled with sunlight, fine furniture, Persian rugs and an assortment of ferns in ornate vases.

"Won't you sit down?" he said.

The Hinsdales took their seats on a red velvet divan as two attendants entered the room. The first carried a sterling silver tea service and the second a tray of crumpets with a variety of jams.

Once the Hinsdales had been served, two orderlies ushered in the kid, outfitted in the trousers and silk shirt he'd worn when he first arrived. The first orderly pulled up a wooden chair, and the second directed the kid to sit in it.

Without emotion the kid said, "Well, isn't this a nice little surprise." Margaret Hinsdale went to him immediately, hugged him and kissed his forehead.

"I brought you a present, dear." She untied the bow on the package.

"I'm afraid we don't allow gifts," MacBride said, "not even from the parents."

She said, "Oh, for heaven's sake, it's just a Bible."

The kid opened the package and said, "See, now that's thoughtful. I sure could use the solace of the good book right about now." He held the Bible in both hands.

MacBride said, "I suppose we can make an exception."

Margaret Hinsdale focused on the kid's face. "Oh, Becket, are you all right, dear? Are you?"

She took a step back and looked at him. His blonde straw-like hair had been combed with a side part.

"Dreadful," she said.

"I know I look ridiculous, Margaret. Don't make it worse."

She whipped her head around to look at MacBride. "Look at those dark circles. My *word*."

Everyone stared at the dark half-moons beneath the kid's eyes.

"What have you done to this boy?" she said.

MacBride cleared his throat. "Some of our residents find it difficult to sleep soundly when they first arrive. There's always a period of adjustment."

"Adjustment? Shit," the kid said. "You try sleepin' in a wooden box in the cellar."

Margaret Hinsdale's face went bright red. "What in god's name?"

MacBride sipped his tea, paused, then said, "Mrs. Hinsdale, I'm afraid it's not unusual for patients to attempt to garner sympathy by spinning yarns, especially during family visits."

"Yarns?" Margaret Hinsdale said.

"Indeed. Fabrications, tall tales."

The kid said, "Tell 'em, doc. Tell 'em how y'all punished me for tryin' t' absquatulate outta here. Tell 'em about that contraption y'all had me stuffed in."

Margaret Hinsdale's eyes brimmed with tears. "Yes, tell us, doctor."

"When Becket first arrived, he did attempt an escape. And I believe the boy is referring to something called a Utica crib. These devices have been employed from time to time in insane asylums, though with no curative success. Perhaps one of the other residents described one to Becket. I can assure there's no such thing on the premises. And under no circumstances would we ever punish a resident."

The kid shook his head and rolled his eyes. "Don't believe him, Margaret. I can show y'all exactly where it is."

"Why don't you show us?" Margaret Hinsdale said.

MacBride turned to Raymond Hinsdale. "I'm afraid, sir, that delusional mendacity is all too typical with your son's kind of madness."

Raymond Hinsdale said, "Why don't we focus on the business at hand?"

He gently took his wife by the elbow. She shrugged it off forcefully and then took her seat.

MacBride said, "Yes, of course. Thank you." He turned to the kid. "Becket, the reason your parents are here is to see if you're ready to go home today."

The kid's expression flattened.

"You seem skeptical. Don't you want to leave?"

"Don't matter."

"Why not?"

"Truth be told, folks in here don't seem no diff'rent from people out there. Not at all. Every last one of us has a situation they're tryin' t' cope with. Real lunatics is you an' that nurse an' them savages there." He jerked his thumb over his shoulder, referring to the orderlies. "Iff'n you ask me, the whole lot of you is evil. An' stone fucking nuts."

"That's enough, Becket!" Raymond Hinsdale gripped the arm of the divan. "Doctor, I don't even have the words to express—"

MacBride looked at him with pity. "No need to apologize, sir. It's therapeutic for the boy to reveal his true emotions and for you to witness the severity of his pathology."

Margaret Hinsdale erupted, "That's not at all what—" Her husband grabbed her hard by the wrist.

"Let's focus on getting him home. Doctor, what must Becket do, and what can we do, in order for him to be discharged?"

MacBride motioned to the orderlies, the first of whom opened the door. The second orderly walked to Margaret Hinsdale and held out his hand.

She said, "I'm not going anywhere."

The kid said, "I'll say whatever you want me to say, answer whatever god damn dumb questions you want me to answer. Just let her stay."

A look passed between MacBride and Raymond Hinsdale.

MacBride said, "So be it."

The first orderly closed the door, and the second backed away from Margaret Hinsdale.

MacBride interlaced his fingers in front of his chest and addressed the Hinsdales. "I've explained to Becket that if he answers my questions truthfully and specifically, we'll know he's on the path to sanity. And while we won't be able to say he's cured, at least he may be well enough for us to consider his return home. Does that make sense to you?"

Raymond and Margaret Hinsdale nodded.

"Becket, do you have any questions?"

The kid shook his head. "No questions, but tell them varmints to skedaddle." He motioned to the orderlies.

MacBride said, "Thank you, gentlemen," dismissing them. "Now, let's begin." The doctor leaned forward in his chair toward the kid.

"Is your real name Abel Truax?"

MacBride and the Hinsdales all pulled in a breath and waited.

The kid said, "No, it's not."

They all exhaled.

"Were you born in West Virginia in 1825?"

"No, I was not."

"Do you believe you were murdered in Bethlehem in 1861 while trying to help a freed slave who'd been wrongfully imprisoned?"

"No, I don't."

MacBride looked at the Hinsdales and said, "This is real progress."

"Finally, he's coming back to us. He's waking up," Raymond Hinsdale said.

MacBride sharpened his focus. "Now, Becket, tell me exactly where Nadine Bauer said she was—"

The kid piped up again. "No, I ain't from West Virginia. An' my real father didn't die handlin' on no snakes."

Raymond Hinsdale said, "He's doing it again."

Margaret Hinsdale said, "Becket, *no.*"

The kid continued, "And I didn't come up here from West Virginia to help my good friend Onesimus Tucks out of a pickle. I wasn't killed by a blow to the back of the neck, and I didn't travel to no heavenly realms and then get sent back to live in no tree and then get born to Ray an' Margaret. No, none of that happened."

Raymond Hinsdale became visibly angry. "Son, when we get home—"

"An' come t' think of it, when I first hit town, I didn't live underneath no whorehouse, neither. An' I didn't see Raymond comin' an' goin' there on a most reg'lar basis."

Margaret Hinsdale lunged across the room and tried to put her hand over the kid's mouth, but he wiggled free.

"No, I never saw Raymond take up with one fine young adventuress in partick'lar, one that I happened to know myself. No, I didn't actually see none of that. An' I especially didn't never hear Raymond moanin' and groanin' up there out an open window, like sin to Moses!"

When Raymond Hinsdale lunged across the room, knocking Margaret Hinsdale aside and reaching for the kid's throat, the kid bolted from the chair and out the door, Bible in hand, with the orderlies close behind.

Raymond Hinsdale stood up, straightened his tie and extended his hand to MacBride, who shook it.

MacBride said, "I'm afraid he'll be staying."

Hinsdale said, "God bless you, doctor. Thank you for helping our son. Our debt of gratitude is immense."

19

Angus didn't need to make a mold, didn't even need to make a fire to heat the iron and hammer it into the shape of a prosthetic toe. After hacksawing the toe cap off Nyx's boots, he simply took a can of matchlock musket balls of varying sizes down from a shelf and found one to replace each of her missing toes. He glued the bullets into the cap of the boot in the correct places, affixing a wad of felt to the bottom of each one so that the stumps were snug against them. He let Nyx try the boots on several times, making minor adjustments each time.

When Nyx was satisfied with the fit, he said, "Now comes the easy part."

Angus attached the prosthetic toes to the sole and then stitching the caps back on. He handed the finished product back to Nyx.

"Get them as tight as you can."

Nyx guided the laces through the eyelets, tied them and stood up. She took a few tentative steps forward, testing her balance with short strides.

She said, "Okay, now I'm going to walk like I used to." Nyx lengthened her gait, striding across the room and finding she could trust the boots. She wobbled only when she tried to push off to run.

"That doesn't feel the same," she said.

"Give it time."

Nyx threw her arms around Angus's neck, pressed herself against him and said, "Thank you, thank you, thank you."

THE LATE MORNING SUN warmed Kamp's feet as he lay on the floor, mind meandering. He recalled the morning he'd returned home from the war, carrying nothing but the Sharps and kicking up dust on the road with the boots he'd worn since the day he'd left. The boots they'd tried to give him were garbage, poorly constructed and unfit even for a Sunday stroll. It occurred to Kamp now that his refusal to wear the standard issue boots was the first in a very long series of gestures of noncompliance that led him on his wayward path to the lunatic asylum.

Kamp's thoughts shifted to the August morning that the kid first came marching up the trail. For the first time in weeks, Kamp remembered that on that day he'd just received the load of planks with which he'd intended to build a slaughterhouse. He remembered, too, his ambivalence regarding the new structure, and while he didn't know from whence the mixed feelings emanated, Kamp knew they were still there. Maybe he'd had enough of killing. He pictured the planks where he'd left them, under a canvas tarp behind the house. They could wait longer. At least until spring.

Kamp felt his thoughts picking up speed and intensity, and from experience he knew that if he didn't start moving, dark rumination would soon overtake him. Following Shaw's wise counsel, namely that involving himself in the crises of others would be more difficult than he'd imagined, Kamp stood up stiffly and looked for his jacket. He could hike the mountain, maybe. His heart started slapping against his ribs, splintered thoughts spinning at him.

It wasn't until he moved for the door that he became aware of the insistent knocking and saw a man standing on the front porch.

"I need to speak with you, Kamp."

He opened the door and saw the prosecutor, Grigg, holding a black leather briefcase.

"Good day. May I come in?"

Kamp stepped out onto the porch, locked the door behind him and headed down the steps.

"Where are you going?"

Kamp disappeared around the back of the house, and Grigg scurried after him, slipping several times on the melting ice and snow. He caught up with Kamp on the trail that led to the mountain.

"I need to speak with you."

"Then you'll have to walk."

"I'm not dressed for it."

"Too bad."

"I can't."

Kamp turned around and saw that Grigg wore his customary three-piece suit, a wool Chesterfield coat with a velvet collar, a cashmere scarf and shiny leather brogans. He carried the briefcase.

"Then wait on the porch."

"How long?"

Kamp disappeared up the trail, and Grigg scrambled up after him, grabbing low branches to steady himself every few steps in order to keep moving.

When he reached the top of the mountain, out of breath, shoes muddy and feet soaked, Grigg found Kamp staring up into the branches of the oak tree.

Grigg unbuckled the briefcase and said, "I need to show you something."

Kamp leaned back and took a deep breath, exhaling it in a great cloud. Still looking up, Kamp said, "My brothers and I used to come up here."

"Is that so?"

"Yah. Long time ago."

Grigg surveyed the landscape and shifted from one foot to the other. "Yes, well, Kamp, if you don't mind I'd like to—"

"When I got back from the war, this was the first place I came. This tree. A safe place, I suppose." He turned to look at Grigg. "This is the tree he said he lived in for two years. The kid."

"Kamp, I spoke with the coroner several days ago. He said you'd visited him a while back."

With his foot Kamp swept away the snow at the base of the tree. "The only difference, when I got back here, the only difference between before and now, is that it seems like nothing grows on the ground here anymore. Used to be grass and flowers. The kid called it a *kyarn*, a dead place."

"Charming. The coroner told me you demanded to see his records from twelve years ago. And he refused."

"So what?"

"So, here they are."

Kamp glanced at the sheaf of papers Grigg pulled from his briefcase. "You're wasting your time."

"How's that?"

"I let it go."

"Really."

"Yah, I'm trying something new." Kamp started back down the mountain.

Grigg laughed. "It's not that easy. Not by a long chalk." He placed the papers back in the briefcase, buckled it, and trailed after Kamp. "They're not going to leave you alone."

"Neither are you, apparently."

"If nothing else, I'm giving you advance warning."

"About what?"

Kamp kept making his way down the trail. Grigg hustled as best he could, slipping to one knee and then getting up and then getting in front of Kamp, stopping him.

Grigg said, "They're coming for you, the Order."

"Why?"

"Three reasons, at least. They believe you're helping Nyx Bau—"

"I'm not helping—"

"They *believe* you are, and they perceive you're a threat to Raymond Hinsdale."

"I'm not."

"Naturally, they have an interest in protecting him. And you did nearly strangle him to death, didn't you?" Kamp tried to push past Grigg, but the prosecutor blocked the way and took a handful of Kamp's jacket. "Face facts. You can try to walk away. They won't let you."

Kamp looked at Grigg's hand on his jacket until the prosecutor let go. "What are they going to do?"

"I don't know what, specifically. I just know they're plotting against you."

"How do you know?"

"I have sources."

"What sources?"

Grigg looked over Kamp's shoulder. "I can't say. I do have one additional bit of information, the professional I told you they sent after Nyx Bauer. I know the individual's name. Adams."

"First name? Last name?"

"That's all I know. Does it ring a bell?"

Kamp rubbed his left temple. "You want to help me, is that right?"

"Yes, I do. Together, we can—"

"Then stay away."

Kamp pushed past Grigg, walked down the trail and into his house, slamming the door behind him.

ANGUS LEFT THAT AFTERNOON, slinging his hunting rifle over his shoulder, strapping on snowshoes and heading out into the woods. He hadn't told Nyx where he was going, saying only, "I'll be back before dark."

He went straight for the first of a half dozen steel claw traps he'd set the day before Nyx appeared at his doorstep. It had snowed several times since then, and Angus didn't hold out much hope for success as he neared the first one. But a cottontail lay dead in its jaws, freshly trapped and unmolested by scavengers. Angus pried the rabbit out, reset the trap and moved onto the next. It, too, held a dead rabbit, which he bagged. Angus hurried to the remaining traps and finding those empty, made a beeline for the cabin. They'd have more than they needed for supper, and Angus's mood, which had been low, owing to Nyx's immanent departure, brightened considerably.

He stepped deftly in the snowshoes, picking up his original tracks and walking back in them. When his cabin came into view through the trees at a distance of a couple hundred yards, Angus saw someone standing on the front porch, peering in the window. His initial impulse was to call out to Nyx and tell her to get back inside, but he stifled the urge. Angus's heart began to thud as he gently lowered the game bag to the ground and slid the rifle strap off his shoulder. He raised the gun and stared down the scope. The figure was a woman, but it wasn't Nyx.

She wore a black cloak with the hood up, and she paced slowly on the porch. Angus took off the snowshoes, picked up the gun and walked soundlessly in a crouch. By the time he got to the edge of the clearing, about fifty feet from the cabin, the woman had begun pounding on the front door. Angus stopped, raised the rifle again and sighted the woman's head.

He curled his first finger around the trigger and said, "Raise your hands. Slow. Don't turn around."

The woman said, "I'm here with the county. Census. I can show you."

"*Ach*, stay still once." Angus approached, keeping the woman in his sights until he reached the first porch step.

"I'm only here to verify that this residence is inhabited, and if so, by how many persons." The woman spoke without fear. "Now, sir, may I know your name?"

"No, ma'am, you may not. What you can do is vacate the premises."

The woman said, "I recommend you answer my questions, but if you insist I'll—"

Angus touched the tip of the barrel to the back of the woman's head. "I insist."

"Well, then, if you'll permit me, I'm going to turn around now so that I may leave."

In a low voice Angus said, "What's your name?"

With her hands still raised, the woman turned a half-circle, and for the first time, Angus saw her face. She had high cheekbones, blue eyes, a fine nose and a square jaw. She stared straight into Angus's eyes and showed nothing soft. No deference.

"I said, what's your name?"

"Adams." The woman glanced at his rifle and said, "Sharpshooter, huh?"

"What of it?"

"My husband was in the war."

Angus lost his focus just enough for the woman to find the blade and sink it into Angus's left thigh. The rifle clattered to the porch as Angus tumbled backward.

From inside the cabin, Nyx yelled, "What is it?"

Angus said, "I'm *g'shtucha!*"

The woman said, "It's all right, Nadine, come outside."

"Go to hell!"

At the moment Angus took up the rifle again and pointed it at the woman, he heard a crack at the tree line and then felt the bullet slam into his left shoulder, knocking him off the porch and onto the ground. The second bullet whistled through his hat, skimming his hairline on its way through. Angus scanned the tree line and saw men in uniforms taking up positions.

The woman leapt off the porch as Nyx swung the front door open and came out firing a shotgun but missing Adams as she fled. Nyx jumped down, hauled Angus back inside and shut the door.

AS SOON AS NYX had heard boot heels on the porch, the same ones she'd heard days before, she'd begun making ready to escape. She packed a bag with a change of clothes, a spare blanket, food, a pistol and a clutch of clean bandages. Then she'd laced up the boots Angus made her, cinching them fast. Nyx set the Henry rifle by the back door, along with three boxes of cartridges. And by the time she'd heard voices on the porch and then the gun shots, Nyx had already loaded the shotgun.

Now, she grabbed Angus under the arms and dragged him backward across the floor of the main room. The first hail of gunfire arrived just as Nyx laid Angus on the kitchen floor. Bullets splintered the window frames and tore into Angus's workbench.

Nyx said, "I'm sorry, Angus, I'm so sorry."

"Ach, what for?"

She threw the back door open and put the Henry, the bag of supplies and the shotgun into the bed of the dray wagon Angus kept in a small barn behind the cabin. Another volley of bullets came through the front of the cabin as Nyx crawled on hands and knees back to where Angus lay.

She said, "You're going to get up and run for the wagon. One, two, three." The pair scrambled out the back door, and Nyx helped Angus into the wagon's bed.

Nyx gestured to the shotgun and said, "It's loaded."

Angus sat up in the wagon and took the gun in his right hand, bracing it against his hip. Nyx took the reins and snapped them hard. The horse bolted out of the barn and onto the path to Long Run Road, rifles cracking behind them, echoes receding.

20

"It's called a douche bath. Otherwise known as hydrotherapy. And it ain't punishment. It's for your own good."

The first orderly talked as he stepped up onto a wooden chair. He held a bucket of water and stood directly over the naked kid, whose arms and legs had been pinned to the ground by the second orderly and three attendants. The scene played out in a small, walled off yard behind the main hospital building.

"Doc MacBride said you need this as part of your treatment. Said you're almost cured, in spite of your fractiousness."

The kid said, "He said that, huh? Yeah, that ol' Doc MacBride, he sure does care about us inma—"

The orderly held the bucket high and dumped the water on the kid's face. "Also said sometimes it's gotta get worse before it gets better."

The kid coughed and sputtered. "Okay, I'm awake now."

Another attendant handed the orderly a second bucket of water. He dumped that one as well and reached for a third.

"Doc MacBride swears there's hope for you. We ain't so sure. And if nothing else, this is one way to keep you from talking."

He emptied the bucket. The kid shut his eyes tight and pursed his lips as the cascade hit him square in the face. He waited, then opened one eye.

The kid said, "You know, boys, Jesus said, iff'n a man slaps your cheek, offer him the other'n as well."

"So?"

"So, I'm here to tell ya, you can keep on, though I prefer you'd stop with this foolishness."

"Ain't up to you."

"Don't worry, though, I don't intend t' exact no revenge. That ain't what I have in mind, not at all."

The orderly said, "What a relief," and the other men laughed. "I heard your parents is rich, too. How in the hell did you end up here?"

The kid raised his voice a notch. "But understand this, I been to the heavenly realms, and I seen what they do in there to evildoers, 'specially them that hurt a child. An' second, Jesus said, 'Better that a man have a millsto—' "

"Christ, just shut *up!*" The orderly dumped another bucket on him.

The kid coughed, cleared his throat, spat on the second orderly's shoes and spoke even louder. "Long as we're down here on this earth, I don't have no truck with you fellas. You're just tryin' t' do a job, awful an' sorry as it is. But when your last moment in this mortal realm arrives, hear this, when the judgment comes on you, it'll come fierce."

"Is that so?"

"You most like won't even hear a trumpet blast to announce it. Bang, an' that's it. An' the lord's payday ain't always on a Friday."

THE PROSECUTOR WAS GONE, but his briefcase remained on the top step of the porch. Kamp saw it there when Shaw and Autumn returned an hour after his conversation with Grigg. Could he trust the man? What if he planted something there to fool Kamp into doing his bidding and undo himself in the process?

"What's that?" Shaw said. She snapped him from his rumination.

Kamp looked at her and at the sleeping child in a sling on her back.

"A briefcase."

She gave him a flat stare. "What's in it?"

"Well, I was told it contains the records of every death handled by the coroner, going back twelve years. I don't want it, though."

She raised her eyebrows slightly and shook her head.

Kamp said, "Honest. I didn't ask him for it."

"Ask who?"

"The prosecutor. He was here. And no, I didn't invite him. He thinks I'm going to help him, but I'm not. Told him to leave."

She stepped close to Kamp and ran her first finger gently across the furrow that ran the width of his forehead and then down his cheek. "Oh, what a noble mind is here o'erthrown."

"Meaning what?"

Shaw put both hands on the back of Kamp's neck and caressed the base of his skull. "The courtier's, soldier's, scholar's, eye, tongue, sword."

"They won't leave us alone. That's what he wanted to tell me. It's starting again."

"Observed of all observers, quite, quite down."

Kamp raised his voice a notch, "You're not listening. They're not going to just—"

"Shh," she said and gestured to Autumn, who'd begun to stir. "Let it go, let it go."

"I can't, you can't."

She began to loose the straps that held their daughter on her back. "Help me with this."

Kamp took the little girl off Shaw's back and walked up the stairs and laid her in bed. When he got back downstairs, Shaw had retrieved the briefcase from the porch and was leafing through the files on the kitchen table.

"How is this organized?" she said.

"What?"

Shaw continued searching the stack of papers. "It's year by year. And alphabetical."

"What happened to 'let it go?' "

She split the stack of papers, setting half to the side. The other half she went through sheet by sheet. Kamp started a cooking fire and ground some coffee beans. By the time he'd fixed himself a cup, Shaw was focusing on a particular record with great interest.

"1863. Here it is." she said.

"What?"

"The missionary."

"What about him?"

"You asked me what happened to him. Here it is." She handed him the sheet of paper.

Kamp sat down at the kitchen table and read it. "Return of a death. Name, Jezek, Daniel J. Occupation, clergy. Cause of death, pneumonia."

"That part is a lie."

Kamp took a sip of coffee and looked up at Shaw. "How do you know?"

"I was there. I saw it happen."

"Where?" He scanned the death certificate. "The place of death is left blank."

"It was in the woods outside Mercy Village, the first one. They didn't want to call it murder."

"Who didn't?"

"My father, my aunt. Jay's father. Just about everyone."

"I don't understand."

She sat down at the table across from Kamp. "A lot of people hated him."

"You didn't."

"I thought he was wonderful. Most of the young people did, too. That was part of the problem. The other missionaries disliked him because he wasn't a good missionary. The Christian Lenapé mistrusted him for that reason as well."

"He was a pariah."

"Some men began plotting. I overheard them talking. One of my cousins, especially. He was jealous."

"What did you do?"

Shaw looked at Kamp and raised her eyebrows. "I tried to stop them. On the night they planned to do it, I took a war hammer and got my cousin first."

"Got him?"

"Yes, but don't bother, you won't find a death certificate in there for that, either. We don't count."

"Lucky for you."

"Well, what I did didn't help Jay. If anything, it made the rest of them angrier. They took him, burned him alive. When they were finished, they came back and gave me this, among other things." She pointed to the crescent-shaped scar above her left eye.

"What do you mean 'among other things?'"

"*Xahònkël.*"

"What's that?"

Shaw could see the color rising in Kamp's face.

She said, "The point is no one, not the Jesus Munsee, not the Moravians, wanted people to know what happened to Jay. They had to keep it secret, pretend it never happened."

"Why?"

"You know about Mercy Village, right?"

"No."

"The first one was the place I just mentioned, in 1755. Missionaries and Indians. The second Mercy Village was in Ohio. Dozens of Lenapé, including women and children, all Christian, none armed, all murdered. Scalped."

"What's your point?"

She rubbed the scar above her eye with her first two fingers. "My point is that all people need is a reason, something they think justifies it. And once they have their reason, it starts. If the people found out Jay had been killed by an Indian, we'd all have been slaughtered."

"At least you did what you could."

She shook her head. "But only by participating in it. If I hadn't done what I did, maybe they'd only have beaten him up and forced him to leave."

Kamp looked at the death certificate one more time. "It says he's buried in the Moravian cemetery in Bethlehem."

"I know."

"Mind if I change the subject?"

Shaw stared out the window, still in the memory.

Kamp continued, "There was one thing Grigg mentioned, something I need to tell you." Shaw turned back to face him. "They've brought someone in to find Nyx."

"They who? The police?"

"Black Feather."

"Jesus Christ."

"Shaw, listen. Her name is—"

"Her?"

"Her name is Adams. Five feet, maybe five two. Thin with blonde hair, blonde in the war anyway. Blue eyes."

"That's a detailed description."

"Well, she's a hunter, very good with a knife. You need to keep an eye out for her. Trust me."

"How do you know her?"

"From the war. I knew her husband. She was the one with the reputation, though."

"Whose side was she on?"

"Hers."

21

Adams heard receding hoof beats and the rifle reports trailing after them, but she didn't feel troubled. Neither did she worry that she wouldn't catch up with the girl soon enough. Instead, she savored the moment when she sank the blade into Angus Kamp's thigh. She'd heard he was smart and dangerous, but not smart enough, as it turned out. Adams took a deep breath and exhaled. Letting them go, or more precisely, sending them scrambling, ensured that they'd lead her to their co-conspirators as well.

She reflected too on the moment Nyx Bauer emerged from the cabin, shotgun blasting. While she found the girl's method clumsy, Adams admired her assertiveness. The front door hung open and Adams went in, while the three armed men stood on the porch.

Without looking at them, she said, "Stay."

Adams assumed that the pair wouldn't have had time to set traps in the cabin before they fled. Still, she wouldn't put it past Angus, given what she'd heard about his skill with firearms and his preference for security. As such, she walked slowly and carefully through the main room. She went to the workbench, where she saw what she expected—black powder, buck shot, cartridge papers and a fine assortment of gunsmithing tools. She noticed a bin of spare and worn out parts, including a loading-lever and a toggle-joint.

In a tin cup Adams also saw fragments of what could only have been bone. She noted the wear on the tools and on the workbench itself. Adams inspected each weapon resting in the gun rack and noticed that the rack wasn't full. Of all the slots, ten had a gun in them. Two were empty.

Adams surveyed the room once more. The breakfast dishes hadn't been cleaned, and the fire in the fireplace still smoldered. She'd surprised them, as she knew she would. On her way into the bedroom, Adams noticed a bedroll on the floor. Angus must have been sleeping there. A selfless act.

Adams inspected the unmade bed, bending low and pressing her nose to the sheets. No perspiration or gunpowder. Only soap and perfume. She pulled the sheets all the way back and saw flecks of blood at the foot of the bed. Nyx hadn't appeared hurt when she came out of the cabin and hauled Angus back in. But when Adams looked through the chest of drawers, she found a variety of clean bandages and anti-septic. She got on her hands and knees and looked under the bed. Amidst the dust bunnies lay an empty, green, grooved bottle. Adams stretched her arm and retrieved it. She stood up and inspected the label:

"Laudanum. Poison."

And underneath the ingredients, at the bottom of the label in small letters, it read:

"Pure Drugs & Chemicals, E. Wyles, Druggist."

Leaving the bedroom, Adams went to the kitchen table and found a game bag that contained two fresh rabbits. Adams turned on her heel and surveyed the cabin's main room one last time. She considered the workbench and the tools, the bedroll on the floor and the blood on the mattress. She reflected on all the care and love Angus must have put into constructing and protecting the cabin, making a safe place for himself, and for fellow refugees.

Adams went back out onto the porch where the men stood waiting.

"Torch it," she said.

THE KID SAT ON THE EDGE of the bed and looked at the cover of the Bible Margaret Hinsdale had given him. When he opened it, between the end of Genesis and the beginning of the Gospel of Matthew, he found that a space had been carved out of the pages. In it, a steel file had been hidden.

"You's a sly one, Margaret. You sure is," he said aloud.

The kid pulled out the file and then looked up at the iron mesh covering the window. He carried the wooden chair to a spot below the window and climbed onto it. He could barely reach the bottom of the window and couldn't get high enough to work on the mesh. The kid got down and tried moving the bed, but it was bolted to the floor. He switched his focus to the door and gently wiggled the file in the lock until he heard a soft click.

KAMP LET THE SUN GO DOWN without having answered any of the questions that taunted him. Long after his family had gone to sleep and eons before the dawn, he sat staring into the darkness outside, a black expanse with wind ripping through it.

He kept falling, tumbling back into fragments of memories, the moment when he first mustered in to his regiment, the moment his brother handed him the red hat, the moment the kid first appeared in his yard, and when the fiend Daniel Knecht went airborne and the noose coils went taut. Kamp couldn't discern the connections among these flashes, nor could he see the machine in his mind that produced the pictures.

Eventually, he closed his eyes and simply listened to the sound of his own breathing. Hours later, but still well before the dawn, he heard footsteps on the porch and then a soft knock at the door.

Kamp went to the front window, and while he could discern the outline of a slight figure, he couldn't tell who it was. He picked up the Sharps, which he now kept leaning next to the front door, tucking the stock against his shoulder, raising the barrel and curling his first finger around the trigger.

"Who is it?"

Kamp saw the figure on the porch shift from one foot to the other. Through the door he heard a girl's voice.

"She needs your help."

He lowered the rifle and swung the door open to find the girl with the corn silk hair and the otherworldly eyes staring at him, without expression.

"Did she say anything else? Is she hurt?"

The girl kept staring. "She didn't say it. I'm saying it. Doctor needs your help."

Kamp pulled on his boots and jacket and followed the girl off the porch to where her horse was tied. She climbed into the saddle, and said, "Get on."

"You sure?"

The horse nickered loudly, while the girl waited in silence. She extended her hand to Kamp, and he put his foot in the stirrup and swung his leg, with difficulty, over the back of his horse and situated himself behind the girl.

He said, "I get dizzy."

"Yah, doctor told me. Hold real tight."

She leaned forward, and the horse started down the path. When they reached the road, she said, "Ya!" and the horse started its gallop. Kamp pressed the side of his head against her back to steady himself, remembering at that moment he'd forgotten to leave Shaw a note.

The girl didn't ease up in the saddle, and the horse didn't slow its run until after they'd crossed the New Street Bridge. Kamp opened his eyes for the first time and looked up and down Third Street, empty in the pre-dawn. He saw the glow from Native Iron and tasted the foul grit that floated down from the stacks. The girl brought the horse to a stop a block away from E. Wyles' pharmacy.

"Get off," she said.

TIPTOEING DOWN THE MAIN HALLWAY, the kid realized that once all the patients had been locked in their rooms for the night, the staff of the hospital disappeared, went back to whatever lives waited for them outside the walls. He stepped lightly all the same, going straight for the first of the three doors that led to the yard. He tried the file in the lock and found that the point was much too big to fit. The kid ran his hand along the iron mesh that covered the window next to the door. Same kind as the one in his room. He scraped the file on the mesh and discovered that while it cut into the iron, the scraping sound echoed loudly up and down the corridor. And it would take much longer than a single night to saw all the way through.

The kid spun on his heel and jogged back in the direction of Dr. MacBride's office. He crouched next to the office door and saw its simple lock, made for a skeleton key.

He whispered, "Jesus, boy, that ain't enough to keep you safe."

With a couple flicks of the file, the lock popped open, and the kid slipped into the office. The moonlight was more than enough for him to see the room clearly. The kid went to the drawer where he'd seen MacBride put the file on Kamp. He opened the drawer and found it still there, labeled: "Kamp, W. W., Capt. US Army." He looked over the part MacBride had read to him before. In the following pages, he found records listing the medals and honors Kamp earned during the war as well as detailed conduct records. He saw that up to a point, Kamp's record was remarkable in terms of meritorious service and that an abrupt change followed. The kid also saw that according to the records, Kamp had been shot in battle.

He turned the page and found a photograph depicting the profile of a man's head, face up and eyes closed. At the temple, there was a ragged hole roughly the size of a silver dollar. In the photograph's white margin in the bottom right corner, it read, "Patient: W.W. Kamp."

A hand-written note had been clipped to the back of the photograph. "December 15, 1862. Fractures of temporal, sphenoid. Removal of bullet fragments (partial). Surgery unsuccessful. Deceased."

The kid shook his head and muttered, "Shee-*it*, son. You's dead, too."

22

Kamp listened to his boot heels clicking on the planks of the wooden sidewalk and heard nothing else. He made his way to E. Wyles' pharmacy and found it intact, including a new storefront window. He saw a dim glow at the back of the store but no movement. He walked to the alley and then to the back door of the pharmacy and found it unlocked. He knocked softly on the door.

"Emma?"

No answer.

Kamp turned the knob, pushed the door open and saw an assortment of bandages in a pile on the floor. By the light of a kerosene lantern hanging on a hook, he saw the wooden surgical case lying open on the counter, and on the other side of the room, the druggist E. Wyles herself, standing at the counter, sleeves rolled up and blood on her hands.

"What are you doing here?" she said.

"I heard you were in trouble."

"No."

"And that you needed help."

Wyles washed her hands in a steaming bowl of water. "You're too late, Kamp. They're already gone."

"Who is?"

"And, no, I don't know where they went."

"Who?"

"Your cousin. And Nyx."

He said, "She told me you were in trouble and that I needed to hurry."

Wyles looked at him for the first time. "Who told you?"

"That kid, the girl with the blonde hair. She came and got me."

Wyles dried her hands and arms and then threw down the towel in order to end the conversation. "Well, I suppose I appreciate her concern, but I assure you that I'm in no—"

A loud knock came at the front door, then a man's voice. "Open this door immediately!"

Kamp said, "Emma, hide."

"What?"

"Let me talk to them."

She shook her head. "They don't want to talk."

"*Go.*"

She reached down, opened a trap door that led to the cellar and started down the steps. "Whatever you do," she said, "don't let them—" Kamp shut the trap door and went to the front room of the pharmacy. He could see lanterns and torches bobbing up and down outside the window like monstrous fireflies.

The voice came again, "By order of the police, we will be forced to gain entry if you do not immediately—"

Kamp swung the door open to find a group of six men in blue wool uniforms, each wearing an angry countenance and holding a pistol. He recognized one of the men as the young officer whom Nyx Bauer had kicked in the shin, though none of the other officers looked familiar.

"What do you need?" Kamp said.

"Where is she?"

"Who?" The young police officer tried to push past Kamp, who stood in his way. "I'm here alone."

The young officer took handfuls of Kamp's jacket, and with the help of the two officers behind him, spun him around and slammed him face first against the door jamb while the remaining policemen filed in. They pinned his head and yanked his hands behind his back.

Kamp said, "Who told you to come here? Adams? Was it Adams?"

"We know Nadine Bauer was here."

"Adams is a liar."

"Yah, we have it on good information that the fugitive Bauer was here, maybe still is." The young officer frisked Kamp while he talked. "And we know that tribadist gave her medical assistance, too."

"That what?"

Kamp shook his head free, and the young officer punched him in the cheek, drawing two shiny beads of blood. The two men holding him turned him back around to face the young officer.

"Your friend the druggist has been rendering aid to Nadine Bauer. And also to that abomination, Agnes."

The young officer pushed his hat back and rubbed his forehead with the back of his hand. "Seems like you're just a magnet for all kinds of scalawags and defectives, say not? Christ, you got enough of your own problems. You better would mind your own business."

The young officer hit Kamp on the jaw with a right cross that put him on the floor, then kicked him in the ribs. "That's for what you did."

Kamp rolled onto his side, breathing hard.

The young officer continued, "Yah, we know what you did. We know you got away with the murder of an assistant chief."

He took a sheet of paper from his vest pocket and unfolded it. "This is an order from your buddy, the Big Judge. It says we have to arrest Emma Wyles." He put it back in his pocket.

The young officer picked up a canister of kerosene from the floor and poured it on Kamp, splashing it over his legs, torso and face.

"Now, I could set this pharmacy alight, starting with you. Call it a mishap. Or you can do the right thing and save the nice store Miss Wyles has here, and spare yourself in the process, say not?"

Kamp propped himself on one elbow, closed his eyes and shook his head, trying to reorient himself. The young officer pulled a match from his pocket and struck it on the counter.

He said, "When I come here before to see about a break-in, I met that Nadine Bauer. I was respectful about it, too. Not that I had to be. After all, she was the one breaking the law. And all I got for being nice? A kick in the shins. Well, that won't happen no more."

Kamp rolled onto his back and stared up at the young man, his square chin, precisely clipped mustache and hard blue eyes. He said, "You don't understand."

The young officer bent low and held the match six inches from Kamp's face.

"Yah, well, *mebbe* there's plenty of things I do understand." The young officer moved the flame closer to Kamp's face. "People tell me you're a smart man, that you was a fine detective. But you don't seem smart to me."

The young officer blew out the match, and a thin curl of smoke twisted into Kamp's nostrils.

The rest of the men filed out the back door, and then the young officer left, calling over his shoulder, "Tell Emma Wyles to report to the police station. Tell her the Judge said so. And have yourself a pleasant evening."

ADAMS SAT ASTRIDE HER HORSE at the end of the alley that went past the back door of the pharmacy. When the door opened, she caught a whiff of kerosene and counted the police officers emerging one by one. She waited to see if perhaps the fugitives had been hiding and would now try to make their escape. As the grey dawn started sifting in with the last of the night, she saw a man, Kamp, stagger out the back door. He bent over and vomited, then pulled in a few ragged breaths and righted himself. He shuffled the opposite way down the alley, and if he'd seen her at the other end, he made no gesture.

WELL BEFORE SUNRISE, the kid returned Kamp's medical file to the desk drawer and retraced the path back to his room, making sure to lock every door behind him. Finally, he returned file to its compartment in the King James Bible as the dawn chorus swelled in the branches of trees in the hospital yard.

KAMP SAW ADAMS sitting in the saddle when he staggered out the back door of the pharmacy. But he didn't much feel like getting reacquainted. He felt tired, sick, pissed off and beaten up. And he knew sooner or later, she'd be coming after him anyway. He pointed himself north and shambled back over the New Street Bridge.

He pieced together what had happened, surmising that Nyx and Angus had fled from Adams to the pharmacy. Kamp assumed that neither Nyx nor Angus had perished, given the absence of a corpse. Kamp willed his own body forward, feeling the old fires in his left temple and right hip as well as the new ones in his ribcage. Kamp found that he could focus on the rhythm of his feet crunching the gravel road and the rapid chuff-chuffing of his breath. He didn't focus on the miles he had to go to get home. Instead, he pulled his slouch hat low, stared at the road in front of his toes and did his broken marionette march out of town.

When Kamp finally hauled himself up the steps onto his porch and tried to bend down to unlace his boots, he discovered that, owing to the pain in his ribs, he couldn't reach down that far. He let his kerosene-soaked jacket fall from his shoulders, then tried to take off his shirt. He couldn't do that, either. Kamp's body went rigid, and an intense fury arose in him. Stifling a scream, he took the deepest breath he could and blew out a sigh.

The front door creaked open, and Shaw stood in the doorway, her eyes welling with tears.

"Come in, love. Come in."

23

The kid hadn't been asleep for more than an hour before the door of his room opened, and the nurse entered.

"Good morning, Becket."

The kid didn't stir.

"Becket, it's time to wake up." She went to him and gently rubbed his shoulder.

He mumbled, "Much obliged," rolled over and went back to sleep.

The nurse pulled the covers all the way down to the foot of the bed and grabbed him under the armpits.

"Becket, we need you to get up."

"For what?"

"An examination."

He rubbed his eyes with the knuckles of his left hand and said, "Christ, what else is there to examine?"

"For heaven's sake, don't take the lord's name in vain. And remember to be polite to the doctors. They're trying to help you."

"Is Doc MacBride going to be there?"

"Why, yes he is."

"Miss Nurse?"

"Yes, Becket."

"May I bring my Bible with me? I find it most comforting to carry the good book when my heart is troubled."

The nurse smiled. "Of course you may, Becket. Of course."

She led him out of the room, down the main hall, past MacBride's office and into a cold room with a wooden table in the center.

"Lie on the table, Becket."

"What's this about?"

"Just lie down."

The kid looked at the nurse and then back at the table. He climbed up and stretched out on his back, clutching the Bible to his chest with both hands.

"Good boy," the nurse said. "Now just wait there."

She left the room, and as soon as he heard her lock the door, the kid jumped down from the table, took out the file and went to the window. He began filing and immediately cut into the lock. In seconds, he'd sawed through the latch as well, but as he swung the metal lattice away from the window, he heard men's voices approaching. He closed the lattice, hopped back onto the table and returned the file to its hiding place.

The two orderlies entered the room and stood on either side of the table. They were followed by MacBride and a tall, skinny bald man with thick eyebrows and a white coat. The kid had never seen the man before.

MacBride said, "Good morning, Becket. Very good to see you."

The group waited for the kid's reply.

"Mornin'." The kid pulled the Bible close to his side.

"Becket, I must say that I'm very encouraged by your progress, and very pleased."

"That so."

"Yes, so much so that I've already begun thinking about your discharge."

"Hell, I got no discharge."

MacBride gave a thin smile. "No, no. Your release. I'm talking about when you can leave."

The kid sat up and swung his legs over the side of the table.

"All righty then, let's go."

The orderlies immediately took him by his shoulders and eased him onto his back.

MacBride said, "I'm sorry. You're not leaving now."

"Ain't I been here long enough?"

"I assure you your health is my utmost—"

"Doc, iff'n one thing's certain, it's that you don't give a squirt o' piss about my—"

"*Ich sage dir wahrlich.*" The man in the white coat spoke in a deep and somber tone that silenced the bickering.

The kid said, "Come again, fella."

The man spoke slowly and approached the kid, "*Ich sage dir wahrlich: Du wirst nicht von dannen herauskommen, bis du auch den letzten Heller bezahlest.*"

The kid looked at MacBride. "Doc, this fella looks as if he's better suited to work in the morgue than in the hospital. No offense."

The man shifted his gaze from the kid's forehead and looked him in the eye. "The last penny. You von't get out until you have paid the last penny."

"Well, shit, I'm broke. So why don't you an' me jus' call it even, and I'll be on my way."

MacBride gestured to the orderlies. The first orderly pressed his full weight onto the kid's chest, while the second buckled the kid to the table, wrists and ankles. Then he cleared his throat.

"Becket, this is Dr. Schultheis."

The kid stared at Schultheis and then back at Mac-Bride. "What kind of doctor?"

"We're delighted and honored that Dr. Schultheis has come. He's very highly regarded on the Continent for perfecting a number of groundbreaking techniques."

"Then where's his shovel?"

MacBride pursed his lips. "There's no need to be impolite, Becket."

Schultheis bent over the table and began massaging the kid's temples and then ran the tips of his fingers softly across the kid's forehead.

He said, "*Gut, gut...sehr gut,*" speaking softly to himself. He said to the kid, "Close, please" and firmly pressed his thumbs against the kid's eyes.

Then he stood up to his full height, looked at MacBride without emotion and said, "The patient is suitable."

"Suitable for what?" The kid squirmed hard enough to push the Bible halfway off the table. When he saw that it was about to fall, he settled down and focused on MacBride. "Suitable for what, Doc?"

Schultheis bent over again and touched the kid's temples with his thumb and forefinger. "The incisions will be here and here."

"Incisions. Christ!"

"*Und* then we will insert the instrument here."

Schultheis pointed to the tear duct of the kid's left eye.

MacBride smiled and extended his hand to Schultheis.

"Thank you, doctor. Thank you."

Schultheis tilted his head slightly in acknowledgement and then left the room.

MacBride looked at the orderlies and said, "Gentlemen, will you excuse us?"

The orderlies left, closing the door behind them.

MacBride patted the kid on the shoulder. "Now, now, Becket. Rest assured. Dr. Schultheis does extraordinary work. Once he's cured you, you'll be on your way home in no time."

The kid let out a long sigh. "What do you want, doc? Just come out with it."

"I'm afraid the time for bargaining has passed, young man."

"I'll say whatever you want. I'll act polite. Whatever you got in mind. Jus' don't scramble my grits."

"Your fear is understandable, Becket. But the severity of your condition demands that we use extreme measures."

The kid took in a deep breath. "Look, doc, I've been lying this whole time. Lying to my parents. I've just been angry at them, and I wanted to hurt them. I've perpetrated a shamnanigan here, and now I see the harm I've caused."

"You do?"

"Yes, sir. And I've lied to you."

"Well, that's—"

"I apologize. I'm sorry."

MacBride studied the kid for several moments and then unbuckled the straps at his ankles and then his wrists.

"Well, Becket, I must say this is a great relief. Not because we were following the wrong course of treatment but because I can see we've finally gotten through to you."

"Yes, sir, and now I can appreciate it." The kid let his body relax, and he lay motionless on the table.

"In that case later today I'm going to ask you a variety of questions, questions regarding Nadine Bauer, her motives and her whereabouts. I'm going to ask you about Wendell Kamp, the ways he's helped her and about other things he may have told you. I'm also going to ask you about some of your father's business dealings."

"That sounds fine, doctor, I'm ready to help you."

"Excellent, Becket. Is there anything else you can think of that we might need to talk about, that you may have been keeping secret from us?"

"No, sir. I intend to come clean. All the way clean."

"That's wonderful."

MacBride held his hand out to the kid. The kid took it, and as he raised himself to sitting, he nudged the Bible off the edge of the table. It fell on its spine and popped open. The file bounced out of its hiding place and clattered loudly on the floor.

MacBride looked at it and then went to the window, where he saw the iron filings on the sill.

He said, "Hmm," before he spun on his heel and walked out of the room.

WHEN SHAW CAME IN the back door, the fire she'd started was going full blaze, burning up the clothes Kamp had been wearing, including the old thin work jacket he loved but that Shaw had been looking for a reason to get rid of.

Kamp sat in the steaming bath Shaw prepared for him in the large metal washtub she'd put next to the fireplace. He crossed his legs at his ankles and hung his arms over the sides.

Without looking at her, he said, "Appears you've been busy."

All of the files, including the murder files from the police station and the death records Grigg brought from the coroner's office covered every flat surface in the room.

She said, "I couldn't sleep, and when I realized you weren't here, I got worried. And then I got bored."

"Worrying about me is boring?"

She stood directly over him and looked down. "So I started looking through all of that ridiculous paper."

"Anything interesting?"

She smiled and raised her eyebrows.

"Like what?" He tilted his head back and closed his eyes.

"First I went through all the records, looking for anyone with a name that sounded anything like Abel Truax."

"And there was nothing."

"Yes. But then I looked for all the records of dead people whose names weren't known."

"John Does."

"I looked up all of them. I wanted to see if there were any details that might show us it was Truax. Or whoever. And I found this."

She handed him a yellowed sheet of paper.

He read aloud. "Return of a Death. Name of Deceased: Doe, John. Color: white. Sex: male. Age: question mark. Cause of death: unknown. Parents, occupation, place of birth: unknown, unknown, unknown." He looked back up at Shaw. "Okay, this man died. No one knew who he was. What's your *shpitza*?"

"Look at the date of death."

He scanned the form. "December fifteen, 1861. So what?" He tried to hand the paper back to Shaw.

"Now the place of death."

Kamp looked again. "County road two, number seven. Where's that?"

Shaw smiled. "That's the church."

"What church?"

"The one right over there. Evilstalk's church."

"Eberstark."

"Yes."

"Then how come it doesn't say church?"

She shrugged. "You're the detective. Think about it."

He sat up straight in the tub and looked at her. "What? I don't see it."

"It's him," she said.

"Who?"

"Abel Truax. This is his death certificate. This is him."

"Ach, I doubt it."

She pulled up a wooden chair and sat down next to him.

"He told us it happened eleven years ago. He told us it happened in the churchyard and that no one knew who he was."

He raised an eyebrow. "So, you're saying the kid's been telling the truth after all?"

He handed the paper to her, and she inspected it again. "No. But maybe he's seen this. Or he heard the story from someone. But even if that's so, this is the person he was talking about."

Kamp stood up and toweled himself off. "Well, we can't ask the kid, and there's no one else to talk to. Coroner won't answer any questions."

"Doesn't matter."

"Why not?"

"The coroner may not even know about this. He didn't sign it."

"So that's a mystery, too."

"No, love. Look. At the bottom." She held out the certificate, and Kamp made out the signature in the lower right-hand corner of the form. He'd seen it hundreds of times on paperwork when he was the city detective.

It read, "S.D., Cons."

KAMP DIDN'T WAIT for morning, didn't wait to call on Sam Druckenmiller at the police station. Instead, hours after Shaw had gone to sleep, he pulled on his boots and went out the front door, locking it behind him. He heard nothing but late winter wind, and he walked in near total darkness under a thin sliver of moon.

He sorted out the implications and possibilities the death certificate raised, while he walked the mile to the High Constable's house. Since Druckenmiller had known about the body, he probably knew additional details surrounding the death. And if in fact a man, Abel Truax or someone else, had been murdered in the churchyard, steps had been taken to obscure the truth from view. And that meant the murderer, or murderers, would have been working all along to keep the secret. And lastly, Kamp surmised, they'd know Druckenmiller would have to be protected, or killed as well. As such, Kamp expected to see at least one guard outside Druckenmiller's house.

He crouched low when he reached the path to the house and saw the cherry of a lit cigarette glowing next to the front door. From its light Kamp discerned the figure of a man sitting on the front steps with a shotgun across his knees. He backtracked and slipped into the woods that wrapped behind Druckenmiller's property. He circled around to the back of the house, crept to the back door and turned the knob. Locked. He ran his fingers along the top of the door until he felt the spare key.

Kamp opened the door, pocketed the key and went inside. He walked to the front of the house to check on the guard, who was still sitting in the same position, stubbing out the first cigarette and then rolling and lighting another one. Kamp turned and started down the hallway to the bedroom. He hadn't brought a pistol and felt its absence now. He knew, though, that given the protection outside his front door, Druckenmiller would feel safe from harm and probably wouldn't have a gun under his pillow.

Even before Kamp cracked the bedroom door, he heard loud, low snoring and from the way it echoed off the walls and ceiling, he discerned that the High Constable was lying on his back.

Having made no sound thus far, Kamp crept closer to the bedside. He extended his arm, and as he reached the bed, he stepped on a board that made a loud creak.

The snoring stopped and Druckenmiller said, "What in the—"

Kamp put his knee on the man's throat and cupped his hand over Druckenmiller's mouth and nose. Druckenmiller writhed under the pressure, but Kamp held him fast.

Kamp leaned close to his ear, "*Shh.* Settle down and listen. Say a word, and that's it. Understand?" Druckenmiller kept struggling. "Think, Sam. Is this how you want it to end?" The High Constable's body went slack. "I have questions for you. All I need is answers and then I'll leave. Do not speak above a whisper. Understand?"

He nodded.

As soon as Kamp pulled his hand away, Druckenmiller hissed, "*Godammit, Kamp.* You know where I work, why in the name of *Yasus Christus* don'tcha just—"

Kamp slammed his hand over Druckenmiller's mouth again. "Sam, shut up and listen. If that guy out there comes inside, it'll be bad for all of us. Got it?" He let go again.

Druckenmiller whispered, "Yah, yah, I got it."

"The rifle in your basement. It didn't belong to you."

"Yah."

"It belonged to a man whose body you found. Is that right?"

"Yah."

"The man was murdered outside Eberstark's church, correct?"

"Don't know."

"But you found him outside the church."

"Yah, but I didn't see it happen."

"What did the man look like?"

"Dead."

"From what?"

"Ach, I don't know."

"Did you see any wounds?"

"Yah, he had such a bruise on the back of his neck. And a cut, too."

"So someone hit him."

"Ach, I'm telling you I don't *know*."

Kamp glanced out the bedroom window and still saw the glow of the guard's cigarette. He turned back to Druckenmiller. "Did you investigate it?"

"Investigate what?"

"How the man died."

"No."

"Why not?"

Druckenmiller took a long pause, then whispered, "Well, if you find some *nix nootz* nobody knows lyin' there stiff and blue, you don't really wonder *nussing*. Not really. I just wrote a certificate for the guy and forgot about it."

"What did Oehler say about it?"

"Who?"

"The coroner."

"He didn't say *nussing* about it. Probably never even heard about it."

"Why not?"

"Well, by the time I went back into the church to find a winding sheet and come back out, he was *fergonga*."

"Gone?"

"Yah, rifle was there. Body was gone. Didn't see no one take it. Coroner only wants to hear about it if there's a body. You know how he is."

"Where do you think it went?"

"Well, Jesus Boom, I don't know. Maybe he just got up and walked away."

"Why were you there, Sam? Why were you at the church in the first place?"

"Ach, leave."

"Why, Sam?"

"There was a concert that night. Orchestra. I went to go see it on my own time. I went outside in the middle of it. That's when I found him."

"Why did you go outside?"

"Oh *gut in himmel*. I was falling asleep. I was bored. Not everything is a goddamned mystery."

"Sure about that?"

"You can leave the way you came. Don't worry, I won't tell 'em you was here." Druckenmiller pulled the blankets up to his chin and rolled over to face the wall. "Christ, you're an asshole."

Kamp left the way he'd come, circling back to the road through the woods, watching the wax and wane of the guard's cigarette as he went.

KAMP DIDN'T BOTHER trying to sleep and instead watched for the dawn. At sunup, he saw the guard walking on the road in the direction of Bethlehem. He waited for him to pass and disappear over the horizon before heading out on the road himself.

Kamp walked the same route he'd taken when last he'd gone to the church, picking his way through the cemetery, passing again the stones that marked the graves of the upright Jonas and Rachel Bauer, already two years gone. He skirted the graves of his own parents and made for the side yard of the church. He went to the three stairs that led to the cellar door, a heavy oaken slab with a padlock, then turned around and tried to imagine the scene where Druckenmiller discovered the body.

He caught the smell of wood smoke and peered up at the sparks popping from the chimney and at the newly-coppered steeple. He went to the back of the building and looked in through the window to the Reverend A.R. Eberstark's office, where he saw the minister sitting down to a breakfast of toast, Bible open on his desk in front of him. He wore plain clothes and no vestments.

When Kamp knocked on the door, Eberstark showed no surprise and smiled when he saw who it was. He waved Kamp in and then offered him a chair opposite his desk.

"*Guten tag, junge. Wie bischt?*"

"Good. You?"

"God is good, god is good." Eberstark took a large bite of toast and washed it down with a long pull from his coffee. Kamp caught a whiff of alcohol. "How may I help you this fine *Morgen?*"

"Reverend, do you remember a concert that was held here a while back, say, in 1861?"

Eberstark tilted his head back, searching his memory. "Why, no, no, I don't believe I was here yet." He continued looking up.

"Who was the reverend—"

"Oh, wait, wait once. I may have been here. When was it?"

"December. 1861."

"Ach, yes. I was here. I just wasn't installed yet." Eberstark saw the confusion on Kamp's face. "I was here, but my predecessor was still the reverend, a fine man by the name of Alcock."

"Do you remember a concert around that time? Orchestra concert?"

Eberstark finished his toast and drained his coffee while he thought. "Why, yes, now I do. I believe I tried to forget it, though."

"What was the concert?"

"Mozart. I hate Mozart."

"Did you attend?"

"I prefer Wagner. If you put these two men—"

"Did you attend the concert?"

Irritation flashed across Eberstark's face. "I did." He leveled his gaze at Kamp. "Reverend Alcock insisted."

"Reverend, do you recall whether anything unusual happened? In particular, was there any commotion outside the building?"

"Outside the building?"

"Yes, do you remember any commotion outside the church? Fighting or anything?"

Eberstark tilted his head back and closed his eyes. "Why, no."

"Do you mind if I look in the cellar?"

The reverend opened his eyes and faced Kamp. "The cellar? What is this about?"

"I believe there may have been a murder on that night. In the churchyard."

Eberstark produced a whiskey bottle from a desk drawer along with two shot glasses. He poured the whiskey and slid one to Kamp.

"No, thanks."

The reverend stared at Kamp with a flat expression until Kamp lifted his glass.

Eberstark said, "To Luther," and they tossed back their shots.

The reverend lit a candle and gestured for Kamp to follow him down the hallway, then down the creaking stairs to the church basement.

Enough morning light slanted in the windows for them to be able to see most of the room, and Eberstark blew out his candle. While he surveyed the cellar, Kamp made sure to keep the reverend in his field of vision at all times. He saw what he expected, namely spare pews and other old furniture along with building materials for maintenance projects past and future.

"Reverend, do you know whether this cellar was ever used for anything besides storage?"

"Such as what?"

"Hiding people."

"What?"

"Runaway slaves."

He watched his words register on the reverend. Eberstark's brow darkened. "Ach, I knew it."

"Knew what?"

"Knew you come to make *troovel*."

Kamp measured the distance between himself and the stairs. He also looked for the door that led from the cellar to the outside.

Eberstark continued, "I will tell you the truth, though. Even though no one else will."

He faced the reverend. "What's that?"

"Reverend Alcock was a fine man. But he was misguided on some things. Important things."

Even in the partial light of the cellar, Kamp saw color blooming in the reverend's face.

"Like what?"

"Ach, he didn't understand Luther, not well enough. He allowed them wretches to secret themselves in this very cellar."

"Wretches."

"Slaves. Them, them *Shwartzes* in full flight from the law. Alcock had no problem with that."

"Why would he?"

"Ach, don't play dumb. Luther knew, I know and you know, we're all slaves in this world. Slaves to *sin*. Slaves to Lucifer. And *Shwartzes*! They can't just do what they want. That's rebellion. Look here."

Eberstark walked to the door that led to the church-yard and opened it. He went to the bottom step, turned around and pointed to the lintel. Kamp stood beside him and looked. Letters had been carved into the wood. The lintel had been painted over, but the letters remained clearly visible.

It read, "*Tutum loco.*"

Eberstark's face twisted in disgust. "*Tutum loco.* Latin. The language of the papists. Do you know what it means?"

"It means safe place."

"Yah, exactly. Coded words. So when them fugitives from justice found this door, they'd know they could hide here and Alcock wouldn't do them no harm."

"Do you think there may have been a runaway slave here the night of that concert?"

Eberstark gave a self-satisfied grin. "I don't just think. I know."

"How?"

"Why, Alcock told me. Thought I'd go along with it."

"What did you do?"

"I told the correct authorities. Not the police. And they put a stop to it. It wasn't safe for them fugitives, not no more. Believe me."

Kamp scratched his forehead. "I thought you said you weren't in charge yet."

"I wasn't."

"Then why would you go against the reverend's wishes? Isn't *that* disobedient?"

Eberstark's anger boiled over. "God will not be mocked! Listen, Luther himself said, 'Man is like a horse. The horse is obedient and accommodates itself to every movement of the rider and goes whither he wills it. Does God throw down the reins? Then Satan leaps upon the back of the animal!' "

"What's your point?"

"It's time for you to go, Kamp. And know that you, too, will answer for your wretchedness. For living in sin. For disobeying. For leading that child astray."

"What child?"

"Why, Becket Hinsdale. You put demonic ideas in his head. There was probably hope for him before that. But now there's none. Do you know what they intend to do to that boy in that so-called hospital?"

"No."

"They're going to cut into his head, his brain. Ach, you can't loose demons that way! But they're going to do just that, I'm told."

"Who told you?"

Ebertstark shook his head violently and then looked at Kamp. "Jesus said, it would be better for you to have a millstone tied around your neck and be thrown in the river than to cause that little one to suffer. It's your fault. You're just a *schnickelfritz* who can't see straight."

"Thank you for your time, reverend." Kamp put on his hat and left the churchyard.

Eberstark's words trailed after him. "I pray for your soul every day, son. Remember that. Every single day."

24

Kamp jogged onto the road to Bethlehem, settling into the fastest pace he could manage, lungs burning, legs getting heavy. It occurred to him that he might be arrested or shot on sight once he reached town, for breaking into Druckenmiller's house, for helping E. Wyles escape, for any number of things. But the kid's situation was dire, maybe hopeless. And his concern outweighed the consternation he might have otherwise felt upon hitting the city limits.

When he came to the toll booth at the entrance to the New Street Bridge, Kamp fired a penny at the toll collector without slowing down. He kept running until he reached the courthouse steps, bounded up three at a time and went inside before the uniformed policeman at the door even recognized him. When he made it to the Judge's chambers, the door was locked. He pounded on it with his fist.

"Judge! Judge! Open the door. I need to talk to you." He heard no reply, though he thought he heard floor-boards creaking inside, so he lowered his shoulder, his good one, and slammed into the door, breaking the lock and forcing it open. He tumbled and rolled on the floor. The Judge stood in the center of his chambers, wearing his court gown and looking down.

Kamp said, "You can't let them do it, Judge. Don't let them."

"Do what?"

He stood up and brushed himself off. "Surgery. Sounds like they're going to kill him. Or turn him into him into some kind of half-wit."

"Who?"

"The kid. Becket Hinsdale."

"It's outside, far outside, my jurisdiction. I could not interfere in such a way, even if I wanted to. Now if you'll excuse me, I won't make you pay for a new door."

"You're responsible, Judge. You sent him there."

"I saved his life, Wendell. They had worse things in mind for him. And for you."

Kamp raised his eyebrows.

The Judge said, "That's right. I'm still looking out for you, my boy. The unseen hand has a mind to slap you down. I'm not letting it."

Kamp studied his face. The Judge appeared haggard, old, and beaten. "Why not?"

"I have my reasons." The Judge turned and walked to the door that led to the courtroom.

"One more question."

"One more, and another, and another."

"Were you aware of people harboring runaway slaves around here during the war?"

"Before, during, after. Yes, I knew about that." He turned the door knob to the courtroom.

"What about at the church? Did you know that was a safe haven?"

"Yes, yes. Come back later. Come back when court's not in session. *Please.*"

Kamp followed the Judge into the courtroom, where everyone—the attorneys, the defendant and the spectators—was standing and waiting for the Judge to sit down. He heard a collective gasp and saw the bailiff put his hand to the pistol at his hip.

Under his breath Kamp said, "Back then, did Eberstark tell you they were sheltering runaways at the church, and to put a stop to it?"

"That fool knows better than to approach me with any of his idiocy. Now, leave immediately, or I will have you shot."

HE MADE IT BACK to his house even faster than he'd run to town, and he formulated a plan along the way. He intended to tell Margaret Hinsdale what Eberstark had told him in the hopes that she'd immediately go to the hospital and have the surgery called off. First, though, he'd stop at home and let Shaw know what was going on.

When Kamp reached the front door of his house and looked through the window, however, he saw the now-familiar figure of Margaret Hinsdale standing inside. Arms crossed, eyes downcast, she accosted him the moment she saw him come in.

"Did you hear what they're planning to do to him?"

"I did."

He looked over his shoulder at Shaw, who stood in the doorway with Autumn crouched behind her, clutching the hem of her dress. Shaw's expression was blank.

Margaret Hinsdale said, "You have to *do* something."

"I am. I'm trying." He looked at her tear-stained face and red eyes. "What does your husband say?"

"About what?"

"About getting Becket out."

"He says it's the best treatment money can buy." Kamp saw the cords in her neck straining as she talked.

Kamp said, "Have you considered riding to the hospital yourself?"

"I can't! It's *stolen*! They stole it."

"What is?"

"Last night someone stole our carriage and all of our horses."

"And you and your husband were there?"

"Of course. We returned home at four-thirty in the afternoon. They must have come in the dead of night."

"What did they take?"

Margaret Hinsdale furrowed her brow and stared at the floor. "An assortment of Raymond's clothing. A suit and some casual clothes, a top hat. One of my dresses, several items from my toilet table."

"What items?"

"Rice powder and hydrogen peroxide. They also took my gold locket and chain. It has a bird on it, a crane. The crane is holding a silver coin in its beak. It was a gift from my mother when she passed."

Kamp said, "But not everything."

"What?"

"They didn't take all your jewelry."

"No. Just the locket."

Margaret Hinsdale sighed deeply and looked out the window and then back at him. She buttoned her long coat. "They're going to take him away from me forever, aren't they?"

He searched for something to say and came up empty. Margaret Hinsdale put her hand on his arm and said, "It's not your fault. You did everything you could."

Kamp stood at the front window and watched her trudge down the path and to the road. Shaw stood next to him, and Autumn tugged at the leg of his pants, asking to be held. Kamp picked up his daughter, kissed her on the forehead and then turned to face Shaw. She could see his wheels turning.

"What is it?"

"Someone took all of their horses and their carriage and all those things from their house, while they were home."

"She's lying. Or she's nuts. Probably both."

He shook his head. "No. Whoever it was broke into their house earlier in the day and then came back and took the carriage later, after they'd gone to sleep."

"None of it matters anyway."

"Unfortunately, it does."

FROM THE DETAILS Margaret Hinsdale provided, Kamp deduced who'd stolen her property and why. He didn't know exactly how it would play out, but he felt certain it would happen soon. And he knew the last train to Philadelphia, the 2-8-4, would be leaving the Third Street yard around midnight and that if he caught the Black Diamond Unlimited into town, he might barely make it.

He reached the tracks in plenty of time to catch out, but the Unlimited was late. One minute, then five, then ten. He felt his chance for getting the Philadelphia train out of Bethlehem drifting away. Then he heard a whistle, faint at first and then the next one louder.

Kamp began jogging, and as the train cars started gliding past, he picked up the pace. By moonlight he saw the first open boxcar and leapt immediately, catching the handrail and then planting his foot in the iron stirrup. He swung his body into the car and landed with a solid thud.

Thirty minutes later the train began to slow on its approach to the train yard. Kamp knew his train was late and that the 2-8-4 would already be pulling out. He leaned out of the boxcar and saw that, in fact, the train to Philadelphia was leaving the yard on the track adjacent to his. Kamp climbed out of the boxcar and onto the roof.

Even with the gaslights in the yard, he couldn't see the tops of the cars on the 2-8-4 very well and from his perch, he couldn't see the sides of the cars at all. He'd hoped to jump onto another boxcar and then climb down inside it and ride all the way to Philadelphia. But given the overall difficulty of jumping from one moving train to another one heading in the opposite direction, he decided a safe landing was more important than a comfortable ride.

The Unlimited lurched now and again while it slowed, and at the same time the 2-8-4 was gaining speed out of the yard. Kamp stood up on the roof of the boxcar, leaned back and then vaulted himself over the gap between the tracks and landed feet first in a coal hopper. He tumbled to the far side of the car, already covered in coal dust. It would be a cold and dirty ride to Philadelphia, but then again, riding in a car with no roof afforded him a perfect view of the stars.

25

"Welcome to Philadelphia." The conductor roused Kamp from a dead sleep by poking him in the throat with a nightstick.

"Where am I?"

"You're in a coal hopper, idiot."

"Where?"

"Broad Street."

Kamp climbed over the side of the car and jumped down to the ground with the conductor following him.

"You know, riding like that is a good way to get yourself killed."

Kamp surveyed the train yard, trying to get his bearings. "Where's the hospital for the insane?"

"The what?"

"The nut bin. Which way is it?"

The conductor pointed across the yard. "West."

Kamp hustled away, and the conductor called after him, "And I hope you have a nice, long stay."

THE KID SAT STRAPPED in a chair outside the operating theater, forced to listen to sounds inside. He'd seen one patient go in already, a young woman. She'd been shrieking and fighting hard against the restraints. Minutes after she'd been carried into the room, the shrieking abruptly stopped. A short while after that, she'd been carried out, eyes closed and smiling at the corners of her mouth, as if enjoying a blissful dream. The only evidence of the operation was a bandage wrapped around the top of her head.

The kid said to an orderly, "I'm feeling a lot better now. Honest. How 'bout we skip this part?"

No one responded. Instead, the orderlies carried in the next patient, a young man missing his left arm.

THE HORSES PULLING THE FINE CARRIAGE trotted to the iron gates of the Pennsylvania Hospital for the Insane and stopped. A uniformed guard emerged from a small cottage carrying a record book and said to the driver, "Good morrow, sir. May I know the purpose of your visit?"

The driver said, "Good morning. My wife requires a doctor. It's most urgent." He wore a topcoat over a grey three-piece suit, and he had delicate features, a slight build and hair combed straight back under a stovepipe hat.

The guard stared at the man for a moment, then said, "May I know your name, sir? So that I can make a record of your visit."

"Augustus Kneff."

The guard looked him over again and then studied the impressive horses and carriage, its shiny brass fittings and black lacquered wood.

"May I see inside, please?"

"Of course."

The guard walked to the side of the carriage and peered through the window. He saw a woman, head down, hair cropped close. The guard stared at the woman's porcelain neck and at the place where it curved and met the base of her skull. The woman snapped her head around to look at the guard. She raised her eyebrows and smirked.

The guard said, "Thank you, Mr. Kneff." He tipped his cap and swung open the gates.

KAMP HAD TO KEEP ASKING for directions as he made his way from the train station to the hospital. Some gave him what seemed to be accurate directions. Others, noting his sooty, disheveled appearance, simply scoffed at him or told him to go back the way he came. But he persisted, picking up the pace and fighting the fear he might get there a moment too late.

ANOTHER PATIENT WENT IN screaming and then emerged half an hour later, same as the first two. Asleep, pacified, bandaged. The orderlies approached the kid.

He said, "Boys, iff'n there's some sort of arrangement we can make, I'd prefer we do it now. At least, let's us make peace."

The orderlies didn't take him into the operating theater. Instead, they walked past, the first orderly saying, "Be patient, fella. It'll be your turn soon enough."

DR. ALISTAIR MACBRIDE SAT at his desk filling out paperwork. He'd told his staff not to bother him, as he had a great many forms to complete. He heard the carriage wheels crunching on the gravel outside, and since he didn't have any meetings scheduled and didn't expect visitors, he tried not to pay attention. A glint of sunlight from a horse's brass throatlatch caught him in the eye, and he looked out the window. He saw the driver in the top hat, coat and expensive wool suit. MacBride remained determined not to be disturbed. He didn't have time for a new admission, and these people, whoever they were, would have to wait.

But MacBride still couldn't help watching the driver clamber down and open the carriage door for the passenger inside. He saw one leg emerge, then the other, and then she appeared. She wore an exquisite silk dress the color of indigo with a low neckline and a hat of the same color, adorned with what MacBride recognized as two feathers from a night heron.

He didn't bother trying not to stare, knowing that the couple couldn't see into his office through the wooden blinds. He watched her mount the stairs, wobbling slightly sideways before the man took her softly by the elbow. MacBride went to the front doors and out onto the portico.

He called to them, "Good morning!"

The couple reached the top of the stairs, and the man took off his top hat with his left hand and extended his right.

"Augustus Kneff. And this is my wife, Nadja."

The doctor shook his hand. "I'm Dr. MacBride." He turned his head to face the woman. "Pleased to meet you."

"Enchanted." She took off her hat, revealing platinum-colored hair.

"Might I say that's a lovely pendant?" MacBride gestured to the locket hanging just above her breasts and leaned forward to get a closer look. It was solid gold with an engraving of a crane standing in water beside cat o' nine tails. The bird held a coin in its beak.

MacBride stood up to his full height and studied her face, her powdered white cheeks, blue eyes, red lips.

Kneff said, "Doctor, may I speak with you in private?"

MacBride snapped to attention. "Yes, yes, of course. Let's go inside."

When they reached his office doors, Augustus Kneff turned to his wife and said, "Wait outside, dear."

MacBride showed her to an overstuffed chair in the lobby. He held her hand, giving it a gentle squeeze as she sat down. She smiled at him and touched the back of her neck.

The doctor turned on his heel and strode back to his office, where the man was already seated in a chair. MacBride closed the door and sat opposite Kneff.

"Now, Mr. Kneff, how may I be of assistance?"

The man removed his top hat and stared down at the floor. "Well, doctor, I'm afraid this is a bit, a bit difficult to discuss." He turned the top hat nervously in his hands. "Well, not just difficult. It's shameful."

"It's quite all right, Mr. Kneff. You're safe here."

Kneff looked up at MacBride. "And I assure you, the difficulty is not financial. I have more than enough money to—"

"I'm certain of that. Please, please, tell me the problem."

The man took a deep breath and let out a long sigh. "It's my wife."

"Yes, I thought so."

"She's mad."

"In what way, Mr. Kneff?"

Kneff looked up at MacBride and then back down at the floor. "I don't want to...I can't say it."

MacBride leaned forward and put his hand on the man's knee. "Mr. Kneff. Augustus. There's no shame here. You can tell me."

Augustus Kneff sat up straight, looked MacBride in the eye and said, "Her madness is sexual excitement. Ungovernable, uncontrollable lust."

MacBride's eyebrows popped up. "Really."

"I mean this woman's hunger knows no bounds. Day and night. Men, women. Why, this very morning I found her—"

MacBride held up his hands. "Mr. Kneff, it's fine, it's fine. Say no more. I understand."

"You do?"

"Yes, I've seen this kind of insanity before. Nymphomania."

"Nymphomania?"

"It's real."

Kneff shook his head and said, "I guess I knew it all along, but I thought marriage would cure it."

"We can help."

"You can?"

"Of course. I suggest we admit her right away. This instant."

Kneff stood up and smiled. "Thank you, doctor. Thank you. What a relief."

"Yes, well, why don't I give you a tour whilst her room is being prepared?"

"Much obliged, doctor. And if you don't mind, I'd like to have Nadja's things brought in as well."

MacBride stiffened. "What things?"

"A trunk. Clothing, a few personal items. It's lashed to the back of the carriage."

"We have all the clothing she'll need. And I'm afraid we don't allow personal items."

Kneff spoke quietly. "Doctor, she refused to stay here unless we brought her things. She was exceedingly concerned that—"

"What is it?" The woman appeared next to MacBride, looking nervous and upset.

"Nothing, sweetheart. It's just that Dr. MacBride said you can't bring your—"

"Oh, I'll allow it," MacBride said, "considering the circumstances." He motioned to two attendants and said, "See that this lady's trunk is brought in immediately." He turned back to the couple. "Now, if you'll kindly follow me."

THE KID HEARD MURMURING inside the operating theater, and the door opened. Another patient was carried out and then the surgeon, Dr. Schultheis, emerged, hands and forearms splattered with blood.

He stared down at the kid and without expression, said, "*Nächste.*"

The kid strained against the straps at his wrists and ankles one more time, and none of them gave. He slumped forward and hung his head. He heard voices at the end of the hallway, one of them belonging to MacBride, who was leading a man and woman toward him.

The kid looked up and focused on the woman and said, "Well, my angel of mercy has finally come to deliver me."

MacBride said, "Master Hinsdale, good to see you this fine morning." He turned to the couple and said, "We offer the newest and most effective moral treatments here. As this boy is about to find out."

The kid looked hard at the woman and recognized her as Nyx Bauer. His eyebrows shot up, and he stifled a grin. Nyx put her first finger to her lips, then said, "What a lucky boy."

MacBride gently moved them along. "There's much more to see."

As the trio departed, the two orderlies appeared, unbuckled the straps and carried the kid into the operating theater.

26

When Margaret Hinsdale said her house had been burgled, Kamp had guessed that Nyx and Angus had done it. And when she'd said the carriage and horses had been stolen as well, he knew why. As the hospital gates came into view, he figured he'd see the Hinsdales' carriage parked at the front steps of the hospital. He'd deduced that Nyx intended to return the favor to the kid and that Angus would gladly help her. Now, peering through the iron bars, he saw the carriage and the horses standing in front of it. He also saw two men unloading a large steamer trunk from the back of the carriage.

What Kamp didn't know was how he'd get in. He approached the guard, who eyed him through the window of the small cottage next to the gates.

Kamp approached the window and waved. "Good morning."

The guard opened the window. "Good morrow, sir."

"I'm here to see my cousin."

"I'm afraid that won't be possible"

"Why not?"

"The residents are not receiving visitors today."

Kamp felt the fire starting at the base of his skull. "I just got to town."

"I'm afraid that doesn't matter."

"It's just that I know it would mean a great deal to him to see me. He hasn't been feeling well. Obviously."

Kamp could see that the front gates were locked and that to get the key, he'd have to assault the guard. Breaking in that way would raise alarms throughout the hospital, putting Nyx and Angus in jeopardy. He also realized that since he was still covered head to toe in coal dust, he'd have no chance of blending in with the hospital staff.

The guard sat up in his chair. "Come back tomorrow, sir."

And he slammed the window shut.

DR. SCHULTHEIS CLOSED THE DOOR behind him as he strode back into the operating theater. The kid couldn't see him, or even turn his head, as the orderlies had secured it fast to the table.

"Say, doc, is there any chance you could go ahead an' knock me out for the next part?"

Schultheis leaned over and stared straight down at the kid. "I'm afraid you must be fully awake."

"What for, if you's just gonna put my lights out."

The doctor turned to the nurse and said, "Make him ready."

WHEN THEY RETURNED TO THE LOBBY, Dr. MacBride turned to face the couple and held out his arms expansively.

He said to Angus, "I think you'll agree, Mr. Kneff, that your wife will be exceedingly well taken care of during her stay here."

Angus said, "Why sure," and pulled a revolver from a shoulder rig under his jacket and put it to MacBride's forehead. Nyx went to the steamer trunk, unlocked it and removed the Henry rifle.

"Take us back to the kid," she said.

"The who?"

"The kid. Becket Hinsdale. Take us to him."

SCHULTHEIS HEARD NOTHING. He'd entered a state of consciousness in which nothing existed apart from the instrument in his hand and the precise location at which he would make the incision, just above the left eyeball. His existence narrowed to the point of the scalpel as it punctured the skin and then went deeper.

The surgeon didn't hear the commotion coming down the hallway, didn't even hear the door fly open. He didn't lose focus on the work at hand until Nyx Bauer caught him across the jaw with the butt of the rifle. He dropped straight to the floor, scalpel clattering to the concrete.

Angus worked quickly to release the kid, who had blood pouring from the cut above his eye.

He said, "Much obliged," then jumped down from the table.

MacBride, for his part, didn't speak. He stood in the far corner of the operating theater, trying not to look directly at anyone but still unable to pull his eyes away. Nyx Bauer raised the rifle and pointed it at his face.

The kid said, "Doc MacBride, I tol' you my deliverance was comin', and now it's here. An' I tol' y'all you ought not have done what you did, 'specially to somebody who appears to be a child."

MacBride held his palms out. "Becket, please. Everything we did was for your own good."

"Like hell it was."

MacBride's entire body began to shake, and he fell to his knees. "Please! Don't!"

The kid said, "You may recall that I don't take no revenge. I been to another place, and I seen how things work there. Revenge ain't no part of it."

"That's right. You said that."

"So in return for us not killing you this fine morning, I expect you to extend mercy, real mercy, to all the lost souls that have the misfortune to pass through here. An' not the bullshit you pass off as mercy, neither. Compassion, real an' honest. Do you know what that means?"

"Yes, yes. I do."

Angus grabbed the kid by the collar and said, "Time to go."

Nyx lowered the rifle and went back out into the hallway, where she saw both orderlies running at them full tilt.

She raised the rifle again and said, "Stop!" But they kept coming. Nyx aimed the repeater and squeezed the trigger three times, hitting the first orderly twice in the center of his chest and once in the face. The second turned and ran.

Nyx, Angus and the kid hustled back up the stairs, stopping at the kid's room and gathering up his clothes. They ran to the main hallway and through the lobby. Angus grabbed the trunk dragged it out with him, following Nyx and the kid. He lashed the trunk to the back of the carriage, then climbed up to the driver's seat, where he was joined by Nyx, rifle still in hand. The kid got inside the carriage and closed the door.

The morning routines of the patients were little, if at all, disturbed by the sight of a man, woman and child scrambling onto a carriage and bolting for the front gate. The staff, too, did less than one might have expected to catch them.

No patient or staff member did anything to impede the progress of the carriage toward the gate, no one except the fastidious guard in his cottage. He saw the carriage coming and decided that it would not leave.

Kamp, who still stood outside the grounds, saw the guard emerge from his building and stand directly in front of the gate. He also saw the carriage approaching and knew that they wouldn't be able to crash through. And then he saw the guard remove a pistol of his own and hold it at his side.

Kamp ran to the wall next to the gate and leapt for the vines that clung to it. Hand over hand, he hauled himself to the top of the wall and first swung one leg and then the other over the iron spikes that jutted from it. He landed hard on the ground on the other side and stood up to see the guard raising his pistol at the oncoming carriage. The guard fired one shot before Kamp slammed into him, knocking him flat. He gripped the guard's throat with his left hand and removed the ring of keys from the man's belt with his right.

Kamp said, "Which one?"

"What?"

"The gate. Which key?"

The man gestured to a large skeleton key. Kamp took the man's gun and ring of keys and ran to the gate. He turned the key in the lock, and it didn't open. He tried a different key. No luck. Kamp turned and looked at the guard who was running to safety.

By this point the carriage had almost reached him, and he could also see a dozen men streaming from the front doors of the hospital and taking up positions within range of the front gate. Kamp tried another key on the ring, and then the next and the next. None worked. Finally, he took the man's pistol and shot the iron padlock until it blew into three pieces and came free.

Kamp swung open the gates just as the horses passed through. He ran alongside the carriage until Nyx and Angus recognized him and then he jumped for the step and the handle and held on tight to the side.

The kid pushed the door open, smiled and said, "C'mon in, son."

AS SOON AS THEY'D MADE IT a mile or so from the hospital, Nyx set the rifle at her feet, put her hat back on and assumed the appearance of a woman simply enjoying the early spring weather.

Inside the carriage Kamp sat facing the kid, looking at the wound above his eye, which had crusted over with dried blood. "You don't look so good," he said.

The kid looked at the dirt and dust covering Kamp head to toe. He said, "You neither," and then laughed. "You know, when me an' Onesimus was breaker boys, we looked like that every day, sunrise to nightfall."

The kid fished a silver case from his pocket. He opened it, took out a cigarette and put it between his lips. He took a box of matches from the other pocket, struck one, lit the cigarette and took a long pull. He tilted his head back, savoring it. He exhaled and looked at Kamp.

The kid said, "I know you don't want me smoking, son, but damned if this don't taste sweet right about now."

"Where'd you get it?"

The kid held the cigarette between his thumb and first finger and inspected it. "Doc MacBride. Stole it off him. From his desk. Want one?"

Kamp shook his head. The kid took another puff and stared out the window. For a moment the carriage fell silent.

The kid said, "I reckon Margaret tol' you 'bout that time she took me to West Virginia, took me to the holler I come from."

Kamp nodded.

"Tol' you how when I seen my father's house, how I jus' went all to splinters."

"Yes, she told me." Kamp saw the color rise in the kid's face and saw his bottom lip begin to twitch.

"I don't mind tellin' you, son, that house was the ramshacklest thing you ever seen, all caved in on itself. Enough to break any man's heart."

"She told me."

The kid stared at his bare feet. "I'll tell you somethin' else, somethin' I never told no one before. Remember how I said my father died from handlin' on snakes?"

"Yes."

"Well, on that day when I seen the spirit drain away outta Martin L. Truax, an' I seen him go cold and blue, I just couldn't take it. I knowed my own world ended right there, much as I loved that man. An' then I didn't want to live myself, no how. So, I took up that same serpent that done it, and I made it bite me, again and again. I made certain I got all the killing power that serpent had left. Made certain it got in my veins. Look here."

The kid turned up his left wrist and held it out to Kamp. He saw a half dozen white spots, scars.

The kid said, "That's right, them scars followed me from one cursed life t' the next."

"But you didn't die from it. The snakebite."

The kid shook his head. "That's the real shit of it. I couldn't, didn't die, much as I wanted to, much as I prayed for it."

"Why not?"

"Why not what?"

"Why do you think you didn't die?"

"That ol' snake was prob'ly low on the venom by the time he got me. Don't matter though, warn't no reason to keep livin' after that. 'Cept I did get to help free my friend Onesimus Tucks. That was a good thing."

"Yes, it was."

"But, hell, then when I finally got killed, they went an' sent me back anyhow. I know, I know, yer gonna say, why, why'd they do it? Don't know, 'cept maybe for one thing."

"What?"

The kid cleared his throat and spat out the window, then fell silent for a long time.

He looked back at Kamp and said, "Glad as I was to see you folks, I apologize for putting you to the trouble. I didn't want to be caught up in none o' this. I don't want to be here, understand? I just want to be rid of all this."

"Makes sense."

The kid tilted his head and studied Kamp. "Say, I come across a paper that says you were in there, in that bughouse. Is that true?"

"Yes."

"Says that you was dead, too. That you perished in the war. What about that?"

Kamp raised his eyebrows, opened his mouth to speak, and then paused.

The kid said, "It's all right, son. There's stories none of us should have to tell." He took in a deep breath and looked out the window again. "There ain't enough like us, son, living or dead. Not nearly enough like you an' me an' Nyx. An' who's that with Nyx?"

"My cousin. Angus."

"Yeah, him too. There oughta be more of us, but there ain't." The kid took another long pause and then focused on Kamp again. "You figure out who killed me yet?"

"I think so. I have to make sure."

"Yeah, I believe I got it figured, too."

27

At a moment well before the sunrise, when her husband walked out the front door and shut it behind him, Margaret Hinsdale awoke from her nightmare, ribs squeezed with fear. She calmed herself by counting silently backward from ten, again and again, listening for the first bird sounds of morning and hearing none. Just before first light, she heard noises at the back of the house that she took to be her husband's return. He must have forgotten something, she thought, as she counted backward once more and drifted into the first real sleep all night.

When she woke up again, hours after the dawn, Margaret Hinsdale heard horses nickering and stomping their hooves. She went to the window and saw the horses and the carriage, exactly where they'd been before they were stolen.

She ran outside and called to them, "You're here, you're here."

She also found the steamer trunk, swung open the lid and saw all of the items that had been taken, including her locket. She picked it up and opened it. The face of her boy in the tiny photograph looked back at her. Inside Raymond's top hat, she found a note handwritten in pencil. It read, "Thank you."

Tears flowed down both her cheeks. Margaret Hinsdale ran in the house and up the stairs to her son's room. She saw his golden head of hair like straw and the rise and fall of his chest under the blankets. She went to the boy and cradled him.

She talked between sobs, "My boy, my boy. You've come back. My sweet boy."

He opened one eye and grinned. "Sure feels good to wake up in my own bed."

KAMP HAD SLEPT in his own bed that night as well, or at least he had tried. Upon returning home, he'd washed his face and hands and had climbed into bed next to Shaw.

"I love you," she'd said, and immediately gone back to sleep. He lay awake for a half hour or so, then gave up. He went downstairs, lit a lantern and ground some coffee beans. When he sat down to drink his cup, he saw a handbill on the kitchen table.

Shaw had written on it, "This."

It read, "One Night Only, the music of Wolfgang Amadeus Mozart at the Lutheran Church, Bethlehem, December the 15ᵗʰ. The Requiem in D minor."

He scanned the rest of the handbill, particularly the small print at the bottom, which named the underwriter of the concert, Native Iron. He turned the handbill over and saw a list of names, written in pencil. He committed the list to memory, folded the handbill and put it in the pocket of his jacket before lacing up his boots, pulling on his slouch hat and leaving again.

RAYMOND HINSDALE DIDN'T HEAR the horses and carriage pull up to the house, because they'd waited until they were certain he was gone for the day. He might not have paid attention even if he had heard the carriage, fixated as he was on getting to the office. He walked the dark road purposefully, head down, not noticing the dawn chorus, not feeling the shift in the weather, a breeze slightly warmer, and not seeing the purple line horizon.

He didn't recognize anything different at all that morning until he unlocked the door of his office, went in, and found Kamp sitting on the edge of his wide, impressive desk.

Hinsdale stood up straight, evaluating Kamp, looking for the man's intention. He held out his hands and said, "I'm not armed."

"Me neither."

"You're trespassing."

"I didn't want to upset them by going to your house."

"Them?"

"Your wife and your son. They're both there."

Hinsdale shook his head, barely concealing rage. "Becket is still—"

"No, he's not. He's at your house right now, probably asleep in his bed."

"Mr. Kamp—"

"Kamp."

"When last we spoke, you assaulted me. Now, you've broken into my office—"

"You need to tell them." Kamp didn't feel anger, didn't change his tone. "They deserve to hear the truth. The lie is killing them."

"What in god's name—"

"You fell in love with the same woman, the prostitute. You and Abel Truax."

"You're insane."

"You saw him as a competitor and a threat. And you knew if he told your secrets, he could destroy you. He was a dangerous man." Kamp watched Hinsdale calculating his next move. "You were working for Native Iron the night of the concert. You were there. And someone, I don't know who, told you Abel Truax was going to be there. And then you realized you could get rid of him and do someone else a favor at the same time."

"Favor?"

"Truax wanted to free a man who'd been wrongfully imprisoned in the church cellar. Someone stood to gain from preventing that man from going free. My guess is that it had to have been someone from Native Iron, from the Order of the Raven. You might've even gotten a promotion for your trouble. Maybe that's why you're in charge of Black Feather Extraction."

"Your facts are wildly inaccurate, as usual."

"You took a pickaxe or a shovel from the shed and stole up on Truax. One swing and it was over."

"Wrong."

"It doesn't matter."

Hinsdale said, "Of course it matters. You're the malefactor here, because you have a vendetta. Against my employer, and therefore against me. If you did in fact kidnap my son from the hospital, you're preventing him from getting the attention he desperately needs."

"Tell them, Raymond."

"Do you tell your family all of your secrets? Do you?"

"Tell them the truth."

Raymond Hinsdale stared down at his hands. "What I share and with whom is my business, of course. And none of yours. Your problem is your mouth and your inability and unwillingness to leave good people in peace."

"Good people."

"Indeed, this city, this region has grown in so many ways that promote the greater good. This region is thriving. People's lives are improving. Detectives like you just want to tear things down, want to hurt others. You need to hurt people because you've been hurt."

Kamp rubbed the bridge of his nose with his thumb and forefinger. "Just tell them."

"They won't allow you to live." Hinsdale took off his coat and hat and put them on the rack.

"Who won't?"

"You want the truth to be known? The truth is that you're an idiot and a fool. It's time you left. Good day."

KAMP HURRIED HOME the way he'd come, assessing the meaning of the conversation he'd just had. He didn't think Raymond Hinsdale would confess but neither did he expect the man, upon hearing his accusations, simply to sit down and commence his daily business. Hinsdale seemed angry but not discomfited in the slightest, and the man's lack of a strong reaction struck him as odd, given that he'd broken into the man's office and accused him of murder.

Then again, he thought, Hinsdale had likely had considerable experience with hiding his misdeeds and burying whatever human emotions may have accompanied them.

Kamp knew Hinsdale's threats were real, and he turned his attention to getting home, making sure Shaw and Autumn were safe. He didn't imagine that anyone would be troubling him or his family on this fine morning, but the knot in his gut told him otherwise. When his house came into view, he saw a man on the front porch, hands cupped around his eyes, peering into the front window.

Kamp broke into a run. "Hey! Hey!" He tried to tell if the man had a gun, but there was no way to know. "Get away from there!"

The man wheeled around, and Kamp saw that it was the prosecutor, Grigg.

Grigg said, "My goodness, you gave me such a fright."

"Yah, me too."

The prosecutor smiled and extended his hand, and Kamp shook it. "You've been busy."

"What brings you here?"

"My briefcase. I need it back."

Kamp went to the front door and unlocked it. When he pushed the door open, he caught the smell of wood smoke and saw a smoldering fire.

"Shaw? Shaw?" No answer.

"I don't think anyone's home. I've been here a good five minutes. I haven't heard anything."

Kamp walked upstairs and checked each room. He came back carrying the briefcase and handed it to Grigg, who said, "I hope you found what you needed."

"And then some." He looked Grigg in the eye. "Thank you."

Grigg said, "I heard Becket Hinsdale escaped from the insane asylum. Authorities said two men and a woman with a rifle broke him out."

"Yah."

"You weren't in Philadelphia yesterday by any chance, were you?"

"Is there some way I can help you, Mr. Grigg?"

"Don't worry. No one has identified you, although I'm sure the Order has already figured it out."

"I wish you well." Kamp gestured to the front door.

Grigg turned to go, then turned back around and said, "The man Nyx Bauer shot at the hospital, the orderly. His name was Mungo Leach. He died. Don't worry about that, either. He didn't have a family. And you heard about Emma Wyles."

"Heard what?"

"She turned herself in to the police."

"For what?"

"Aiding and abetting a fugitive. Or two. Your cousin was with Nyx Bauer when they went to her shop, correct?"

Kamp shrugged his shoulders.

"Yes, well. She's still in jail. One bit of advice. Let her get herself out."

Grigg buttoned his coat, picked up his briefcase, bowed slightly to Kamp and went to the door. He put his hand on the doorknob and said, "The coroner was furious that I took his files, but if it ultimately helps bring justice, then of course it was worth it."

"And I owe you one."

Grigg smiled, "At least one. Goodbye."

Kamp closed the door and turned to see Autumn standing at his feet, arms raised.

"Daddy's home," she said.

He picked her up, kissed her on the forehead and said, "Yes, he is."

LONG AFTER his family had gone to sleep that night, Kamp checked and rechecked all the house's doors and windows to be sure they were locked tight. If someone were to attack, it would most certainly be Adams. He intended to lie awake until dawn, but a powerful relaxation overtook him immediately, and he began to dream.

He dreamt of the mountain behind his house, and in the dream he was flying and looking down at the mountaintop. He saw his brothers down there, and himself. Pulling up and soaring into the sky and clouds, Kamp descended into the first deep sleep he'd known in years.

28

Once she was certain Kamp had gone to bed, Adams started inspecting the locks, jiggling each slightly to see if it would give and to what extent it would be amenable to being picked. She stepped silently across the porch, going to the first window, then the door, then the next window, patiently and precisely searching for a way in. When she finished, she went to the back of the house and checked all those locks as well.

Knowing that Kamp was exceedingly vigilant and likely an insomniac, Adams exercised extreme caution. She believed she could cut him down in a knife fight if necessary, but she didn't want commotion. She wanted to bleed him right in the bed next to his woman, without a sound. Adams wanted a way in, but the locks were too tight.

She went around the side of the house and found the bulkhead doors lit by bright moonlight. Even as she approached, she could see that the padlock was open and that the chain had been removed. She lifted the right-hand door to test it. The door was well-oiled and swung freely. Adams steadied herself and slowly inched it open further. She had no flame or lantern and couldn't afford the risk of lighting one, so she let her steps guide her down into the darkness. Besides, she didn't need to hurry. The moment would come soon enough.

Adams reached the bottom step and felt for the dirt floor with her right foot, planting it on solid ground. She let the blade slip from the sleeve of her jacket and began moving across the floor to where the base of the stairs would be, in the center of the cellar.

Kamp snapped from his dream, heart slamming in his chest. A stifling fear hit him, but he couldn't find its origin. He forced himself to lie still and let it come to him, while he listened to the gentle sounds of Shaw's breathing.

The pitch darkness intensified Adams' other senses. She smelled the damp earth and the dried vegetables and herbs, garlic the most. She caught another smell, an animal smell. Rats in the cellar, she thought.

Kamp's heart didn't slow and in fact raced even faster. His thoughts swirled in a great cyclone until the realization finally came. He'd forgotten to lock the bulkhead doors, and now she was in the house. He felt certain of it.

Adams made out the dim outline of the staircase and moved for it. The animal smell, which had been faint before now filled both nostrils. She recognized the presence of a being in the cellar, though she couldn't see it.

She readied her blade and took another step, placing her foot squarely on the neck of the hibernating bear. The animal roared from its slumber, and when, from instinct, Adams slashed with the knife, the bear caught her wrist in its jaws, biting down with the force of nature.

The bear pulled Adams' hand deeper into her jaws, chewing and working the wrist with her back teeth. Adams brought her fist down atop the bear's head, angering the beast further. Adams pulled until her forearm came free, hand and wrist gone.

Adams scrambled out the bulkhead doors, cradling her arm which sprayed blood. The bear, famished from the long sleep, crunched all the bones and swallowed before standing up stiffly and departing the cellar as well.

Kamp heard what he thought might be a growl and then a thump in the cellar. He swung his legs over the side of the bed, crept downstairs and stood in the kitchen, listening for several minutes. He heard nothing but the first robin of the new morning. He lit a candle, and as soon as he opened the cellar door, a strong breeze blew it out. His heart began pounding anew. She was there after all, or had been.

When he reached the bottom step, he went to where he knew the bear was hibernating, though he couldn't hear her. Kamp put his hand to the warm, wet ground and rubbed his fingers together until they became sticky. Blood, not piss. He kept feeling along the floor, realizing what had happened. Kamp wasn't surprised when his fingers brushed a very sharp blade.

He walked back upstairs and inspected the weapon, a Bowie knife with an elk handle. Indian, Kamp knew. He turned over the blade and saw engraved there the face of a figure, smiling and wearing a cap in the Phrygian style.

"THE GIRL CANNOT BE CONSOLED," Shaw said.

Kamp went to Autumn, who sat in the corner by the front window, sobbing.

"She left. She left!"

He sat down next to her. "I know, sweetheart. She's gone, but she had to leave. It's spring. That's how bears are."

The tears slowed, and then Autumn looked at him and said, "She'll come back, won't she?"

Kamp's mind went to the trail of blood leading from the cellar. Adams had been mauled, that was certain. But it was possible she'd delivered a mortal wound as well.

The little girl stood up, threw her arms around Kamp's neck and then ran out the front door. Kamp stood up and waited for the soreness in his hip to abate.

"Do you think she'll be back?" Shaw said.

"The bear?"

"Adams."

Kamp and Shaw stood side by side, watching their daughter walking toward the tree line.

"Eventually, maybe. Not soon."

He pulled on his boots, jacket and slouch hat.

"You're not—"

"No, I'm not going anywhere. Just outside."

KAMP PULLED THE TARP OFF THE PLANKS, precisely where he'd left them the day after the kid first appeared in his yard. He counted the boards and measured them, making adjustments in his mind based on his new plan.

He allowed himself to focus solely on the task at hand, sorting materials and imagining the structure he intended to build. The exertion loosened his joints and muscles, and soon Kamp ditched his jacket and hat and rolled up his sleeves. Winter had conceded, and it felt good to be warmer, to be working, and to be at home.

He knew the kid would appear and suspected he knew the reason for his visit. And so Kamp didn't look up from his labor when he heard footfalls crunching on the trail to his house.

"Son, it's good to see you takin' the fresh air and doin' honest work."

"Good morning. How can I help you?"

There was a pause until Kamp stopped working and looked at the kid, who said, "Well, I don't believe you can help me, not this time."

The kid wasn't clad in the familiar velvet trousers and jacket. Instead, he wore a cotton shirt, canvas pants, work boots and no cap atop of his head of straw-like hair. He carried nothing, no haversack and no bindle.

Kamp stood up straight, tilted his head back and wiped the sweat from his brow with the back of his hand. "Why not?"

"You already helped me in a lot of ways."

"But I never told you who killed you."

The kid gave him a sad smile. "No, I figured it out while I was lyin' there in that box they stuffed me into in the hospital. Probably knew all along. Just din't wanna believe it."

"I'm sorry they put you—"

"They're not evil, son, no. Confused, maybe."

"Yah, well, that doesn't—"

"Truth is, I jus' needed to know one bitty thing from Raymond, and he did tell me, the thing I had to know so I can be on my way."

"What was it?"

"What was what?"

"The one thing you needed to know."

The kid turned back and looked at the road and then the path up the mountain.

The kid said, "Last thing I need t' say." His bottom lip started to tremble. "You been a most worthy and upright friend to this ol' West Virginia boy. An' I ain't ashamed to tell you, son, I love you. I really do."

Tears streamed down the kid's face as he threw his arms around Kamp, hugging him and then letting go. He straightened up and said, "Look at me, a grown man, cryin' like a child."

Kamp waited for the kid to compose himself and said, "I decided not to build a new slaughterhouse after all."

"How come?"

Kamp felt his own throat catch. "I don't know."

"But it appears you're fixin' to build something anyhow."

Kamp surveyed the materials and the site he'd chosen. "Yah, another house. Once it's ready, you're welcome to live there."

The kid let out a sigh and tilted his head. "That is most kind, though my business is settled, and it's time for me to go."

"But what was the one thing you needed to know?"

"You's curious, son, and most tenacious. That's another thing I'll miss about you. You'll get word soon enough, along with due recompense."

"I don't need any recom—"

"Goodbye, son." The kid held out his hand and Kamp shook it. Then he walked past Kamp to the tree line and onto the trail up the mountain.

He called over his shoulder, "First off, remember that he that shall endure unto the end, the same shall be saved. And second, when you meet Onesimus Tucks, iff'n you ever do, tell 'im, they ain't broke us an' they never will."

And the kid was gone.

THE NEXT DAY Kamp heard hooves on the road and then saw Margaret Hinsdale riding up the path to his house. She dismounted, tied up the horse and took a package from one of the saddle bags. Kamp walked to the front porch to meet her.

"Good morning," he said.

She said, "May I come in?" and went straight past him and into the house.

Margaret Hinsdale set down her package on the wooden table in the front room. Then, she turned to face him. Her hair was pulled back, revealing all her features.

She said, "He's gone, isn't he?"

"Who?"

"My son."

"I don't know."

"When was he here last?"

"May I offer you a drink, Mrs. Hinsdale?" Kamp started for the kitchen.

"When!"

He stopped. "Yesterday."

Margaret Hinsdale stood straight, arms crossed and shoulders stiff. "Where did he go when he left?"

"Up the trail."

"Did you try to stop him?"

"No."

She stared at the floor, crossed her arms tighter and pursed her lips as if to hold back an explosion.

"Then he's gone."

"Mrs. Hinsdale, do you know who your son is? Did you ever consider that he might be—"

"That he might be a ghost, or some kind of...goddamned freak?"

"No, simply that it's—"

She gritted her teeth. "Shut up. Just shut *up*." Margaret Hinsdale untied the red silk ribbon on the bundle and spread out the materials on the table. "I found all of this under his bed. Look. See for yourself."

It was a collection of books, magazines and newspapers. Kamp looked at the cover of one of the books, a penny dreadful. It was entitled, *West Virginia Tales: Life in the Holler.* The next one, a newspaper, bore the headline, "Snakes Alive! Preacher Dies from Rattler Bite." And the next was a novel, *Runaway Slave: A Tale of Murderous Intrigue!* The cover depicted a scene in a churchyard, apparently the failed rescue attempt of a runaway slave. In the picture the men accompanying the slave appeared to have shot the would-be rescuer. The last item Kamp saw, another penny dreadful, was called, *Breaker Boys: The Low Life of Coal Kids.*

Margaret Hinsdale hissed, "*That's* Abel Truax. Cut from whole cloth. Every detail he ever told you is there."

"Do you think it's possible that he gathered this material because it reminded him—"

"Becket read every one of those stories he told you."

"It wasn't just stories, Mrs. Hinsdale. He knew things, specific facts, details a boy his age couldn't have known. The birthmarks on his wrist and on the back of his neck correspond with—"

She shook her head slowly. "You've been duped by a child. Accept it. I have."

He rubbed his forehead with both hands and said, "Why would he create an elaborate and false version of himself?"

Margaret Hinsdale let out a long sigh. "Why would a child reject his parents?"

Kamp went to the kitchen, poured a glass of water and handed it to Margaret Hinsdale. She set it down without taking a sip and then lit a cigarette.

He said, "Perhaps he was angry. Perhaps he felt as if he needed to escape."

Margaret Hinsdale took a long pull on the cigarette and then let the smoke cascade from her lips as she spoke.

"What could have angered that child? We gave him everything. He wanted for nothing."

"Maybe he felt the tension, the frustration and the rage, your husband's and your own."

"About *what*!"

"Did your husband tell you that—"

"That he killed a man? You can't hurt me with your shocking revelations, Kamp. You're disgusting."

"Carrying that kind of secret is a terrible burden."

"Well, you ought to know. How many people have you killed? How do *you* sleep at night?"

"I suggest that you and your husband consider the implications of your actions."

"Well, that's private business, isn't it?" She took one more drag on the cigarette and then dropped it to the floor, crushing it with the heel of her black riding boot. She gestured once more to the items on the table and said, "You can keep all of this garbage. I certainly don't need it."

KAMP TOOK A LONG WALK later that day to clear his mind, to try to quell the demons. He'd inspected the writings on the table and found that, indeed, all of them corresponded directly or indirectly to the stories the kid had told. He began to ask himself questions and then to ruminate. Soon, the war erupted in his mind anew. He'd told Shaw he'd be back soon, though he knew it would take hours of walking to settle down.

He walked in the forest behind his house. When he reached the far side of the mountain, Kamp happened upon a pile of bear shit. In the center of the pile, he caught a glint of metal, and when he bent down to inspect it, he found a gold ring. He plucked it out and looked at the inscription inside the band, "To My Love, 1861." He pocketed the ring and smiled at the thought of going home and telling Autumn that her bear was still alive.

Kamp walked home on the road, passing the stone mansion where Raymond and Margaret Hinsdale lived. He saw the fine carriage parked behind the house and all the horses in the stable. He kept walking, and just before he reached the path to his house, a police wagon flew past him in the opposite direction, horses going full gallop.

After Autumn had been put to bed, Shaw found Kamp sitting at the kitchen table, staring out the back window. She rubbed his shoulders, working out the knots.

She sang softly, "And will he not come again?"

He let his shoulders relax. "That's good. Right there."

She said, "I read all those things on the table."

"And?"

"He was a troubled boy. He wanted to get away, so he lived in his stories, and now he's gone."

"Just like the missionary, Daniel Jezek. Just like me."

"Let him go. Let them all go." She continued massaging his shoulders and neck and singing, "He is gone, he is gone. And we cast away moan."

EPILOGUE

Kamp decided to put the new cabin far back from the road, even farther than his own house, and he worked alone as much as possible. Throughout that spring and summer and into the fall, Kamp built the structure nail by nail, plank by plank. He intended the place to be a sanctuary, a safe place, though for whom he didn't know yet.

The only visitor was Grigg, who told him that Raymond Hinsdale had died in the kitchen of his home. The cause of death, the prosecutor said, was head trauma, almost certainly caused by a cast iron skillet in the hand of his wife, Margaret Hinsdale. He added that despite the force and accuracy of the blow, it had been ruled an accident.

One hazy morning in early fall, as Kamp finished the cabin roof, he saw a man walking on the road. The man paused, scanned the property and the mountain behind it

341

and then started up the path. Kamp climbed down from the roof to meet him.

The man was lanky, taller than Kamp, and thin. From a distance he looked at Kamp but didn't call out. When the man came within a few steps, he stopped and produced a sheet of paper from the vest pocket of his plain coat. Kamp noticed the man wore a wool forager's hat, and he saw gold hair like straw poking out at angles underneath it.

The man slowly unfolded the paper, cleared his throat and said, "I received this letter two weeks ago, dated one month before that. The letter is from my brother, Abel Thomas Truax." The man looked down and read from the paper, "Dear Brother, first off, go ahead and find Kamp."

The man stopped reading and looked up. "That's you, ain't?"

Kamp nodded.

He started reading again. "Second, tell him you've come to collect my bones and take them back. Third, don't forget to introduce yourself." The man extended his hand. "My name is John Truax. Folks call me J.B."

Kamp shook Truax's hand. "Where should we look?"

"For what?"

"For your brother's bones. I don't know where they are. Do you?"

J.B. Truax squinted and then looked back down at the letter.

He read, "An' another thing, Kamp's gonna say he don't know where I'm buried. Tell him, yes, he does."

Kamp tilted his head back and looked at the sky. He thought back to his conversations with the kid and found his answer. "Follow me," he said.

They walked around the back of the house to the tool shed and Kamp removed a pick ax and a spade shovel.

"Better let's get us a winding sheet, too," Truax said.

Kamp went in the house and came back out carrying a bed sheet. He carried the ax as well, handed the spade to Truax and then the pair set off for the tree line. As he reached the trail that led up the mountain, Kamp called over his shoulder, "Does it seem strange to you that your brother would send you a letter after he's dead?"

After a long pause, Truax said, "You had to know Abel."

Kamp went to the oak tree at the top of the mountain. The ground at the base of the tree, the place the kid had called a *kyarn*, the dead place, was devoid of life no more. It was thickly covered with mushrooms.

Kamp raised the pick ax high over his head for the first swing.

"Hold on, hold on, son."

J.B. Truax stepped in front of him and bent down. He picked one of the mushrooms between his thumb and first finger. It was black with a funnel shape that expanded outward and curled at the top.

"The French call this here 'trompette de la mort.'"

"What?"

"Trumpet of the dead."

Kamp reached down, picked one and inspected it.

Truax said, "Best eatin-est mushrooms you'll find. Valuable, too."

He popped it in his mouth and savored it for a moment, then took off his jacket and harvested the rest of the mushrooms. He bundled them in the jacket, tied it with the sleeves and set it aside. "Okay, go 'head."

With a few hard swings, Kamp broke up the ground, and Truax shoveled the dirt. Soon, they were a few feet down. Truax sank the blade and stopped.

"That's it," he said.

The two men carefully, reverently scooped out the ground around the corpse, the stench of decay hitting them full in the nostrils. They unearthed the feet and legs and then the torso.

"Threw 'im in head first," Truax said to himself.

Lastly, they found the head detached from the body, blonde hair matted with chunks of mud to the skull. Kamp lifted the head gently from the hole and set it on the ground.

J.B. Truax gathered his brother's remains on the winding sheet he'd spread out on the ground. He peeled the jacket from the torso of the corpse and felt along its seams.

"What is it?"

Truax's fingers kept searching and then stopped. He produced a pocket knife and sliced open the fabric.

"Legal tender. Tens and twenties."

Truax pulled out a thin stack of bills, then another. He counted the money, split it, and handed one half to Kamp. "It's still good," he said.

"I can't take his money, or yours."

"Shee-*it*, son, he don't need it. Truth be told, I don't neither. But he told me to give you due recompense. And that's that."

Kamp pocketed the bills, while Truax climbed back in the hole.

"Now what?" Kamp said.

Truax sliced through the dirt at the bottom of the hole until he hit metal. He got on his knees, dug out the object, and held it up to Kamp.

"My knife. Abel stole it from me right before he lit out." He shook his head and said, "Little brothers."

Truax picked up the winding sheet and the bundle of mushrooms, slung them both over his shoulder and said, "One more thing."

"What's that?"

"Abel told me to tell you your hat, that red felt number. He said you stuffed it in a notch in this here tree, part way up."

J.B. Truax started back down the trail and was gone. Kamp stared up into the tree at the spot he'd climbed to on the day he'd learned of his oldest brother's death. He jumped, arms stretched above him, and caught the first low bough, then swung his left leg over it. He soon righted himself on the bough and stood up and ascended until he reached the large notch. He scraped away the years of detritus that had collected there and eventually touched felt. He took a handful and pulled out his beloved hat, misshapen and dyed dark brown by the disintegration of dead leaves.

He climbed down from the tree, clutching the hat, tears filling his eyes. Kamp gathered up the ax and spade and walked down the mountain home.

20653411R00213

Made in the USA
Middletown, DE
04 June 2015